GOODBYE PARADISE

goodbye
PARADISE

SARINA BOWEN

Tuxbury Publishing LLC

PART I

CHAPTER ONE

Josh

Autumn

It should have been just another ordinary day of work and prayer, followed by more work, followed by more prayer. I had endured almost twenty years of those days already. But this one would turn out to be very different.

Also, I had a headache.

It was a crisp November afternoon, and we were out in the dry bean field, gathering in the crop. This was, hands down, my least favorite chore. Every fall we stood out here in the wind, fingertips sliced to bits by the sharp-edged bean hulls, the dried stems clattering in the breeze.

The throbbing at the base of my skull put an extra special twist on the whole experience. Hooray and hallelujah.

When I was a boy, we had a machine to hull the beans. I'd loved that crazy old diesel-fueled hunk of metal. The men had pitched the dried sheaves into one end, and the machine shook them senseless. Beans (and dust) came shooting into a hopper on one side. All the chaff was chucked out of the back, and the work went ten times as fast.

That machine wore out, though. And our Divine Pastor did not replace it. Why would he? It wasn't his fingers bleeding on the beanstalks.

To entertain myself during our long days of labor, I often took over the compound in my mind — all two thousand acres of dusty Wyoming ranch land. The first thing I always planned (after excommunicating all the assholes) was to invest in farm machinery, tripling the acreage for our cash crops. In my mind, I built us a shiny, efficient operation, diversified to minimize the risk of crop failure.

I enjoyed these fantasies while standing in that row of beans wearing torn trousers and hand-me-down boots a half size too small. Not a soul at the compound would ever listen to my plans, even if I were stupid enough to share them. I'd learned at an early age never to point out the foolishness of our leadership, or the inefficiencies of our operation.

Nobody wanted to hear this from the skinny kid with slow hands.

Beside me — just a few feet away — stood the other object of my fantasies. Caleb Smith was my best friend. We'd been close since we could barely toddle. There wasn't a day of my life when I hadn't counted the faded spray of freckles which stretched across his nose, or admired his slightly crooked smile.

While my elders might have little patience for my farming fantasies, the thoughts I had about Caleb were a punishable sin. He was the last one I saw before I closed my eyes at night and the first person I looked for when I opened them again in the morning.

Even now, as he leaned over the next plant, I coveted his broad chest and fine shoulders. He was quicker than I was at tearing the bean pods off the stalks and liberating the beans with his thumb. They dropped into his bucket with a satisfying clatter. My own slowness was probably due to my habit of stopping to admire Caleb's rugged-looking hands.

At night, in my bunk all alone, Caleb's hands made frequent appearances in all my best dreams.

Again, I pushed aside my sinful fantasies and tried to pick faster. It was my lot in life to be always two steps behind the other young men. For a long time I assumed that I would grow out of my dreamy nature. That I would someday be quick with farm tools and chores. But now that my nineteenth birthday had passed, it was obvious that my skills on the compound would never be praised.

I'd come to accept a lot of things about myself, actually. It's just that I could never speak any of them aloud.

We had reached the end of a row. Caleb leaned down to yank his bucket around the end of it. But at the last second, he grabbed the handle of *mine* instead. Before I could even protest, he and my bucket had disappeared around the corner.

His bucket remained at my feet. And it was nearly full to the top.

With my face burning, I did the only conceivable thing. I hefted it, swinging it around the corner, setting it down at my feet, as if I'd picked all those beans myself.

Beside me, Caleb dropped more beans into the bucket formerly known as mine, his tanned hands threading into the dried sheaves the way I'd always wanted them to tangle in my hair.

Biting back a sigh, I grabbed a pod and cracked it in my hand. Discomfort and shame were my constant companions. Caleb covered for my mediocrity as best he could. My best friend had saved my backside too many times to count. And how did I repay him? With sinful, lusty thoughts.

Just another day in Paradise. That's what they called this place where we lived and worked and prayed when they told us to.

Depressingly, the little kids of The Paradise Ranch didn't even *know* that the rest of the world was not like this place. Sometimes I peered into the window of the little schoolhouse where the children were learning to read the Bible. (Only the Bible, and a book about our Divine Pastor. There weren't any other texts. Poor little souls.)

Until the third grade, Caleb and I went to a real school in Casper. We all did. And man, I loved that place. Teachers pressed books into my hands and told me I was a wonderful student. School was my refuge.

But then, ten years ago, our Divine Pastor decided that the public school was a bad influence, because we came back to Paradise asking for Go-Gurt and Jell-O and Harry Potter. We came home corrupt, wanting things from the sinners' world.

The elders didn't like it. So they built the schoolhouse (which is really just a drafty pole barn) and taught us exactly what they wanted us to learn, which is almost nothing.

I haven't been off the Paradise Ranch since then.

Caleb sees the outside world, though. He's the first born grandson of an elder, and therefore has a much better standing than I do. He has a valid birth certificate and — even better — a driver's license. Once a week or so the elders send him out to the post office or to the feed store. Once they sent him to Wal-Mart, and he came back with lots of colorful stories of what he saw there. Bright television screens (we didn't have any at Paradise, but we'd seen them when we were younger), crazy clothing, and all kinds of food in plastic packages.

There were no stories for me today, though. We couldn't gossip on a bean harvest day, because there were too many others around to hear us. Though it was nice to be near Caleb. I could even hear the tune he kept humming under his breath.

Singing was not allowed. Caleb was very good at following the rules, but music was his downfall. Some of the compound trucks still had their radios. And since Caleb was handy with engines (and branding cattle, and the ancient tractor, and all the stuff I could never seem to manage) he was often asked to do mechanical maintenance. Even though it was risky, when he worked alone he would sometimes play the radio.

I couldn't tell which tune he had stuck in his head today, because only little bits of it escaped. But even those breathy sounds made me want to lean in. I wished I could put a hand on his chest and feel the vibration when he hummed.

My head gave a brand new throb of pain, and I dropped some flaky pieces of chaff into the bucket, and had to fish them out.

THE DAY ENDED before the never-ending bean field, which meant that we'd have to come back again tomorrow. Carrying my last ungainly bucket, I felt oddly exhausted. I stumbled, nearly spilling all those ill-gotten beans on the ground.

Ezra, the evilest of the bachelors, came running over — but not to help. Instead, he laughed in my face. "The little faggot can't even carry the beans."

Do not react, I cautioned myself.

Ezra used the word *faggot* whenever he felt like it, and not always on me. But I knew what it meant, and when he said it I always felt transparent.

That's when Caleb arrived at my side, setting down his own bucket without a word. He just loomed there, a quiet wall of support.

Ezra grinned in that mean way he had. "Why do you help the little faggot, anyway? People gonna talk."

My blood was ice, then. Our whole lives, Caleb had been taking heat for helping me. To hear such ugliness come from Ezra's mouth terrified me. Because if, even for a second, people believed the things that he had just implied about Caleb? I would *die* of unhappiness. My sin was my own, and I couldn't stand to see that ugliness tainting my friend.

Luckily, Caleb had both parentage and competence on his side. He always shook off Ezra's taunts. When he spoke, his tone was mild. "I help everyone, Ezra," he said. "Even you. Christian charity? You ever heard of that? You been sleeping through Sunday mass?"

At that, Caleb picked up *both* our buckets and carried them to the truck. He lifted them as if they weighed no more than two chickens.

~

THEN IT WAS DINNER TIME, thank the Lord. My headache had spread down my neck and across my shoulders. For once in my stupid life, food did not even sound very appealing.

But I took my seat as usual at the end of a bench in our bunkhouse common room.

All the bachelors lived together. Usually around age sixteen, boys moved out of their family houses and into the bunkhouse. There were, at present, twenty-seven family houses on the compound, though the number went up by one or two houses each year. Each house held one man's family, which meant they were crowded. Since each man had several wives, there were lots of children, too.

Teenage boys were very useful for farm work, of course. But the men did not like having their grown sons in the house. They took up too much space, for one. But also, it was not fit to have lusty young men share a roof with so many women. Since the girls in Paradise were married off at seventeen or eighteen, that meant that the youngest wives were often the same age as the bachelors.

Boys, on the other hand, could never marry as teenagers. The difficulty with polygamy was the imbalance. I had worked this out at a very young age, and naturally kept my conclusions to myself. But if a man deserves four or five wives, and women have boys fifty percent of the time, there are always far too many boys.

A boy in Paradise could expect to wait until he was in his

twenties to marry. That gave the compound more than a decade of his farm labor while he tried desperately to prove himself worthy of his own wife and home.

Evil Ezra was twenty-four already, and probably the next in line to settle down. (I couldn't wait to see him go, even though he wouldn't go far.) In our bunkhouse there were twelve men over the age of twenty. Caleb turned twenty last month. I would turn twenty come springtime. There were a slew of teens, too.

Owing to the math, many of us would never get the chance to marry. But neither would we be welcome to stay on. Five years from now, quite a few of my bunkhouse roommates would be gone from Paradise. Some would run away, but many would be kicked out.

Nobody spoke of this practice, of course. There were many, many idiosyncrasies at Paradise that were not to be mentioned aloud, but the throwing away of half our young men was the ugliest one.

And here's a sad thing—it often took Caleb and me a day or two to *notice* that someone had gone missing. We might hear a bachelor say at lunch, "where has Zachariah been today?"

And the question would be met with deep silence.

Then, a day or two later, a story would begin to circulate. Zachariah had been caught behind the tool shed with one of the daughters. Or, Zachariah had worshipped the devil. There was always a crime that was responsible for his downfall. And the crime did not need to sound original, or even plausible.

Those who disappeared weren't around to defend themselves. The ones who disappeared, however, were often the most dispensable among us. The weak and the slow. The ones whose labor would not be missed too badly.

The boys who disappeared looked a lot like me.

Caleb sat down on the bench beside me, folding his big hands in a typical gesture of patience. Whereas I was a pile of nerves, he was a calm giant. His body language was always serene. It was only when I looked into his eyes that I sometimes saw anxiety flickering there. That always gave me a start.

In those rare moments when I caught Caleb wearing a pained expression, he always looked away. Whatever it was that bothered him, it was something he did not want me to see.

And I always had a strong desire to comfort him, which would never be tolerated, of course.

When we were at prayer, I spent a good portion of my time praying for his safekeeping and happiness. The other portion was spent apologizing to God for my sinful preoccupation with him.

As they did before every dinnertime, daughters began to file into the room, each one of them bearing a pan or a dish. It was the families' job to feed the bachelors three times each day. During an ordinary work week, mealtimes were the only moments when the daughters and the bachelors saw one another.

There was always supervision. Even now, Elder Michael stood at the head of the table, his serious eyes watching the proceedings, vigilant in the face of possible sin.

The swish of skirts continued. Since the daughters were made to dress alike, in long, roomy pastel dresses of identical design, all the swishes sounded the same.

A plate, napkin, and cutlery were placed in front of me. And I saw a particularly succulent chicken casserole land on the table as well. I kept my eye on it, even though someone quicker than I would probably reach it first, just after the prayer.

There was never quite enough to eat in the bunkhouse. More than two dozen hungry farm workers can put away an awful lot of food. None of us was ever truly full. And nobody *ever* got fat. Only married men had that privilege. In the family houses, a man was king, with a small army of women and children who were all vying to be the one who pleased him best.

That's what the Ezras and Calebs of the bunkhouse were working toward — their own little promised land.

One particular skirt swished to a stop behind us. "Evening Caleb," a soft voice said.

I did not look up for two reasons. In the first place, I did not need my eyes to identify Miriam. She had been a part of our lives since I could remember. Our mothers were all friends. As children, the three of us had climbed onto the school bus together back when that was allowed.

Miriam and Caleb always seemed meant for one another, too. It wasn't something we talked about. It just *was*. Caleb showed Miriam the same favor as he showed me, helping her whenever possible. He even had a special smile for Miriam, which I coveted. It was a smile that knew secrets.

The other reason I did not turn around to greet Miriam was as a favor to them both. My lack of notice helped them have a brief and whispered conversation. It was the only sort of conversation they could have, except on those rare occasions when there was some sort of party. A barn raising, or a christening, maybe. Otherwise, the daughters and the bachelors were kept apart.

"I need to speak with you," she said in the lowest possible tone.

Caleb answered under his breath. "After supper I'll change the oil on the Tacoma."

With the message received, Miriam darted away without another word.

Elder Michael began to say a prayer, so I bowed my head. And then there were "amens" and the passing of dishes.

I did, in fact, secure a chunk of the chicken casserole, as well as a rice dish and some potato. This I forced myself to eat, even though I felt ill. Because you did not pass up food in Paradise.

TWO HOURS LATER, I lay in my bed, shaking. From fear, not illness.

In front of me, I held my Bible. Quiet prayer was one of the few activities acceptable just before curfew. So I often sat here with the heavy book on my lap, thinking.

Or worrying. And tonight I was definitely doing that.

After our meal, our Divine Pastor had walked into the bunkhouse common room. All conversation stopped, of course. He was accompanied by Elder Michael and two others.

"It has come to our attention that a handgun has gone missing from the tool shed," our Divine Pastor said.

I'd felt Caleb's body go completely still beside me.

"I must ask," our Divine Pastor continued, "Which of you was the last to perform an inventory of our supply of tools?"

Lord in heaven. My stomach cramped in distress. Slowly, I raised a shaking hand into the air.

"Joshua," our Divine Pastor barked. "When was this?"

"T...two weeks ago," I quavered. "After the pumpkins were in." I always volunteered for inventory jobs, because it meant brainwork instead of outdoor labor.

"Did you perform the inventory piece by piece? Or do you keep an old list as a guide? I am trying to discern how easily you might have erred. Which might, in turn, help me learn when the gun went missing."

"I..." I cleared my dry throat, feeling every pair of eyes on me. "I never use my old lists, because if there are new tools then I'd miss them."

"So. You make a new list each time?"

"Yessir," I choked out.

"The missing weapon was part of your recent inventory," Elder Michael said, pinning me with his gaze.

I nodded. It was silent in that room. Nobody even breathed. Because no one else dared draw the attention of an angry elder.

"Do you have anything to say for where it might be?" he asked.

Of course I did not. And *many* people had access to that storage room. But I would not point this out, because it would sound as if I were desperate to shift blame. "I have no idea, sir," I said. It was not a great defense, but it was my only move. "I remember the gun. It was new in August."

The portly elder frowned. "Well then. Tomorrow, first thing, you will come with us to the tool shed and look again at the inventory. We need to know what else may be missing."

"Yessir," I'd said.

My stomach had remained in knots ever since.

I had no idea what would happen tomorrow. None at all. It was possible that they really only wanted my assistance. But an inventory was an easy thing to read, with or without help.

My fear was that someone had stolen the gun, knowing the theft would be pinned on me. There was nothing I could do about it. A man cannot prove his innocence. He can only prove another's guilt.

I had, of course, no idea who took the gun. And it did not matter a whit that I had no *reason* to take a gun. I had no way to sell it, or curry favor with another for handing it over.

But you must never look for logic in Paradise.

Stewing over the problem wasn't going to help. It's just that I didn't have anything better to think about. Caleb was not here in our room. He was in the garage, changing the oil in the Tacoma.

And kissing Miriam, maybe.

Someday it would happen for real. Caleb would marry a woman. He was just the sort of bachelor who would eventually be granted a wife. When the time came, I would watch the ceremony with horror in my heart. And I would lie awake in the bunkhouse that night, wild with jealousy as he made his bride into a woman.

I forced myself to imagine it from time to time, if only to maintain my grip on reality. Caleb building a house for his bride. Caleb in a wedding suit.

Caleb removing all his clothes, and spilling his seed into a woman.

When I was twelve, I had seen the act done. I'd been home at an odd time of day, because my mother had asked me to change a couple of lightbulbs after lunch. With my task finished, I'd walked quietly along the upstairs hallway of our house.

At the end of the corridor was the youngest wife's room. The door had been open a crack. I paused there because I heard the strangest sounds coming from within.

My real father had died when I was four, when he overturned a tractor. The man I'd called "father" ever since had married two of my birth father's wives, including my mother. His name was Seth.

Seth's hairy ass was the thing I saw first when I peered into that room.

It took me a moment to realize what I was witnessing. But even when I understood, I could not look away.

It was fascinating.

The breathy grunts he made washed over me like steam. And the way his powerful thighs flexed through each thrust was beautiful to me. He growled and he groaned, and finally he shook. With a cry, he collapsed onto the wife that I'd barely noticed was underneath him. Coming to my senses, I'd snuck away.

Someday, that would be Caleb. And no amount of wishing otherwise would help.

I stared at the page of my Bible until the letters blurred together.

PERHAPS TWO HOURS LATER, I woke in the dark. The Bible was gone from my hands, but I spotted it on the bedside table. Someone had placed it there for me.

Caleb.

Even in the darkness, I could see his large form in bed across the room that we shared with two others. He lay on his back, hands clasped behind his head.

Strong and confident, even in his sleep.

There were snores coming from Ezekiel's and David's corners of the room, My head did not ache so much now, but I felt hot and irritable. To ease myself, I focused on Caleb's silent form. His shoulders were wide, taking up a goodly portion of the narrow bed. His legs were long and solid under the quilt.

I wished I could spread my body out on top of his, sinking into all that muscle. I wanted to bury my face in the hollow between his shoulder and neck, breathing in his cottony clean scent.

I wanted so, so many things that I would never have.

My cock began to feel full between my legs.

Lying there, I squeezed my ass together a few times. It had been such an awful, scary day. I deserved a little comfort, didn't I? Unbidden, my hand slipped beneath the waistband of my boxers. Touching myself was risky. It was a sin, of course, although surely everyone did it sometimes. Even Caleb.

In fact, once when we were sixteen, he asked me to stand guard. We were out by the cow shed, sitting on the hay bales in between jobs. "Can I ask a favor?"

"Sure?"

"I need five minutes alone. Would you stand at the fencepost and wait for me? If somebody comes, just talk to them, and I'll know to cover up."

"Okay," I'd said, "but why?"

He'd rolled his eyes at me. "I have to jerk. It's a desperate situation. You can take a turn after I do."

"Oh."

Oh.

Do not *look at his dick*, I'd ordered myself, scandalized. *Do not.* I'd marched away immediately, where it was safe. Then I'd stood at that fence post like a sentry, ready to holler at the first sign of anyone.

But not a soul had wandered by. And all the while my ears were peeled, desperately hopeful that I'd hear him come. And I did, though it was just a quick gasp, over practically before it began.

"Your turn?" he asked me about two minutes later.

"Nope, I'm good," I stammered, my face the color of a tomato.

"Suit yourself. But if I were you, I'd stay out of the tall grass back there for a day or so." He'd laughed at this joke, and so I did too.

That was the extent of my sexual experience—watching my step-father plow a teenage wife and listening to my best friend jerk.

And touching myself, of course, which I was doing now. I closed my eyes and ran my hand slowly up and down my shaft. When I did this, I made it a point never to stare at my best friend. He wouldn't like being the center of my sexual fantasies. And it wasn't his fault that I was a pervert.

But who was I kidding? The faceless bodies in my dreams all matched his. And it was his full lips that I so badly wanted to kiss...

I clamped my mouth shut, to avoid making noise. And I sank into my mattress, silently coaxing my body toward climax. I pictured Caleb smiling at me. And I heard him whisper my name...

"Joshua!"

My hand went stock still. Because that whisper was not part of my imagination.

I opened my eyes to see Caleb moving through the shadows. He tiptoed silently to my bed, sitting down on the edge. In the dark, I could see his blue eyes roll at me. *Stop it*, he mouthed.

Then, as my heart shimmied with surprise, he put an elbow down on my pillow and leaned down, his lips skimming my ear.

My entire brain short-circuited. And then I realized that he was just trying to talk to me in the only way possible at this hour.

"Move over," he whispered directly into my ear.

Immediately, I rolled onto my side, away from him. Not only did this make room on the mattress, but it pointed my traitorous dick as far away from him as possible. *God have mercy on me*, I inwardly begged. My friend caught me stroking myself while I was thinking of him.

Hell was waiting for me. No question.

Caleb cupped one of his big hands over my ear, and I had to bite the inside of my cheek to hide my reaction. "How can you jerk at a time like this?" he asked, while my heart spasmed. "We need a plan. Like, yesterday."

"Sorry," I mouthed, stupidly. I wished the mattress would roll up and swallow me whole.

Caleb gave me a little punch to the shoulder, like he always did. But then he put his hand on my bicep and squeezed. He was always touching me. Caleb was a toucher. That was just his way. It made me crazy half the time, because I wanted those touches to *mean* something. (They never did.)

"I'm worried," he said into my ear. "This isn't good."

That snapped me out of my own head, and quickly. Because Caleb wasn't a worrier. In fact, I craned my neck to see just how serious he was.

The most familiar set of eyes blinked back at me from inches away. He beckoned to me, and I put my ear up against his mouth again. "Tomorrow, I need you to be prepared. Just in case. Can you do a few things for me?"

I gave him a little nod.

"Okay, listen. I need you to put on your newest clothes in the morning," he breathed. "Anything valuable you have, put it in your pockets."

A chill snaked down my spine. "Really?" I mouthed.

He gave a sad sigh, his warm breath sweeping sweetly down my neck. "Maybe I'm being paranoid. But I'm afraid they're going to..." he didn't finish the sentence. Caleb couldn't stand to say it. *Throw you out.*

I shivered.

With another sigh, he put his hand on my chest, right in the center. "Do *not* panic. Maybe it won't happen tomorrow. But Joshy, it's coming. And I need you to listen to my instructions."

Nobody had called me Joshy since we were seven, and eating cookies in his mom's kitchen. And now my throat was tight.

It's coming, he'd said. Not only was this terrifying, it meant that I was just as pathetic as I'd always feared. Caleb knew I was useless. He *saw.*

"*Sh sh sh sh sh,*" he said into my ear. His hand closed over mine. "Are you listening? This is important."

I squeezed his hand to tell him that I was.

"I'm not sure where they'd take you. If I had to guess, I'd say the bus station in Casper. They'd pick somewhere far enough away that you wouldn't try to walk back and steal anything. If it wasn't Casper, it would be Riverton. Either way, you and I are going to meet up in *Casper.* Whether this happens tomorrow, or any other time, I need you to get to Casper. Hitchhike if you have to."

My heart skipped an actual beat, and I spent the next few seconds trying to figure out if I'd heard him right. Slowly, I turned my head on the pillow so that I could see Caleb's eyes.

We? I mouthed.

Slowly, he nodded. Then he pushed my chin aside so that he could get to my ear again. "We're going together. But if they toss you one morning and I don't see it happen, I have to know where to find you."

All my insides did a nauseous, crazy dance. It was the maddest thing I'd ever heard, and I really did not trust that I'd understood him. I whipped my head to the side again. *WHY?* I mouthed.

He put his lips so close to my ear that I could feel them tickling my skin. "I have to get out of here. There's no life for me here. I've been saving money, but I don't have enough yet. I could really use a little more time."

I'd never been so surprised. Caleb was set up to do very well in Paradise. He would someday be married and have his own house. Everyone liked him, except the jealous ones. And he'd managed to steer clear of trouble even from them. And...

There was one question that I had to ask. I pushed an elbow into the bed and rose up to get near his ear. "What about Miriam?"

Caleb flinched. He whispered to me again. "Elder Asher wants her."

Oh no! I mouthed.

He gave me a sad nod.

I felt a stab of pain in my chest for Miriam. Asher was not a nice man. At sixty-something years old, he had five wives already. And two others had died, while one had run away. In fact, it was Miriam's own sister who had escaped from him. One morning she was just gone. Nobody knew where she went.

What Asher wanted, Asher got. He was the half-brother of our Divine Pastor. If Asher wanted Miriam... I shuddered.

I turned to study Caleb's serious profile. It was hard to make sense of everything I'd just heard. My best friend thought that I would be taken out like so much garbage tomorrow. Into a world where I knew literally nobody. Penniless, too. And Caleb wanted to run away?

If he couldn't have Miriam, that made a tiny kernel of sense. I'd always dreaded the thought of him in another's arms. Perhaps it was the same for him. If he could not stand to watch Miriam marry another man...

I put my hand close to his ear. "You could ask for Miriam first."

The expression on his face then was hard to read. It was *disappointed*, maybe. "She *wants* me to ask," he whispered. "But I know it will never work." The pain on his face doubled, and so I did not ask more questions. The fact that Caleb wouldn't even *try* was a shock to me, though. He was loyal to a fault.

Abruptly, the snoring from Ezekiel's corner of our room came to a halt.

I felt Caleb go absolutely still beside me. We could *not* be caught like this, lying on the same bed. Plotting together was nearly as great a sin as whatever else they might imagine we were doing.

For many long seconds, we lay there like statues. I still had a hold of Caleb's hand, though, and I squeezed it. He squeezed back, too.

No matter what happened, I would always remember this night.

An agonizing minute later, Ezekiel began to snore again. Beside me, Caleb relaxed. Then he gripped my hand one more time. Into my ear he said, "the bus station in Casper." And then he stole silently across the room to his own bed.

CHAPTER TWO

Josh

When the wake-up bell rang, my eyes flew open. My first emotion of the day was fear. And the second one was shame. I was afraid, and I was *ashamed* to be afraid.

That's how it always was with me.

I got up, stumbling into my clothes. Mindful of Caleb's instructions, I put on my good pair of Carhartts, and a clean undershirt.

"Josh." I looked up to see Caleb watching me. "Catch," he said. Then he tossed me something.

It was a new pair of socks. The woolen kind. His mother knitted them for him every winter.

My mother did nothing like that for me. Ever. Even my own mother valued me at zero.

I sat down on the bed to pull on Caleb's socks. My hands were shaking now. And maybe for nothing, right? If Caleb was wrong, I could give him the socks back after laundry day.

One of my flannel shirts had no holes, so I wore that one. Then I added a wool sweater that had been my father's, and my canvas work jacket.

The last thing I did was slip a pocketknife into my trousers.

That too had been my father's. My mother gave it to me when I'd turned ten, before it became too obvious that I would not be a leader of our community.

The bell rang again to call us to breakfast and Ezekiel and David ran out of our room. Caleb waited, though. There was a moment of silence, and I could feel him holding back until all the other bachelors assembled in the common room where the food was.

"Josh..." he whispered.

But he was cut off by another voice yelling my name from the hallway. "Josh!" David stuck his head back into our room. "Elder Michael is waiting outside. He wants you at the tool shed right away."

My heart plunged. David was watching me, so I didn't risk a look in Caleb's direction. Though I wanted to. I wanted one more glance at his beautiful face, for courage.

I didn't see Caleb again, but I did hear his voice. "Bus station" he whispered as I left the room.

Bus station, I repeated to myself as I stepped into the cold morning. I walked quickly toward the tool shed. I was practically racing there, which made no sense. Why hurry to your own execution?

Bus station, I chanted inside my head. *Bus station.* My own little descent into hell would be accompanied by two words for a place I'd never been, and really had no wish to see.

But they were words that Caleb gave me, and that was something.

Bus station, I whispered as I saw not one but four men waiting near the toolshed. Elder Michael was there, but also Evil Ezra and two of his cronies.

It got worse, too. The Tundra was idling nearby.

Still, I stepped closer, trying to keep the fear off my face. "Good morning," I said.

Four grim faces were silent in return. That's when I knew. That's when I was sure that Caleb was right.

Elder Michael pointed at the door to the tool shed, which confused me for a moment. Were we going through with the charade of performing another inventory?

I went to open it, turning the knob.

Locked. So...?

My forehead bounced off the wooden door then, stunning me. Someone grabbed me by the ankles, which meant I was going down hard.

Bus station...! My chest hit the ground, my forehead bouncing once on the gravel surface.

"Get his hands," someone grunted. I recognized the voice as belonging to my step-father, Seth.

My own family was helping to throw me away.

My head throbbed anew, and my heart quaked. On the ground, I tasted dirt, and as my arms were roughly yanked back, I felt my bowels loosen with fear.

But *no*. I was *not* going to totally lose it. Because Ezra would enjoy that too much. And I didn't want to make this fun for him.

Many hands lifted me up, then rolled me onto the bed of the Tundra. I heard the clang of the tailgate.

"You know what to do," Elder Michael said.

"Yessir," said Ezra's voice and another one that I did not catch. Two truck doors opened and shut. And then we began to roll.

Bus station. Bus station. Bus station.

Bus station. Bus station.

Bus station.

SIX HOURS LATER, I wasn't chanting anymore.

The bumpy ride toward Casper had seemed to last forever.

Bouncing around the dirty metal truck, it might have been twenty minutes, or twice that long.

At last we rolled to a stop. I could hear cars going by on a nearby road. The tailgate was suddenly jerked away, and Ezra's face appeared in mine.

He started the conversation by slapping my face. "You little faggot. Don't you dare come back. And don't even think about going to the police. They'll only lock you up for stealing a gun."

But I didn't steal it. I did not say this out loud, because I knew he didn't care.

Ezra snaked a hand toward my body, and I flinched. But he was only jamming something in the back pocket of my Carhartts. "Use this to get on a bus," he said. "There's a homeless shelter in Cheyenne."

I said nothing. I just watched his lips move. Because I was trying to get over the idea that they were going to leave me by the side of the road. This road, which I did not recognize.

The thing was, part of me always knew I'd be one of the boys who disappeared. I *knew.* It's just that a little piece of me always hoped that it wouldn't turn out this way.

"Do I make myself clear?" Ezra demanded.

Swallowing every bit of my stinking pride, I whispered, "Yessir."

He reached into his jeans and took out a knife, at which point my heart nearly failed again. But he only used it to slice the tape that was tying my hands.

"Out," he said, grabbing me by the arms. Since my feet were still taped together, I went down like a sack of potatoes, landing on my ass in the dirt.

The engine still ran, blowing exhaust into my face. I began to cough.

Ezra moved away, his feet crunching on the gravel. Then I heard the truck's door open and shut.

Then they drove away.

For a little while I sat there, stunned and wheezing. The cold seeped into my trousers, and the wind whistled past.

Eventually, I began to tug at the tape on my ankles. When it was all torn off, I finally stood. I found myself in a weedy field, about fifty yards from the roadway. And in the distance, I saw buildings which made up the outskirts of Casper. It had been ten years since I'd come through here for school. But I recognized the approach into town.

Putting one foot in front of the other, I walked into town. The bus station was on a windblown strip behind a gas station and across the street from a hotel.

I went inside, where there was a ticket window and a few benches. Feeling self-conscious, I sat down to wait.

For a long time, there was nobody else in the room except for my new friend, the constant headache. (And, thanks to Ezra, I also had a lump on my forehead from hitting the tool shed door.)

As the day wore on, people began to collect in the room. There were young men with backpacks, and a family of four. They made me feel less conspicuous, until a bus pulled up, and they all got on. After that, I was alone again, and probably looking more suspicious by the minute.

Eventually, a security guard I'd seen passing through twice before came to stand in front of me. "Are you a passenger?" he asked me.

Somehow I found my voice. "I will be. I'm waiting for someone."

It sounded ridiculous, I was sure. But even so, he seemed to accept that answer, and he walked away.

But for how much longer?

I was afraid to leave the waiting area, because I had no idea when Caleb might turn up. I'd never asked for the details of his plan, which now seemed stupid. I didn't even know if he planned to come today, or not.

Eventually I got up and went into the men's room. Washing

SARINA BOWEN

up as best I could, I wished I'd brought a toothbrush. And then that errant desire made me smile in the mirror. Of all the things I could wish for in the world, like a home to go back to or even a hot meal, I was missing my *toothbrush*?

And I used to think I was so smart.

Back in the waiting room, I kept the vigil. My stomach growled, but I ignored it as best I could. The envelope that Ezra had shoved into my pocket contained exactly $50. If I was running away with Caleb, I would need all of it.

The afternoon wore into early evening, and the light began to fade, taking with it my bravado. If it was five o'clock, that meant I'd last seen Caleb ten hours ago.

Was that right? My head was cloudy, and my throat burned. I took another trip to the men's room to gulp water out of my palm. On the way back, I felt unsteady on my feet. It was probably because I hadn't eaten.

Or had I? Somehow, the details weren't as clear as they should have been.

"You," someone said, kicking my foot. "The place is closing."

My head snapped up. I'd fallen asleep in my hands. Where was I? It was dark outside, and a man in a uniform was staring down at me. Police? No. He didn't have a gun. But he had a mean face.

"I'm going," I said, rising quickly. The room swam, and I put a hand out to catch myself on the wall.

The man gave an angry grunt. "You can't sleep it off here. Don't come back tomorrow."

Pulling myself together, I headed out the door. It was surprisingly cold outside. Still unsteady, I kept one hand on the cinderblock wall. Where was I headed? No place, that's where. And I was just so *tired*.

Bus station, Caleb had said. But I *was* at the bus station.

Stumbling, I followed the wall around, to the rear of the building. There was nothing there but an empty parking lot, and a few scrubby bushes. With the wall at my back, I sank down on my haunches. I needed a plan. But first I needed to rest...

～

MY DREAMS WERE CRAZY. Later I'd realize they were fever dreams. But at the time they were terrifying. Ezra showed up to slap me in the face again.

And then the devil taunted me. I couldn't see him, but I could hear his sinister voice. *Sinner*, he hissed. *You are deserted because you are a worthless faggot. Everyone knows. Caleb isn't coming for you. Nobody ever will.*

Slipping in and out of consciousness, I was sometimes aware of a clicking noise, which turned out to be the sound of my own teeth chattering.

As always, I endured.

The fever dreams finally went away, and I was deep under. That's why I really didn't appreciate the fact that someone was trying to hoist me up again. In fact, I curled an arm over my face to protect myself against the onslaught.

The bothersome person was talking at top speed, too. Talking and begging. "Josh, come on. Come on. Come back to me. You have to wake up, because I'm fucking scared now. Wake *up*."

I groaned to express my displeasure.

"Yes! Come on now. Sit up for me."

That was asking too much. But I did open my eyes. And the sight of Caleb's familiar face in the darkness lifted me like nothing else ever could.

He hooked a hand under my arm pit and yanked me into a sitting position. Then he pulled me right into his arms. "Shit. Shit," he said, pressing his face into my cheek. "You are so fucking cold. I'm sorry. I'm so sorry."

That got my attention. "Why?" He'd come for me. It was all I ever wanted him to do.

He put two hands on my head and held me close, our faces still pressed together. His nose felt warm against my frigid cheek. "We have got to get you inside. I need you to stand up, Josh. There is a Motor Inn right over there." He pointed across the lot.

I simply shivered. My teeth started their dance, again.

"You walk, or I'll carry you," he said firmly.

We couldn't have that. So I pressed a hand down and tried to rise. I got vertical. But my knees weren't having it, and I ended up right back in the dirt a second later.

"Shit!" Caleb swore. That was four or five curses in four or five minutes. So something must be very wrong. I didn't care what it was, though, because I was just too sleepy.

"If I carry you into that lobby, they'll never give us a room," Caleb said. "Goddamnit."

I drowsed, while he fumed beside me.

"Josh," he patted my cheek. "Josh, listen."

"Yeah," I managed.

"I'm getting a room, and you're going to wait here."

"'Kay."

"I swear to the Lord in heaven that if you're not here when I get back in ten minutes, I will have a coronary. Because I'm already fucking scared enough."

I dozed.

THE NEXT TIME I regained consciousness, I was on a warm, soft surface. And Caleb was removing my clothes.

That should have been exciting, but I was too tired to care.

"That's it," he said as gentle hands tugged my trousers off. It got cooler again when he removed my socks. And there was a tussle over my undershirt, because I did not want to give it up.

"You've sweated through everything," he said quietly. "Damp

clothes aren't helping. Trust me, Joshy. You'll be warm in a minute."

But that was a lie.

Sure, he shifted me into a bed—a softer one than I'd ever had for my own. And sheets and blankets were laid upon me. But my teeth just wouldn't quit chattering, and I was shaking so hard my muscles were sore. "S...so cold," I complained.

"That's your fever talking," he said.

But then the bastard put something cold and wet on my forehead. "No," I argued, pushing it off.

"But I don't know what to *do*," he whispered. "I don't know how to help you. Don't you dare die, or I'll kill you myself."

I tried to decide whether that made any sense, and came to no conclusions. And then that cold thing hit my head again, and I gave a holler of protest.

"Sorry, baby," he whispered. "So sorry."

"Cold," I complained. "Please." I was begging, but I didn't even know what for. "Please. Please."

"Okay," he relented, tossing the cold thing away. "Okay. I'm sorry. I really am. This is all my fault."

I heard him moving around while I tried not to shake. It came in waves, actually. I could calm my body down for a minute or two. And then I found myself clenched up again and shaking like that old bean separator that I'd loved to watch. I shook and shook.

One more blanket landed on my body. And then the covers shifted, and the most glorious warmth settled at my back. I leaned in, where Caleb's warm body met mine. *Yes.* This was heaven. His skin pressed up against mine, his strong arms came around my chest and pulled me in.

I relaxed on a sigh and let sleep take me yet again.

CHAPTER THREE

Josh

When I woke up, I was in an unfamiliar room, where a set of ugly drapes blocked out most of the light. Slowly, several other facts began to present themselves to my foggy brain.

For one, I was naked in bed. Secondly, I was naked in bed with a very naked Caleb. And furthermore, his morning erection was poking me in the ass.

It was a scenario I'd been dreaming about all my life. But poor Caleb! He would be mortified.

Assorted memories of the night before were swirling through my sluggish head like a broken kaleidoscope. I remembered the shaking and some of the worried things he'd said. The bus station. The cold outdoors.

He'd been trying to keep me warm. *I'm so sorry*, he'd said.

It was a lot to take in. But it wouldn't be right to lie there with him any longer, now that I wasn't delirious.

Slowly, I slipped from his arms and out of the bed. Toward the back of the dim little room I spied a bathroom, and I headed for it. When I flipped the switch inside, the light came on, revealing all of my clothing and Caleb's, hanging from the shower bar.

When I touched these things, they were mostly dry. But not quite.

I pulled down the clothes and carried them out into the bedroom, where I laid them quietly on the heater under the window.

Caleb did not wake, or else he pretended not to.

I snuck back into the bathroom and turned on the shower, which rained down with a pleasant force.

At the Compound, there was never enough hot water for more than a quick shower. But now I washed my hair and body with a little bottle of shampoo I found in the hotel's shower stall, while the hot water came pouring down on me. After I was finished, I lingered awhile, basking in it. Because there was nobody to yell at me to get moving.

Then, feeling more refreshed than I had in a long time, I toweled off, listening to my stomach growl. There was a big mirror over the sink, which I found fascinating. We didn't have mirrors at the Compound, except for tiny ones in the shower, meant for shaving. Because vanity is a sin.

Except for the occasional reflection off of a window, I hadn't seen myself properly in years. I thought of myself as a scrawny thing. So I was surprised to find that my shoulders were much broader than they used to be. I looked stronger and more solid than I'd thought.

My face wasn't the same as I remembered, either. I saw a squarer jaw then I used to have, and my hair was bleached out from the summer's sunshine. *Not half bad*, I realized.

Standing there, I looked a long time at myself. Which was precisely why there were no mirrors in Paradise.

Wearing a towel, I tiptoed back in the room, testing the seams of my clothing again.

"They're not dry, I'll bet," Caleb said sleepily.

"Not quite," I said, keeping my voice low, though there was nobody else here to eavesdrop on us. I wasn't used to being alone

31

with Caleb. It seemed impossibly luxurious. Even better than a long shower.

If I'd thought he would be embarrassed to wake up in that bed with me, I'd thought wrong. He raised his arms up over his head, which made more of his fine chest visible, and smiled at me. "Happy to see you on your feet. Come here." He patted the empty bed beside him.

Feeling self-conscious, I padded over there and perched on the edge.

Caleb sat up, and I put all my focus on keeping my eyes where they should be, and not letting them wander down his bare chest. Ever since we were fifteen, and he began to fill out, the ridges and valleys of his abs have fascinated me. I've had to be very disciplined with myself, or I'd always be staring at them.

He reached up and put a palm on my forehead. "Well, you just got out of the shower, which should heat you up. But I think..." he leaned in and pressed his lips to my forehead, the way my mother used to check for fever when I was small.

All my blood stopped circulating.

"Hmm," he said, backing off a few inches. "You kicked it, didn't you? The fever broke?"

But speaking now would have been impossible. Because I was just too aware of his body, and the way his pecs had brushed mine when he'd (sort of) kissed me. So a shrug was all I could manage.

"We have to wait for our clothes to dry. Yours were coated in dirt," he said, grabbing his pillow and punching it against the headboard. He sat back. "Bring that knapsack over here, would you? I have a little food."

I shot up and practically sprinted across the room, needing a little distance. Sure enough, a sporty backpack sat on the floor. "That's Ezra's," I said, whirling around in shock.

Caleb chuckled. "It *was* Ezra's. As were the twenty-dollar bills I found inside it." Then his smile faded. "I shouldn't have taken so long at the compound, though. Trying to get supplies slowed me down. And then I had to hide near the gate for hours, because Abloom and Isaac were working on the irrigation line. I didn't know you'd be lying on the *ground*." He closed his eyes. "I didn't know."

"I'm okay," I said quickly. I brought him the backpack, then walked around the bed to my side.

"Can you eat? I have Miriam's corn bread." He pulled a loaf out of the bag. It was wrapped in wax paper.

I stared at that package. "She gave you the whole thing?"

He gave me a sad nod. "I went to say goodbye to her. It was only fair."

Wow. I couldn't imagine what that had been like. Saying goodbye forever to the girl you wanted to marry? "What did she say?"

Caleb blew out an unhappy breath. "She cried. And she said she didn't blame me." He shook his head, miserable. "She's the only thing that could even make me feel bad about leaving."

"I'll bet," I said. "You're in love with her."

Caleb tipped his head back and stared at the ceiling. "Is that what you think?"

"Well... yeah." *Wasn't he?*

"Never was," he said, his voice flat. "But I wanted people to think so."

"Why?"

He brought both hands up, draping them over his head. "If you don't know, I'll tell you sometime."

Okayyy. It wasn't like Caleb to be mysterious. But I didn't press him. "Can we eat cornbread now?"

With a sad grin, he said, "sure."

33

CHAPTER FOUR

Josh

"Check-out time is eleven o'clock," Caleb said, stepping into his jeans. "And we can't afford to stay another night. We couldn't really afford last night, either. But it was an emergency."

"How much did it cost?"

"Forty dollars. Which means I have about sixty left."

"I have fifty," I volunteered.

"I know. I found it in your filthy pants. Your money's in the knapsack now. Where'd you get fifty bucks?"

"They gave it to me. Told me to get on a bus and don't come back."

Caleb's scowl was fierce. "They gave you fifty bucks for a bus ticket, so that you wouldn't hang around here, and end up telling the police what happened to you. Those *assholes*."

I burst out laughing.

"What?"

"You're cursing. All the time! It's funny."

"I'm not living by any of their rules anymore, Josh. I'm not kidding. They think God doesn't like it when you curse? But God is *just fine* with throwing you out by the side of the *road?* Do you *hear* how messed up that is?"

The laughter died in my throat. I did hear it. And I didn't want to. My memories of the time I spent in the back of that truck getting tossed around like hay bales were too ugly to contemplate.

In spite of how lonely the hours afterward had been, I was glad that Caleb had not been there to see my humiliation—my most pathetic moment. There was a stain on my heart now, and I would never be able to remember my last minutes at the Compound without feeling low.

"Here," Caleb said, handing me my shirt. "Let's go find out how much bus tickets cost."

"To where?" I asked. Funny how I'd just gotten around to asking the most important question. It had been such a relief to find myself safe and with Caleb that I'd forgotten to worry that we had nothing and no one.

"Western Massachusetts," he said immediately. He shook out his sweater, another hand-made item from his mother.

"Where?"

"Remember Maggie?"

"Miriam's sister?"

He nodded. "She lives in Massachusetts with her husband." My mouth dropped open, and Caleb laughed. "You should see your face. It's true—her family knows where she is. They didn't hear from her for two years after she left. Then Maggie sent a UPS package to her father, disguised as a tool delivery." Their father was a metalsmith. "And there was a letter from her inside."

"So..." I cleared my throat. "Will we be welcome there?"

"Yeah, I think so. The letter said to send anyone their way who needed to leave."

"Even us?" I asked softly. He had to know what I meant. The boy who had just abandoned Miriam couldn't easily ask for help from her sister.

Caleb sighed. "Even us, okay? Because I think Maggie would want news from her sister. Even if it's bad. And did it ever occur to you that maybe I can help Miriam *more* from the outside?" His voice took on a gruff, irritated tone, which frightened me. Because Caleb never got angry with me.

"Okay," I said quickly. And I knew he'd try to help her. It's just that he and I weren't in the position to help anybody, and I didn't see how we would be, anytime soon.

"Let's go." He stuffed the last of our things into the backpack and zipped it up.

THE CLERK behind the ticket window at the bus station dashed our hopes in ten seconds flat. "Two hundred and forty-one dollars," she said.

"For both of us?" I asked, hopefully.

She shook her head. "Each."

"God *damn* it," Caleb muttered. That was the worst curse he'd said yet.

We turned away, disgusted. "Plan B is hitchhiking, I suppose," I said.

He grunted. "We could ask how far fifty dollars gets us. But that would leave us with almost nothing, and we're going to need food."

Outside, we turned toward the East, and started walking. Because that was the only logical thing to do. Logical, and yet ridiculous. Because we could not walk to Massachusetts.

"If we can't make it all the way there yet," I reasoned, "we could do farm work somewhere until we earned two hundred and forty one dollars. Each."

"In November?" Caleb asked.

Right. In April my plan might work. Or in August. But not November. It would snow here any day now.

We walked in silence for awhile, just trying on the idea of how bad things were. "I'm sorry," I said eventually.

Caleb stopped. "No, okay? You have nothing to be sorry for. *I'm* sorry."

"Why?"

"I just am. Leaving was always the plan, but I wasn't ready, and I should have been."

"It was *always* the plan? How long was always?"

"I dunno. A nice long time. I knew we had to go eventually."

"The two of us," I said, still not quite sure I believed him.

"Yes, Joshy, I always wanted to leave. With you."

"Why?"

Caleb groaned. "For a smart guy, you're kind of an idiot. I'll show you later. Right now, we need some kind soul to pick us up. Try to look safe and friendly."

"I *am* safe and friendly."

He turned to me with a chuckle, and then squeezed my arm. "I *know* that. But other people don't. So, smile!"

FOR HOURS, nobody picked us up. Caleb put his thumb in the air a million times. "You try it for a bit," he said. "You're better looking, anyway."

"Or at least less intimidating," I suggested. Nobody was better looking than Caleb, with his sparkling eyes and sculpted cheek bones.

The funny thing was, only five minutes passed before a pickup rumbled to a stop beside us. The passenger window lowered, and an old woman's face looked out. "It wouldn't be too comfortable, but you could ride in the truck bed if you want. We're heading to Cheyenne."

"Thank you so much," Caleb said immediately. "My brother and I are in a bit of a bind."

My brother and I. The thoughts I had about Caleb weren't

exactly brotherly. But I still liked hearing it. He'd claimed me, when others had not.

She got down out of the cab slowly, while her elderly husband gave us a squinty-eyed inspection. "Come on, then," she said.

Their truck had a shell on it. So she popped that open, and Caleb lowered the tailgate. We climbed in, and the woman hefted the gate and closed us in. There were rakes and shovels lining one side of the truck, so we sat on the other, our backs to the side.

"Well," Caleb said. "This was either a lucky break, or they're cannibals who are planning a barbecue right now."

I laughed, but my head was feeling woozy. With a groan, I tipped my head back against the side. "I still feel off," I said.

Caleb put a hand on my knee. "I'll bet you do. We'll get you some real food in Cheyenne. That will help."

The truck began to move, and I concentrated on the warmth of Caleb's hand, which miraculously was still on my leg. I drifted, waking frequently when the motion of the truck moved my body. My head was too heavy. There was no place I could rest it where it wouldn't bounce around and wake me up.

"Relax," Caleb whispered. He took my head in his hands, pinning it to the center of his chest with one hand.

That felt insanely good. And I was too sleepy to care that it wasn't really the way two friends were supposed to sit beside one another. I fell into a satisfying slumber.

"WAKE UP, BABY," someone said, rubbing my head with a big hand.

No thank you.

"Come on. They're going to open the doors. So you have to get off of me."

That got my attention. Even so, waking up hurt me. In the first place, I was completely comfortable, nestled in Caleb's arms.

Not only did I not want to be awake, I also did not want to deal with the embarrassment of waking up cuddling my best friend.

But he didn't say a word.

Lifting my head was difficult, but manageable. Caleb helped, by shifting my weight off his body. And just in time, because the tailgate creaked open, and the elderly driver appeared.

"Thank you so much," Caleb said in his most polite voice. *That* was the voice I recognized, far more than the new, cursing Caleb. For years, I'd heard him make nice to the elders, and to the other bachelors when he wanted to pacify someone.

"You're welcome," the old woman said, joining her husband and Caleb climbed out. "I hope you and your brother have safe travels. Please be careful."

"We will," Caleb said, shaking her hand. "And you too! God be with you."

She smiled a wrinkled smile, and I followed Caleb out of the truck. We were at a gas station, the biggest one I'd ever seen.

Caleb didn't say anything for a minute until we were well out of earshot. "My ass is numb," he complained.

"Sorry," I mumbled. My mouth felt like paste. "Do you have any water?"

"Sure." Caleb went into his backpack and pulled out a bottle, handing it to me. "This is a truck stop," he said, turning around. "A big one. That might be good."

"Yeah?"

"They might have a pawn shop. I have a couple things I could sell."

"You do?"

"Sure. But also — you never know. We could find somebody who was heading east, and offer them a hundred bucks to take the both of us. I mean, they're going anyway."

"That would be lucky. If they have room."

"Let's try it," he said, taking the water and downing a gulp for himself. "Put on that friendly face again."

But it was a no go.

Caleb approached maybe ten different guys as they waited for their massive tractor trailers to refuel. He got variations on one answer: "even if I was headed your way, it's against my truck line's policy to pick up hitchhikers."

I became thoroughly discouraged.

"It only takes one," Caleb reasoned. "Let's ask a couple more times. Then we'll take a break for supper. I'm starved. And a truck stop has to have food."

Caleb approached the mangiest looking guy we'd seen yet. He had stringy hair and a cigarette hanging out of his mouth. "Excuse me, sir. Is there any chance you're headed east?"

The guy looked up from the diesel pump and gave Caleb a crooked grin. "Might be. Who wants to know?"

"My brother and I are stranded. We've only got a hundred dollars, and we need to get as close to Massachusetts as we can."

"Is that right?" He shifted the cigarette from one side of his mouth to the other. Then he checked over his shoulder before speaking again. "I'll make you an offer. I'll get you as far as New York..."

"New York is good," Caleb said quickly.

"...But I need a favor from each of you. One favor a day until we get there."

Caleb's eyes went stormy, and I didn't know why.

"What favor?" I asked.

The greasy man laughed, shaking his head. "Blow jobs, moron."

Beside me, Caleb's jaw tightened. "No deal," he said through clenched teeth.

"Wait," I said. "What if..." But Caleb grabbed my arm and literally dragged me away, around the fuel pumps, and over to the side of the building.

It was getting dark already, but I didn't need any light to see the fury on Caleb's face. "Are you *crazy?* Do you even know what a blow job is?"

"Of *course* I know what a blow job is! But he's the only one who said he'd help us."

"No he did *not!*" Caleb hollered. We were toe to toe, and both of us angry, which never happened. "You can't *trust* a man who offers to drive you somewhere for blow jobs! And there are *diseases*, Josh. Bad ones."

He had a point. And I did not want to have anything to do with that freaky guy's body. But my whole life I'd been tortured by my craving for dicks. (Or at least one dick, anyway.) And it was almost as if God sent this other one into my path as some sort of cross to bear. If it solved our problem, I knew I could get through it. "I just thought..." I sighed. "You wouldn't have to watch."

Caleb's face contorted with disgust. He put two hands on my shoulders. "No. You're not going *near* that fucker. Over my dead body."

I did not point out that dead bodies were an increasing possibility if we did not find some kind of ride, job, or shelter soon.

"Boys." We looked up to see an older black man standing a few yards further down the wall. He was smoking a cigar. Removing it from his mouth, he pointed the cigar at Caleb. "He's right. There are guys who prey on young people out here. And you two look a little wet behind the ears."

I had no idea what *that* meant.

The man went back to smoking his cigar and looking the other direction, as if he was done with us.

"Caleb," I said, "let's not fight."

He took a deep breath and let it out again. "Okay. It's just that you keep scaring me to death."

"Don't mean to."

"I know."

"Hey. We're in Cheyenne, right?"

"Yeah. Just outside of it."

"The last thing Ezra said to me before he left me by the side of the road with my ankles taped together, was that there's a homeless shelter in Cheyenne. Maybe we should find it."

"He taped your *ankles* together?"

Once again, Caleb was getting off topic. "And my wrists, big brother. But he gave me that little piece of advice, too. Did you hear me?"

"I'm going to strangle that fucker."

I sighed. "No you're not. You're going to eat dinner with me, and then we're going to find a homeless shelter, whatever that is. And in the morning, we'll try some more hitchhiking."

"Okay," he said heavily. "At this rate, we're never getting to Massachusetts."

"That's the spirit."

Caleb smiled at me, which was always my downfall. So I didn't notice that the black man had come closer. "Boys," he said again. "I may be able to help you."

"Really?" I asked, hopeful for the first time all day.

He stubbed out his cigar on the wall. "It's against the rules. But you two sound like you need a break. Runaways, right?"

"No," I said, at the same time Caleb said "Yes."

The black man laughed. "I see."

"We were both honest," I explained. "He is a runaway, actually. But I got tossed."

The other man's eyebrows lifted, so Caleb tried to explain. "We grew up not too far from here, in a religious type of place."

"A cult," the man said.

I didn't know that word, but Caleb nodded.

"Polygamist?" he asked with a sour look on his face.

"Yeah," Caleb confirmed.

"Peachy," the man snorted. "The name's Washington." He held out a hand.

"Nice to meet you, Washington," Caleb said, shaking, "I'm Caleb and my brother is Josh."

"Your brother?" Washington asked, shaking my hand. "You two don't look alike."

"We get that a lot," Caleb said.

"Well, Caleb and Josh. I'm going to Albany. That's real close to Massachusetts. But before we get started, we're going to eat dinner."

I HAD NEVER BEEN inside a restaurant.

The place was oddly bright, but it smelled wonderful. I hadn't eaten a real meal in forty-eight hours. Miriam's cornbread was great, but we'd finished it eight hours ago.

A woman led us over to a table which had two bench seats facing inward. It was like sitting in a small room within a bigger room. I liked it immediately. Even better, she slid a glossy card onto the table in front of me, which listed everything under the sun. There was a whole section just for soups, and one beneath that for sandwiches. On the second page, there were "dinners." Just reading the card, I thought I'd expire from hunger. I wanted one of everything.

Then I noticed the prices, and scaled back my expectations. The steak was $19.99. Wow. And why didn't they just write $20? It wasn't like I was fooled.

When the waitress came back, Washington ordered a hamburger with French fries. Then she turned to me.

"A cup of chicken noodle soup," I said. Because it was only $1.99. And the menu promised crackers.

Caleb eyed me over the top of his menu. "Really?"

I nodded.

"Fine. I'll have two hamburgers with fries. And two Cokes."

The waitress took our menus and went away. "Two?" I had to ask.

Caleb rolled his eyes. "One is for you, genius. You haven't eaten in two days, and I didn't feel like arguing with you."

Oh. "I was trying to save money."

"I get that. But if you pass out, I have to carry your ass. Which I've done recently. And you're heavier than you look."

Well *that* was mortifying.

Washington didn't say anything, but his eyes laughed. He was sitting by himself on the opposite side of our table. I studied him, because it was either that or pinch Caleb, who had embarrassed me. (Pinching was our favorite form of silent retribution. Unlike a slap, a pinch could be accomplished without gaining unwanted attention from teachers, pastors, etc.)

Our new friend was interesting looking. There weren't any black men at Paradise. I'd met a few people with brown skin when we were little and went to school. But none of the elders ever had anything nice to say about black people. (Or about *me*, come to think of it.) This man had a trustworthy face, and kind eyes. I couldn't pin down his age, though. His skin was unwrinkled, but there was gray in his hair.

"What?" he asked me after a minute. "Do I have spinach in my teeth?"

"Sorry," I said. "I was just trying to figure out how old you are."

He grinned. "Fifty-seven. Got no children of my own, but I have nephews about your age." He paused while the waitress put two glasses and a cup of coffee on the table. "They're in college now," he said when she left.

"Lucky," Caleb said.

Washington shrugged. "You're young. Maybe a year from now, or two, you'll go to college."

"You never know," Caleb said, in a voice which did not sound all that optimistic.

"You finish high school?" Washington asked.

Caleb and I laughed at the same time.

"I guess that's a no."

"Weren't allowed to go to school with all the sinners," Caleb said. "God forbid we learn something that makes us less obedient."

"That's just sad, boy," Washington said. "You're better off away from that kind of place."

"I *know* that," Caleb said, with a glance at me. "But the dismount is pretty painful. Now, Josh. Try this." He pushed one of the glasses to me.

There was a brown liquid inside, and I could see bubbles clinging to the side of the glass. "Coffee?"

"Better," Caleb insisted. "It's Coke."

I took a sip, but ended up coughing because the bubbles tickled my nose.

Watching me, Caleb burst out laughing. "Man, we are going to have to work our way up to beer, I think." This set Washington off, too, so now they were both having a chuckle at my expense.

I didn't mind, though. Because the dark liquid was both tangy and sweet. I loved it. And since I was starving, the sugar felt like nectar going down.

"Wow," Washington said, shaking his head. "I'm sorry to laugh, but how have you never had a Coke?"

"Think of him as a prisoner released from jail, and you won't be far off."

"But you're not?" Washington asked.

I was wondering the same thing.

Caleb shook his head. "My grandpa was somebody important in the hierarchy. So they gave me a lot of the good jobs. I got to drive their trucks around, picking up things they needed. Did some errands. I got good at pinching a little of the change for a drink, or a candy bar. The best part was just being out in the world. I went to the public library in Casper sometimes to read the newspaper. I listened to the news on the radio, which is forbidden. I got just enough to know what I was missing."

Now I was just staring at him, my mouth hanging open. "You never told me most of that."

He looked sheepish. "It would have been mean, right? I did all this fun stuff today, I tried Coke. I ate a Twix bar and a taco." He shook his head. "I never brought anything back. I never even got into the truck with so much as a napkin or a wrapper. Too dangerous."

I didn't know how I felt about that. There was a time not too long ago when he and I told each other *everything*. And I was sad to hear all these things I hadn't known.

Yet I'd been hiding something huge and awful from Caleb for years, hadn't I? He'd have to eat a whole lot of sweets to make up for all my sins of omission.

The waitress reappeared with three plates on her two arms. And the next ten minutes were lost to me as I worshiped at the altar of my first truck stop burger with all the fixings, with giant slabs of fried potato.

Wow.

With a full belly, I found it possible to believe that everything just might be okay. Maybe.

CHAPTER FIVE

Josh

After dinner, we climbed into Washington's *giant* truck. I had wondered how Caleb and I were going to fit onto one passenger seat. I was picturing the overturned milk crate that we used on the compound between the seats of our flatbed truck cab.

But Washington's truck was roomy and gleaming. And there was even a bunk in the back.

"Somebody sits on the sleeper," the man said, waving a hand at the bed. "And somebody sits here and talks to me."

"Sit on the bed," Caleb ordered. "You look bushed."

"We'll take turns," I promised as Washington cranked the engine, and the big truck hummed to life. The bed was comfortable, though. I scooted back until my spine met the wall, leaving my legs sticking out.

The cab began to move, but I couldn't see out of the windows from where I sat.

"Where'd you grow up?" Caleb asked.

"Kentucky," Washington said. "Used to be a tobacco farmer, but trucking pays better…"

I'll bet we didn't travel two miles before I fell asleep.

47

～

WHEN I NEXT TUNED IN to the voices in the cab, I'd slumped over, with my head on the mattress. Washington's voice droned on in the driver's seat. I couldn't make myself pay attention until I heard him say, "is your brother okay?"

Caleb didn't answer right away. "He's had a rough couple of days. I'd be exhausted, too."

That was a good answer. It sounded better than, "he's getting over a flu, and breathing all over your bed."

"Can't imagine why someone throws away his own child," Washington muttered.

"That's... yeah," Caleb sighed. "His real father died young, so he didn't have a protector. That's who gets thrown out. It's all about the pecking order."

"Makes sense."

"I mean... if you ask Josh, he might tell you that he's not a good farmer, or not as strong as some. They've been telling him that all his life. But that's crap. Every year, perfectly good workers get tossed out. And all because the older guys each want four wives."

Washington gave an unhappy grunt. "I dunno. One wife seems like plenty most of the time."

They both laughed. But I was stuck on what Caleb had said. That we were here right now because of politics, and not because I couldn't throw a fifty pound bag of chicken feed onto a truck bed.

"You're not really brothers," Washington observed.

"Well," Caleb hedged. "Pretty close, though. Our mothers were friends. I never went a day of my life without sitting next to him."

"Hmm. You two had a kinda fucked up life. But most people don't have friends so close. Real community is rare now most places."

48

"Yeah? I never thought about it that way."

"You know," Washington said, "you ain't the first kids I ever helped. Usually I don't pick nobody up if he isn't real young. Like a teenager. And I never picked up two at once. But you two just don't smell like criminals."

"I don't know, Washington," Caleb teased. "Earlier I confessed to stealing candy money from the till." They had another chuckle, and the truck seemed to slow down. "Where are we stopping?"

"North Platte, Nebraska."

"Cool. My first time out of Wyoming."

"Christ, boy. Really?"

"Yessir."

"You amuse me. Both of you. First thing I ever heard you two talk about was whether your brother knew what a blow job was." He laughed, but then Washington's tone got more serious. "Imma get a room at that hotel right over there, and you two can sleep in the truck."

That prompted me to speak up for the first time in hours. "We can't take your bed."

Washington waved a dismissive hand. "I only spend every *other* night in that bunk, because I'm not a youngster anymore. There's a travel budget, and I haven't hit it too hard lately. I save up for emergencies, and this is one."

"I'll pay," I volunteered.

He shook his dark head. "Don't you worry. I get to watch some TV and take a long shower. Can't do that at a truck stop. But listen, I have some rules. I gotta take the keys with me, which means you two are going to visit the men's room now and take care of business while I fuel up. Then I lock you in."

"Okay," Caleb agreed.

"You have an emergency, you can leave the truck one at a time. Always stay in well-lit areas, okay? Truck stops are not all so great. This one is decent, but you never know. And *nobody* gets in this truck except for you."

"Sure," I said. "But who would want to?"

He chuckled. "Nobody you need to talk to. Lot lizards, for one. Those are prostitutes, and don't be tempted. Druggies, most of them, with angry pimps. Not safe. If anybody knocks who ain't me, that's bad news. They want to sell you drugs or pussy."

"That is not our way," Caleb promised.

"I'm sure that's true, but I gotta say it anyway. You two've never seen the good things in this country, but I'll bet you haven't seen the bad ones, neither. Trust *nobody*."

"Except for you. And us," Caleb joked.

Washington smiled. "My truck better be here when I get back. Don't steal from me. I like you guys."

"Never," Caleb said. "You're the first person who's been nice to us, pretty much ever."

"That's not true," I said as a reflex. "Your mother loves you. And Miriam."

"My mother never protected me from the men who used me like a cart horse. And Miriam can't help herself, because I'm awesome."

"Poor kid got no self-esteem," Washington joked. Then we all got out of the truck.

IN THE TRUCK stop men's room, I used Caleb's toothbrush and refilled his water bottle.

Washington was waiting for us beside the cab. "Sleep tight, and be safe," he said as we climbed in. "There's a blanket above the bunk. If you put that on the floor, one of you could stretch out there."

"You don't have to worry about us," I told him. "And we won't even touch the doors."

"I know. I'll come back around seven so we can get some

breakfast. Can't drive until eight, because there's a mandated ten hours off."

"See you at seven."

He slammed the door, and I watched him walk toward the hotel. When he disappeared, I turned to Caleb. "He's an angel in disguise."

"Something like that. You take the bed."

"No can do. I already slept there, some. You stretch out."

"You've been ill."

"I'm *not* an invalid, okay? Lie down."

Grumbling a little, he did. I sat in the roomy passenger seat, my stocking feet on the dash. A peaceful silence descended on us. Caleb was probably tired, but my nap had perked me up, and now my mind was busy just trying to process everything that had happened since yesterday morning.

Could things get any weirder?

For the first time in my life, I was a long way away from the compound. But it was weird to picture our room in the bunkhouse right now. Ezekiel and David would still be there, lying in their bunks like any other night. Were our two bunks empty? Or had they wasted no time moving two teenage boys into our spots?

That's probably what they'd done. *Cover up the violence. Nothing to see here.*

I wondered if my mother had been told. And I wondered if she cared. Caleb's mother would. And Miriam. "Poor Miriam," I said aloud. "I wonder when Asher will marry her."

From the bunk, Caleb groaned. "You're killing me, you know that?"

"Sorry."

"It's not like I don't feel guilty. But Josh, I couldn't save her."

"I understand," I said quickly.

But he wasn't finished. "See, I don't think you *do* understand.

51

Even if I asked for Miriam's hand, and by some miracle they allowed us to marry, it still wouldn't work."

"Why not?"

"A *lot* of reasons. Even if we got married, and somehow I'm able to build her a house, even though there isn't any more money for new houses..."

"There isn't?"

"No. That's why Ezra doesn't have a wife. The compound is broke. But even if all that weren't standing in the way, Miriam would still end up hating me."

"She would *never*."

Caleb thumped his hand on the mattress. "Yeah, she would. Because do you think they'd let me be the one guy with only one wife?"

I hadn't thought that far ahead. "I guess not."

"Right. So imagine I have two wives, then three. Miriam, plus a couple of poor young things who played with dolls when you and I were already working the farm. And it's the usual henhouse crap, everybody trying to figure out who's the favorite wife. Instead of saving Miriam, I get to be the guy who helps *break her soul*. Hooray for me."

"Oh," I said softly.

"Yeah. Not such a pretty picture, right? I don't want three wives. I don't even want one."

"You don't? Why?"

From the bunk came a big sigh. "No more talking tonight, okay? I can barely keep my eyes open."

Soon, soft snores came from the bed.

I sat up a long time, watching trucks pull in and out of the lot. And when I finally fell asleep, I dreamt about Caleb warming me up in the hotel bed the previous night. But the dream was a whole lot more interesting than the reality had been.

∾

BY MORNING, I had a cramped neck and stiff legs.

"You didn't stretch out?" Caleb asked. "I would have switched places with you."

"Didn't think of it," I lied. When I woke in the night, he'd looked so peaceful on the bunk that I didn't want to disturb him.

Breakfast was the Two Egg Special in the truck stop diner, a bargain at $2.99. I tried coffee, which I did not like, until Washington suggested adding some half and half. Then I liked it so well I drank every drop.

We saddled up at eight o'clock to drive all day. Caleb sat in front for awhile, while I napped on the bed. When we switched places, I enjoyed watching the scenery roll past the window. We passed Lincoln, and I made Washington laugh by remarking that it was a big city. Soon after, we passed Omaha, and then Des Moines, which both put Lincoln to shame.

We stopped for lunch (another heavenly burger) and dinner (a bowl of soup, because I wasn't very hungry for real this time.)

Washington bought a newspaper, and asked Caleb to read him the sports section out loud. I didn't understand half of what he was reading. First down? Punt? Touch back? It was like a different language.

When night fell, we hit Chicago, which was fascinating. And Washington said we weren't even in the *real* Chicago—just passing a lot of the sprawl to the south of it. But I still couldn't believe it. The nighttime lights seemed to stretch on forever. The sky wasn't even black here, it was a sort of orange color. You couldn't see any stars, because Chicago was just too bright.

I was staring at the strange sky when the truck bobbled a little, and something began to beep on the dashboard.

"Aw, shit," Washington said, gripping the big steering wheel tightly. "Hang on, boys!"

The road got very rough for a minute, and Washington braked hard, steering us down a shadowed exit ramp.

"What's the matter?" Caleb asked when we finally stopped moving. "Did you really just get a flat?"

"Sure did."

"Hell. Can we change it ourselves? Those big rims are probably dangerous."

"Correct, son. We gotta call a tire shop to come out and do it for us." He reached for his phone and dropped it into his shirt pocket. Then he unhooked his seatbelt.

"Is this gonna set you back?" Caleb worried. "I know you keep a tight schedule."

"Sure will. But that ain't the biggest problem. This is *not* in a good place to be stranded. And I gotta set flares, it's a safety regulation." He removed a molded plastic box from under the driver's seat and popped it open. "Imma be right back. Now stay in the truck, you hear? This here is a *shitty* neighborhood. With a capital 'shit.' You sit tight."

When Washington left the truck, Caleb slid into the driver's seat, watching from the rear-view mirror. After the flares were set, Washington stood in front of his truck, making his phone call. Then he took a walk around the truck again to look at the tire.

Although this stretch of road was awfully quiet, before long, a car stopped, pulling up in front of us.

"That is *not* the tire truck. That guy looks like a real punk," Caleb said unhappily. "And why would you park right there, if you weren't trying to look intimidating?"

I looked, and saw that *two* guys got out of the sedan. Both of them were all muscle, wearing T-shirts with the arms ripped off, and bandanas tied on their heads.

Slowly, as if trying not to make any noise, Caleb eased the driver's door open a couple of inches so that he could listen.

The men walked slowly toward Washington, their eyes roaming the truck.

"Get down," Caleb hissed. He and I dipped our heads to avoid attention.

"What you hauling, old man?" one of the men asked Washington. "You need some help?"

"No thank you. I already called roadside assistance. They're on the way."

"Why don't you show us what's in the truck?"

All the hair stood up on the back of my neck.

Washington's voice was calm, though. "Can't do that, son. Against the rules. I need this job. The load is for a paper company, though. Couldn't be nothing too interesting."

That was a lie, though. Washington had told us last night that he was hauling a whole lot of bottled wine for a California distributor.

Caleb ducked down, grabbing his backpack off the floor.

"What are you doing?" I whispered.

He didn't answer me.

Outside, the men had stepped even closer to Washington, and now I was sweating. "Where your keys at?" the bigger man pressed.

"Don't do that," Washington warned. "Roadside is going to pull up, anyway."

"I don't see nobody coming."

I couldn't see Washington now, I could only hear his voice. But the next thing he said was, "*get* your hands off me!"

"Where's your wallet, pops? Is it in your cab? *Yo*. Check the cab!"

And now I was in a full panic.

Caleb grabbed my wrist. "Josh," he hissed. "Don't *move* from your seat unless one of those guys is climbing in here." The next second he disappeared out the door.

I held my breath, wondering what he thought he was going to do to help. And that's when I heard the cock of a gun.

My heart seized as I pictured Caleb at the wrong end of the gun.

But it was his voice that shouted, "Get the *fuck* away from him before I *fuck* you both up!"

I couldn't see him, though, so my heart was in my throat until the two men reappeared in my line of vision, hurrying back into the car.

Seconds later, they pulled away, tires squealing.

Caleb climbed back into the cab, followed by Washington, who looked as if might explode. I scooted into the back to make room for both of them. The driver slammed the door, then rounded on Caleb. "What the fuck was that? You have a *gun* in my cab?"

Caleb pointed the weapon at the floor and offered it to Washington. "Take a look. It's not loaded."

Washington palmed the gun and then inspected it, and all the while his face was a raging storm.

"I'm sorry," Caleb said. "I stole it from the Compound because it has value. I wanted to pawn it." His guilty eyes weren't looking at Washington anymore, though. They flicked to *me*.

"This could get us in *buckets* of trouble," Washington spat. "Could get *me* in trouble! Right now, if the police pull up to see why I'm stopped, and they search this place? I got a weapon and no license? I'm arrested."

"I'm so sorry."

"You got anything else in that bag?"

Caleb kicked it over to Washington. "Not a thing. Look for yourself."

"Am I going to find the ammo?"

"I didn't steal the ammo. It's heavy, and I didn't know if it was valuable."

Washington groaned. "Boy, are you shitting me right now? Because you just *looked* like you knew your way around a gun. That's why those punks ran off."

"I *do* know my way around a gun. Been shooting coyotes since I was twelve. Most of our acreage was cattle. I've never shot at anything on two legs, though, unless you count the paper cut-out at target practice."

With a sigh, Washington buried his forehead in his hand. "You better pray the police don't show their faces. I'm not taking the rap for this."

"Yessir."

"Yessir," Washington muttered. "Such a *nice* boy — with an unlicensed handgun. You swear there's nothing else in here that can get a guy locked up? Weed? Blow?"

"No sir."

Maybe Washington was over it already, but I wasn't. "Do *I* get to look in the backpack?" I was disgusted with all that I'd just learned.

Caleb trained his weary eyes on mine. "I'm *sorry*, Josh. I should have told you about the gun."

I felt the inconvenient sting of tears hit the back of my throat. "You got me thrown out of the compound for stealing something you took!"

He sighed. "Everything is *so* fucked up. I took that gun to get some cash, so I could leave with you."

"*With me*," I spat. "Are you sure?"

He looked stricken. "Of *course* I'm sure!"

"I don't believe you."

"Why the hell not?"

Washington was watching our drama play out, but I didn't care. "You felt *guilty* about getting me tossed. That's why you left."

"The timing sucked, Josh. I won't argue with that. And I *forgot* that you always did that fucking inventory, okay? I took the gun because neither one of us had ever used it. But it was just my shitty luck that they noticed right away. I didn't even steal it but one day before! And then the fucking *inventory*." He put his head in his hands.

I rolled to face the wall, shutting Caleb out, trying to think.

Suddenly, everything looked so different to me. Caleb never meant to leave Miriam behind at all. But he'd had to, because he'd inadvertently got me tossed. He obviously thought I couldn't manage to stay alive by myself. He couldn't have that on his conscience.

The truth settled into my stomach like a chunk of lead.

It was so quiet in the truck right then that you could hear the engine cooling. But finally the tire guys arrived, and Washington and Caleb got out of the truck. I stayed behind, curled into a ball on the bunk.

The tire was changed, somehow. I didn't watch. And when Caleb and Washington returned to the truck, Caleb came into the back to see me. He sat down and put a hand on my back. "I'm sorry," he said gently.

I ignored him.

But I was sorry, too. So sorry to be so useless all the time.

After a little while Caleb gave up the vigil and went back to sit in the passenger seat.

"We're stopping for the night at the next exit," Washington said eventually. "You two can wash up, and then stay in the truck again. Same rules as last night."

"Thank you sir," Caleb said quietly.

CHAPTER SIX

Josh

When Washington left us to go to his hotel, I was still snubbing Caleb. The truck door was locked, but I hadn't spoken to him yet. I slid into the passenger seat and looked out the side window.

"Have the bunk," Caleb offered. He was still trying to get me to say something.

"No thanks," I mumbled.

Caleb sat down on the bunk with a long sigh. "I don't get why you're so pissed at me. We couldn't stay at the Compound, anyway. If it wasn't now, they would have tossed you some other time. And it wasn't just *you*, Josh. Suppose my grandfather died? Or one of his allies stabbed him in the back? They would have tossed me, too. We were *always* going to end up where we are right now. Gun or no gun."

For every word that he added to his excuses, my heart ached. "Stop, okay? Just *stop* trying to make me believe you. If you keep pretending that you *meant* to run away with me, I just feel worse."

"Josh," he gasped. "I'm not pretending. It's my life, and I wasn't going to spend it in that little fucking *wasteland*."

"I get that. But I think you meant to run with Miriam."

"Oh good *God*," he thundered. "That's just not true! How many times do I have to say it?"

"You can stop anytime," I said miserably. For two days, I'd been so happy he was with me. Being with Caleb was all I ever wanted, even if I couldn't have him the *way* that I wanted. And now I was sure it was all a big mistake.

For a few minutes it was very, very quiet.

"Josh," he said eventually, his voice thick. "I didn't want to do this here. In a truck, at a gas station."

"Do what?"

He took a deep breath and let it out. "Come here."

I'd been feeling so sullen that I almost didn't obey. But since it was almost impossible for me to refuse Caleb anything, I swung out of the passenger's seat and went over to the bunk. Caleb sat up, patting the edge of the mattress.

I perched on the edge, and Caleb tilted his head, studying me. I let myself look into his eyes. It was allowed, because that's what he was doing. "I'm going to try something, and hopefully you won't freak out."

"Okay?" That was a strange thing to say. But even though I had no clue what came next, I wasn't nervous. I could never be afraid of Caleb. It just wasn't possible. I could be angry at him sometimes. But never afraid.

"Turn toward me."

I shifted my knees so that I faced him more directly.

Caleb reached a hand up to cup the side of my face, dragging his rough thumb across my top lip.

I stopped breathing.

His lips parted. Then he slowly leaned in, until his face was an inch from mine. His thumb still stroked my face. I was having an out of body experience, probably. Or dreaming. But it felt so real. And then...

My brain flickered out as his lips brushed mine. I heard a gasp, which had come from my own chest. And then Caleb *kissed* me.

His mouth slanted over mine, and the moistness of his lips was too real to be a dream. Too sweet to be a hallucination.

I moaned, leaning into the kiss. My whole life I'd wanted this impossible thing. And I didn't know why it was happening now. But it was everything I'd ever wanted. One kiss led to another. And another! Without my permission, my shaking hands made their way onto the flannel covering Caleb's chest. And I pressed my palms against those pecs that I'd been admiring since we were fifteen. His chest felt as broad and solid as I'd always known it would. Caleb groaned, and I felt the vibration under my wandering fingers.

Strong arms snaked around my waist, and Caleb pulled me closer. One of his hands wandered down my back, leaving tingles in its wake. That big palm ended its journey on my ass, where it gave me a squeeze.

I moaned again. *More. More, more, more.* That became my new chant.

Just when I didn't think it could get any better, Caleb's tongue swept into my mouth. That's when all thought became impossible. There was just Caleb, and the sweet taste of his mouth, and the fire in my heart for this man. His whiskers scratched my face, made my lips raw. And I *loved* it. Every huff of breath. Every foreign sensation. He was in my arms, and I was never letting go.

Except then he gave a low, masculine growl and began to suck on my tongue. That sweet suction was overwhelming. It was so good. So, so good. *Too* good. I felt my balls tighten in a dangerous way.

I yanked myself back. "Stop," I gasped. I was panting like a farm dog after a good run through the brush.

Caleb froze. His arms released me immediately. He placed a single hand in the center of my chest. "I'm sorry, baby. That was too much. I'm sorry. It's just... I..."

I'd never heard Caleb stammer before, and my lust-filled brain couldn't really handle anymore talking right now. I put a hand up, sloppily, and covered his mouth. "Shh... it's just. It's..." I took a deep breath and tried to clear my head. "I don't understand."

With a sigh, he pulled me toward him again, but this time we landed in a hug. He put his chin on my shoulder. "I know. Didn't mean to shock you. But... I know you've thought about this before."

"You do?" I asked. He *knew?*

His big palm began to rub sweet circles into my back. "Yeah. You're not very good at hiding it."

"I'm not?" I began to panic. Because hiding was essential. It could save my life.

"Not from me, you aren't. You're always staring at my ass when you think I'm not looking."

"Not true," I argued. I would argue this point until the day I died. Because it was *essential* to avoid being transparent.

He pulled back, tilting his head to the side, considering me with a look of amusement. "Really? I could swear you had my ass memorized."

The look on his face was so soft that I wanted to put it in my pocket and keep it forever. "Not true. Sometimes," I swallowed. "Sometimes I'm staring at your chest. Or your face."

He grinned.

"But..." now that my heart rate had begun to decline back into the safe zone, I was actually more confused. "You never stare at *me*." What did it all mean, anyway? I couldn't wrap my head around anything that had just happened on this bunk. I'd just... revealed my true self. And for what?

"Josh, I only let people see what I want them to see," he whispered.

"Lucky."

He shook his head. "I haven't been honest with anyone for years. I don't feel so lucky."

"So you..." I cleared my throat, because this wasn't easy to say out loud. In fact, I'd never said it out loud, about anyone. "Like men?"

He put a hand on my chest again. "Yeah. Especially this one."

The warmth of his hand was divine. But my head still rang with questions. "How do I not know this?" I'd just spent the last several years cowering from this secret. *Miserable* over it. And he knew?

He spread his fingers on my pecs, which felt mighty fine, even if I was still confused. "What was I supposed to say? If we'd talked about it, that would only make us sad. And doing anything about it would only have put us in danger. You *know* that."

He wasn't wrong. But it was still difficult to process. "I thought you wanted Miriam." My head was spinning. I had to reorganize my understanding of my *whole life*, now. It didn't seem possible.

He closed his eyes. "Don't make me talk about her again."

"*Why?* If you don't love her."

"Because she *guessed*, okay? A couple of years ago she asked me if I was in love with you. I guess I wasn't as good an actor as I thought. Because she was only fifteen, and she figured it out. That was a tricky conversation. But then last month she said, 'please, let's get married. We understand each other. This way, we won't end up with people who'll hurt us.'"

"Oh." Miriam was smarter than I was, obviously. Just like everyone.

"Hey," Caleb cupped my cheek again. "I never want you to feel bad. We get to be honest with each other now. I've been *dying*, Josh. Wanting you. Wanting to tell you. I'm sorry if I scared you just now."

"You didn't. You never could," I said. His thumb continued to trace a sensuous path around my face. It swept my cheekbones, then my nose. I just wanted to close my eyes and sink back into him.

"Then why did you stop me before?" he asked, removing that thumb that I loved so much.

"Because," I whispered. "I was about to..." I let out a shuddering breath. "...And we can't make a mess in Washington's bunk."

Caleb let out a bark of laughter. Then he kissed me on the cheek. Then he did it again, because once wasn't enough. "Come to bed with me. I won't let you make a mess."

Now my body was on *fire,* just because he said the word *bed.* "Don't know if that's possible," I stammered.

Still laughing, he pulled off my sweater. "Trust me, okay?"

Trust me, he said. The thing was, I'd trusted him my whole life. And, if this night was to be believed, the Caleb I'd trusted was a different one than I thought.

I did not know how to feel about that.

Yet his fingers brushed my chest as he began to unbutton my shirt. And then Caleb began removing *his* shirt. My Caleb. He shucked it off, and then he stood up and stripped down to his boxer shorts right in front of my eyes. And—God have mercy on my soul — his erection tented the front of his boxer shorts. I stared and stared.

With a chuckle, Caleb caught me under the chin with his hand. "You're catching flies," he said.

I slammed my jaw shut.

"Come on, now," he said, patting my cheek. "Get in bed with me."

Still feeling shaky, I kicked off my shoes, and took off my trousers. I left my T-shirt and briefs on.

"Put the blanket on the floor, like he told us to," Caleb suggested. "If we hear him at the door, one of us can roll down like we'd been there all night."

"You are sneaky."

"You have no idea." He got into the bunk and held the covers aside for me.

I followed him, lying down on my side. *Getting into bed with Caleb.* I shivered, just from excitement.

He didn't make me wait. Caleb pulled me into his arms and kissed me. And I was *gone*. There was nothing better than this. I pushed my tongue into his mouth to taste him. And he pushed it out, chasing me into my mouth, tangling his tongue with mine. I was moaning already, and I didn't think I could stop.

The reality of kissing him was so much better than my daydreams. My fantasies never had much to go on. I'd always just had a vague idea that I wanted his skin on mine, and his hands on my body. But my poor daydreams had never accounted for the sweet slide of his soft lips against mine, or the rough feeling of his two-day beard on my neck.

It was all amazing — every little sensation. But they were coming on with more speed than I could even process. We were cocooned into each other. His hard body bumped and tussled with mine. The rest of the world ceased to exist.

Nobody had ever thrown me away.

There were no mistakes.

No lies.

There was only the heat of his mouth and the exquisite stroke of a hard cock bumping against mine. I wanted to touch it so badly. And the wanting made me crazy.

Again, I pulled back. "We have to stop. I can't take it."

His teeth flashed with a smile in the dark. Then he reached down and eased the elastic of my briefs over the throbbing head of my erection.

"Caleb!" I gasped. "What are you doing?"

"Told you I wouldn't let you make a mess. Gonna use my mouth on you. I'm going to suck you off, and swallow everything you've got."

A wave of burning hot lust shot down my spine. I flexed my hips upward, because I just had to.

Caleb yanked down my underwear and moved, until he was

kneeling over my body. And before I could even prepare myself, he'd bent his head down to lap his tongue against my cockhead.

My shout of approval could probably be heard all over Nebraska.

A big hand grasped the base of my shaft. Then, he began to bathe my dick in kisses. Wet, sloppy kisses *everywhere*.

My hips began shaking with excitement. "Oh, Caleb. I can't..."

He opened his mouth and sucked me down.

I never felt anything so amazing in my life. His mouth was tight and wet all around me. He gave a good hard suck. Just one. And then I was coming. And Caleb was swallowing. My whole body shook with joy. Caleb moaned and he cupped my balls in one hand and I'd forgotten to breathe for entirely too long...

A few seconds later I lay gasping for air. I draped an arm over my eyes, because I was depleted and there were so many things I could not face. Like Caleb, for starters.

"Mmm," he said, still stroking my sac with his thumb. "You have a beautiful cock. And now I know how you taste."

I wanted to die of shame.

"Baby, are you okay?"

No. Not at all. But please feel free to call me 'baby' again. Anytime you want.

"Josh?" He crept back up and lay beside me. "Didn't you like it?"

I peeked at him from under my hand. He was still the same, calm Caleb that I'd always known. "I never liked anything more," I admitted. "But we shouldn't have done it."

Maybe another man would have gotten mad. But Caleb just reached up a hand and pushed the damp hair off my forehead. "I wanted to wait until we were somewhere more... secure," he said. "But I'm not going to feel guilty about this. And I hope you won't, either."

I squeezed my eyes shut. "It's a sin."

"No," he whispered, still stroking my face. "Hurting someone is a sin. Did I hurt you?"

"No."

"Does this hurt someone else? Are you going to marry a woman, Josh? Am I keeping you from that?"

"No," I sighed. It was funny, but I'd always known I wouldn't marry a woman. A wife would never be found for me at Paradise. And not once had I felt bad about it.

"I know it hasn't even been forty-eight hours," he said quietly. "It's going to take you a while to leave that place behind. I'm sorry. I should have waited. I'm just so tired of holding it all at bay."

I really didn't want him apologizing to me. I reached up, circling him in my arms, pulling him down beside me. "I love you." I could say that without guilt. Because loving someone wasn't a sin. Other things... sure. But love could never be a crime.

"Aw," he whispered, curling into my body. "I love you, too. So much. That's what I've been trying to tell you. Except I sucked your dick instead."

Pushing my face into his neck, I laughed. He kissed me on the ear. Then he nibbled my jaw. "Hang on a second," he said, sliding off the bed. I heard him fumbling around in the backpack. He took out the water bottle and gulped some of it down.

"I expect you'd need that," I muttered.

He tossed the bottle down and put a knee onto the little bed, looming over me. Then he put his wet mouth onto mine and kissed me long and hard. "Gonna be a lot of work, getting you over all your hang-ups," he said. "But I'm just the man for the job. Now move over some."

I rolled onto my side, facing the wall. He curled his bigger body around me, which felt ridiculously good. I pressed back against him, looking for even more contact. But then his very hard cock ended up between my ass cheeks.

He pushed his hips against me once, then groaned. "Okay.

That's a game for a different day." Then he settled onto his back instead.

I swiveled, too, until I was facing him. Caleb put an arm around me, pulling me part-way on his body, my head on his shoulder. I draped one leg over his muscular one. But I was careful to say clear of his crotch. "I'm, um, sorry that you're still..." I could not finish that sentence aloud.

"Horny?" he chuckled. "I've been horny my whole life. What's one more night? Or ten."

"Are you..." I cleared my throat. "A virgin?" Some of the boys weren't, even though they were supposed to be.

"Of course. You're the only one I ever wanted to fuck."

And my face was on fire again.

"Remember when we were young, and I asked you to stand guard while I jerked?"

"I'll never forget it."

"Yeah? Well I was hoping to make a habit of it. I wanted you to play along. I don't know. I think I wanted to ease you into the idea that we could have sex. But I freaked you out, didn't I? You looked like you'd seen the devil."

I groaned into Caleb's shoulder. "I was hard for a month afterwards. I used to save up paper napkins from dinner so I'd have something to wipe up all my messes."

Caleb snorted. "I'm pretty sure every boy who ever slept in that bunkhouse did the same thing. It's just that they were thinking about the daughters when they yanked it."

My head was now filled with the image of a dozen bachelors lying on their bunks stroking their penises. Naturally, mine began to harden against Caleb's hip.

He rubbed my back. "You want me," he said simply. "It's just that you don't *want* to want me."

"I've always wanted you. And I've always tried not to."

"What if you stopped trying?" He pinched my ass for emphasis. "Never mind. We have forever to think about this. Right now, we should sleep."

"I don't know if I can."

"Do you want me to move?"

"No," I said immediately, tucking my ear against his chest. "Don't move. Not ever."

He kissed me on top of the head.

It took awhile. But eventually Caleb's breathing became long and even. I lay there for hours, filled with wonder, having no idea what was supposed to happen next. Nothing had ever felt better than lying in Caleb's arms.

My whole life I'd wished for things. But I'd never known how confusing it might be to see my wishes come true. And then there was the problem of our complete destitution...

"Caleb," I whispered softly.

"Mmm?"

"What's going to happen to us?"

"Dunno," he mumbled. "'Cept we're going to stay together while we figure it out. No matter what."

"Okay," I breathed.

"Sleep now," he ordered.

So I did.

CHAPTER SEVEN

Josh

I woke up because Caleb rolled off the bed. At first, I thought he'd fallen. I shook off my sleep to peer over the edge to see if he was okay.

But he was already struggling into his jeans down there, and that was when I heard the sound of the truck's door levering open. "Morning," Washington's voice called out.

"Morning," I said quickly, to cover the sounds of Caleb's fumbling.

"Everybody decent?" he asked.

"Mostly. Caleb, are my trousers down there with you?"

"Think so," he mumbled, sounding sleepy. "Here."

I threw my legs over the side and slid into them. "We're good."

Washington pulled himself into the cab and shut the door against the chill. "Ain't the heater on? It's cold in here again."

"Not really," I said quickly.

"Don't think we needed it last night," Caleb added.

My neck got hot. We did not, in fact, need the heater. Because we'd spent the night in each other's arms. I was mortified by the idea. And yet I couldn't wait to do it again.

Washington held out a card that read *Motor Days Motel* on it. "You two can have a shower. Room 302. Just make it quick."

"Thank you sir," Caleb said.

I followed him out of the truck.

CALEB and I each took a quick shower. I entirely avoided looking at his body during that fifteen minute stretch. Because I was still shocked by what we'd done. I had to tuck the idea of going to bed with Caleb away into a corner of my mind, if only to allow the rest of my brain to function properly.

We met Washington on the sidewalk outside the restaurant. "Okay, here's the plan," he said. "Josh and I are sittin' down to breakfast. And you're going to go into that little store..." he pointed a cocoa finger at a sign reading *Pat's Pawn Shop*. "They'll take that gun off your hands. You won't get a lot of money for it, but you won't be carrying an unlicensed gun around, either."

"Okay," Caleb said sheepishly.

"Whatever price they quote, you name a slightly higher one," Washington said. "Say, aw come on. This is worth double. You should pay at least twenty five bucks more."

Caleb grinned. "Good plan. Wish me luck."

In the diner, Washington and I got a table, and I ordered breakfast for both Caleb and myself.

"You know what he likes, huh?" Washington asked, passing me the half and half for my coffee.

"Um..." I shrugged, my face hot. I felt different today. Marked. As if anyone could look at me and know what had happened between us last night. "There was never quite enough food where we lived, and we never got to choose anything. The two egg breakfast has bacon, anyway, which we don't usually get. Not at breakfast, that's for sure."

Washington shook his head. "You can have two wives, but no bacon for breakfast."

"The men who are married can have anything they want," I corrected him. "The bachelors just take whatever the families send along. We did the work they told us to, and ate the food they felt like bringing us."

"That is a bum deal," Washington said.

"Yes sir, it is. It *was*."

He grinned.

Caleb slid onto the bench beside me, also smiling. "Got $250. Maybe he ripped me off, but I'll never know."

"They make you sign a bunch of papers?"

"Yeah," Caleb grunted. "If the gun was used in a crime, they could trace it back to the Compound. But it was only in that tool-shed a couple of weeks. I don't think there's a risk."

This time, when the breakfast check came, Caleb did not bother to calculate our share. He just put down money for the whole thing. "Our treat," he said. "It's not much of a contribution, but..."

Washington shook his head and deposited a five dollar bill in front of Caleb. "You can't treat until we get you sorted out. By tonight we'll be in Albany. So it's time for you to make a phone call."

"We, uh..." Caleb looked sheepish. "Our friend is somewhere in Western Massachusetts. We're just going to have to go there and look around."

"We don't know her number," I clarified.

"Naw," Washington protested. "That's not how we do things in the twenty-first century. We can Google her. What's the name?" He pulled out his phone. It had no buttons, only a slick shiny surface. I thought it was the most beautiful thing I'd ever seen. "Hope her name's not Jane Smith. If it's something unusual, that helps."

"It's Magdalene, but she goes by Maggie. And her last name is Beaufort, unless she changed it."

Washington winked at me. "There can't be too many Magdalene Beaufort's in New England. Spell it for me." He tapped the letters into a little keyboard that appeared on the screen as Caleb spelled them out.

"Uh huh," Washington said, and a smile spread across his face. "That's right! I got a hit in Cheshire, Mass."

Caleb snapped his fingers. "That's it. I remember thinking that it sounded like something from *Alice in Wonderland*."

Washington tapped on the screen a couple more times. "The name comes up on a website for a farm. It's called the Runaway Dairy. Strange name for a farm."

"She *was* a runaway, though," I said. "I think that's intentional."

Washington took the last sip of his coffee. "You mean, she *wants* to be found?"

"Yeah," Caleb agreed. "She wants her family to find her if they need her."

"Are you family?" Washington asked. "Because it's time to make the call. The number is right here."

I saw Caleb swallow hard. "I guess I'm about to find out if I'm family." He put his palm out, and Washington tapped the screen one more time, then handed the phone over.

Caleb put the phone to his ear and closed his eyes.

Under the table I put my knee against his, and he pressed back against me. I waited, holding my breath.

"Uh, hello sir? I was hoping to speak to Maggie Beaufort?" He cleared his throat. "Yes, this is... a friend of her sister Miriam's. Thank you, sir." He looked sideways at me. "I think I just spoke to Maggie's husband."

"Wow." My stomach bottomed out from nerves. What if she told us not to come?

"Maggie? This is Caleb Smith. Do you remember me?" An

73

audible squeal came from the phone's tiny speaker, and Caleb grinned. "I'm well! And you?" He listened for a minute, then took a deep breath. "So, I've left the Compound, and I'm with Joshua Royce. Do you remember h...?" Another squeal, and Caleb grinned. "We wouldn't want to inconvenience you too bad, but were hoping you could help us get on our feet."

As I watched Caleb, he put his head in his hand, dropping his eyes to the table. "That would be..." he choked on the words a little bit. "That would be great. Thank you, Maggie. You don't know how much we... yeah. Okay. Thank you. We've got ourselves a ride toward Albany. From a trucker. A trucker we owe big. And he said we'd get there some time after midnight. Not sure how we'll get to Massachusetts, yet."

He blinked, and I saw that his eyes were glistening. I'm positive I never saw Caleb tear up before. "We thought about busses, but they're pretty expensive... The route? I'm not sure. Hold on just one second." He looked up at Washington. "What route are you taking? I'm sorry."

Washington winked. "May I speak to your friend?"

Caleb handed over the phone.

"Good day, Miss Maggie," Washington said, grinning. "I have two fine young men here who need a little help."

I nudged Caleb. "What did she *say?*"

"She said they keep an extra room in their house, just hoping that somebody from the Compound turns up."

"That's... wow."

"I know."

"What about Fishkill, New York?" Washington was saying. "That's right off 84. Uh huh. Exactly. Bunch of little hotels right there. Holiday Inn Express is one. It's not a bad spot. I've stayed there. Okay. It's a deal. Thank you, ma'am."

He handed the phone back to Caleb. "Hello? Okay. In Fishkill? If you say so. I don't know where that is." He grinned. "Wow. Tomorrow morning. That's amazing. Okay, Maggie. I can't wait to see you. We'll tell you everything we know. Thank you!"

He hung up, and then smiled. "They're going to drive down for us in the morning, after they milk the cows. It's two hours, so she said that would be about ten."

Washington slapped the table and grinned.

I smiled too, because it was contagious. "Maggie has milkers? No way!" We were going to see Miriam's sister. And Massachusetts. And there was a room for people who needed a room.

Astonishing.

Caleb pushed his leg against mine again, and I'd never felt so optimistic in my life as I did right then.

I COULD BARELY TOLERATE that day's ten hours of driving, because I just wanted to get there so bad. But Caleb was in a lively mood, sitting up front playing a guessing game with Washington. This came about when Washington had expressed dismay that Caleb and I had learned so little after the third grade. Caleb had joked that he wished there were a way to earn a living reciting the good book, because he and I could clean up.

So the two of them were trying to stump each other, and Caleb had just scored a point for: "my soul melteth for heaviness."

Washington couldn't guess it, so I called out "Psalm 119," from the bunk.

"Eh," Washington complained. "The King James version is the problem. I know that verse as 'my soul is wasted with sorrow.' Just figures that your people would pick the ugliest translation there is."

It did, in fact, just figure.

About a year later (although I may be exaggerating) we finally exited the highway in Fishkill, New York. Washington pulled the truck over on the shoulder. "I'm not gonna be able to park at that hotel, boys. So Imma gonna say goodbye to you right now." He fished his wallet out of his back pocket and pulled out a card. "This is my home address, and my cell phone number. You have a problem finding your friends, you call me. But I don't expect that to happen. I *do* expect, however, to get a letter from y'all after you get settled."

"Thank you, Washington," I said quietly. "Thank you for saving us."

"You boys gonna save yourselves. I just helped a little bit."

"We do appreciate it, though," Caleb said.

"I know." He put the truck in gear. "See that sign lit up ahead? You're going into the Holiday Inn. Maggie made a reservation in Caleb's name. If you have any trouble, call me quick, so I'm not too far down the road when the phone rings."

"We'll be fine," I assured him.

"I know it. Your friend Maggie sounded like the best kind of lady. Now you two get ready to hop out, before I get all emotional."

Caleb laughed as the truck slowed to a stop on the street in front of the hotel. "We'll write you," he promised opening the door.

"You'd better."

Caleb moved aside, which allowed me to jump down first. After a moment, he followed me. But I saw him drop something onto the seat before he slammed the big door.

"What was that?" I asked.

"Two hundred bucks from the pawn shop money," he said.

"Sneaky."

"Wish I had more to give him."

So did I.

~

THE HOTEL LOBBY was shinier than the other two hotels I'd seen on our journey. The woman behind the desk found our reservation right away. "Your room has been pre-paid. Let's see... we've assigned you number 112, which has two double beds."

"Awesome," Caleb said.

The discussion of beds gave me a twinge of discomfort. I was used to hiding my desires from the world. But now Caleb was my accomplice.

We were told where to find the restaurant, and that check-out time was noon. Then we went to find room number 112.

CHAPTER EIGHT

Josh

The door opened with a click. We walked inside, and Caleb shut it behind us. Then he leaned on the door and sighed. "How lucky are we?"

"So lucky that it cannot be measured," I said, looking around the tidy room. I kicked off my shoes, and then thought better of it. "Should we go eat something? Are you hungry?"

Caleb gave me a wolfish grin. "Not for food."

Oh. A dangerous tingle settled into my groin, just from the look on his face. I looked away. I took off my jacket, and stripped off my sweater. I was tired of wearing the same less-than-clean clothes. "Tomorrow we can do laundry, maybe," I said. It wasn't that I wanted to discuss laundry. But I was feeling self-conscious all of a sudden, now that I was alone in a bedroom with Caleb.

If Caleb had an opinion about laundry, I didn't hear it. He walked over to one of the beds, yanking down the covers, exposing the sheets. Then he began to methodically remove all his clothes. He didn't stop at the sweater, like I had. His shirt, T-shirt, jeans and socks all hit the deck.

I swallowed hard as he removed his boxers, tossing them

aside. He lay down on his back, gloriously naked. I just stood there, while my mouth went dry and my dick went hard at the same time.

Caleb put a hand down to his semi-hard cock and gave it a slow stroke. Then he raised smoky eyes to mine and smiled. "Josh, I know you're not as comfortable with the idea of touching me as I am with the idea of touching you. But I need to get off. I've been hard for twenty-four hours. Or twenty years, depending on how you count. So I'm going to take care of that problem whether you help or not."

I took a long blink.

He chuckled. Then, with one hand, he teased his own nipple. "Mmm," he said, shifting suggestively. "Sometimes I think about you sucking on me right here. And right here," he moved his hand languidly across his chest, tweaking his other nipple.

Lord help me. I wanted to do exactly what he suggested. But I wasn't sure I should. Slowly, I removed my trousers, leaving my boxers on.

With his other hand, Caleb cupped his balls. "You could touch me here, sometime," he said. "And here." He moved his hand onto his cock. "Yeah, just like that," he said, stroking. I'd never actually seen Caleb erect before. We'd changed in the same room many times, but usually I tried to look away. And last night he had stayed covered up.

So this was the first time I'd ever seen what I'd been dreaming about for years. He was beautiful—so thick and blush-colored, with a fat cock head that I just wanted to lick.

And it was pointing at me.

I found myself dipping a hand into my own boxer shorts. Just from watching him, my own dick was as hard as a fencepost. I gave it a squeeze. And you couldn't have paid me to look away from Caleb as he slowly touched himself. There wasn't enough money in the world.

But my feet were still rooted to the hotel carpeting, even as I began to match him stroke for stroke. He turned lazy eyes to my body and grinned. "Maybe you're not ready to touch me tonight. But if you're going to jerk, I need you to lose the boxers. I want to watch you come."

Letting out a hot breath, I dropped my boxers onto the floor. And I shucked off my T-shirt, as well.

When I turned toward him, naked now, Caleb groaned. His eyes raked over my body, and he began stroking himself faster. "You are so beautiful, baby. I know you're worried about sin. I get it. But those idiots who taught you to be afraid? They say touching *yourself* is a sin. And touching *me* is a sin. So why is one so much worse than the other?"

The man made a very good point.

"Josh," he rasped, slowing down his strokes. His hips were canting off the bed with each languorous touch. "Will you please kiss me while I come?" His eyes had gone glassy, the lids hooded. "Please," he begged, stroking himself. "Maybe I'm a sinner, but it feels so good."

With a groan, I gave in. I scrambled onto the bed, then stretched my body out on top of his, the way I'd always wanted to. He was hot, solid muscle beneath me. And our cocks lined up beside each other, like they were meant to be there.

"Oh, yeah..." he moaned. "Want you so bad." He arched his neck to lean in for the kiss, which went hot and wild, right away. He jammed his tongue in my mouth, moaning. Our dicks scraped together, and it was the best thing I'd ever felt.

"Caleb," I panted, just because I wanted to say his name. Everywhere under me was his skin. His big hands grabbed my hips, which were already moving. Every time I pushed hard against him, I thought I might die of joy.

"That's it," he panted. "Fuck yourself against me until you come. I want you to spray all over my belly."

"I don't..." I gasped between kisses, "want it to end."

"Yeah you do. Come like you need to. You can have me again whenever you want." He reached a hand down between our bodies, taking both of our pricks in his big hand. "Oh, fuck. *Mouth*, baby."

I kissed him hard, and he gave me his tongue. Straining against him, I let all my inhibitions go. And a few minutes later, we were both moaning and erupting into Caleb's hand. He slicked us both with our warm seed. It was beautiful and shocking all at once.

Finally, I collapsed onto his sticky body, and he wrapped both his arms around my back. "Thank you," he whispered. "I needed that so much. When I get to touch you, every awful day we've survived seems worth it."

For me, speech wasn't even possible yet. I'd never come so hard. Since I couldn't make conversation, I kissed him slowly. I trailed my tongue along his scruffy jaw. I sucked his earlobe into my mouth. Meanwhile, he ran a hand up and down my back.

I touched him as much as I wanted, but I did not let myself think about the consequences of what we'd just done. The guilt would kick in later, anyway.

It always did.

"We need a shower," Caleb said eventually.

"Yeah."

He pinched my ass. "Let's go together."

UNDER THE WARM SPRAY, he soaped up my chest with his hands, touching me gently. Then he shampooed my hair. It felt so good. It was so *tender*. Nobody had taken so much care of me before. It was embarrassing how much I enjoyed it. Of course, I got to return the favor. We stayed in there a long time, just letting our hands travel everywhere they'd always wanted to go.

I was hard again by the time we got out. So I wrapped a towel around my waist, but Caleb pulled it off. "This is as much privacy as we're going to have for a long time. Don't cover yourself."

Caleb walked naked into the bedroom and got between the sheets. I followed him, wondering which bed I should sleep in.

"Get over here," he said, patting the mattress.

"I thought you might want to stretch out." Sleeping in the truck hadn't been all that comfortable.

He grinned. "I want to stretch out on you."

I got into bed feeling both aroused and euphoric. Sleep seemed impossible. Caleb rolled onto his side, curving his bigger body around mine. Once again, his hard dick bumped my ass. "Someday I want to fuck you," he announced. "I know you're not ready."

Truly, I wasn't.

He began massaging my back, his big hands soothing my weary muscles again and again.

"I love you, Caleb," I said.

He kissed the back of my neck. "I love you, too. And that's never going to change."

I grinned into the pillow.

EVENTUALLY SLEEP CAME FOR ME. The soft bed and the heat of Caleb's body put me under. When I opened my eyes hours later, there were two unfamiliar sights. The first was the hotel room. The second was Caleb's hard cock, which appeared right in front of my eyes. Upside down.

It took me a groggy moment to realize that Caleb had turned the wrong way around on the bed, and was nuzzling my balls with his lips. A warm tongue began licking the base of my morning erection.

"Oh, Lord," I gasped.

A muffled chuckle came from my groin. "Somebody swore."

I had, too. And I thought I was probably going to do it again. Because that *tongue*. It was shameless. My cock was bathed in wet licks and kisses.

In front of me, maybe a foot away, I saw a bead of milky liquid appear on the tip of Caleb's cock. He was hard and leaking for me.

Reaching out, I closed my hand around him. He gave a happy gasp as I began to stroke. The only dick I'd ever held before was mine. His was hot and throbbing under my hand, the way I'd always hoped he would be.

"Good morning," Caleb whispered from below.

My answer was a shout, because he chose that second to suck me all the way into his mouth. "Ahh!" I gasped. I'd never get used to that. It was heaven.

Caleb moaned, and the vibration made my cock practically sing. I began to thrust my hips gently, because I was lying on my side, and holding still seemed impossible. In my hand, Caleb's dick was undulating gently, the darkened tip only a couple of inches of my mouth.

Feeling impossibly bold, I opened my mouth, allowing that pretty cock to hit my tongue when I drew it near.

His moan was loud enough to wake the neighborhood. So I got bolder and took more of him in my mouth, taking care to keep my teeth away.

But he was too thick. I gagged immediately when his cock hit the back of my tongue.

Caleb stilled his hips, reaching up to put a hand on my hip. "Easy, baby. Try just taking the tip."

That was much better. I wrapped my hand around the base of him, and sucked on the top half. And that was fun, because Caleb began moaning up a storm. So I did it again. Harder. I loved the musky, slightly salty taste of him. Pure Caleb.

"Oh God!" he gasped. "Oh, shit. I..." he pulled his hips back. "Look out."

But I didn't want to look out. I went up onto one elbow and leaned over his body, bathing his cock with my mouth.

The first salty spurt still took me by surprise, so I swallowed on instinct. Then I just kept swallowing, keeping up with all the creamy seed he gave me. And Caleb made noises like the world was ending. And it occurred to me that nobody had ever done this for him before. Maybe I'd craved him all my life, but I was *his* first, too. I felt powerful because of it.

By the time it was over, Caleb lay spread-eagled on the sheets, his chest heaving. His eyes were shut, but he spoke. "All right. If I died right now, I'd still have lived a very full life."

That just made me smile. "Don't, though," I said, dropping a hand onto his muscular thigh.

He grabbed my wrist and tugged me down, onto his chest. "That was..." he groaned instead of finishing the sentence. "There aren't words."

I snuggled into his neck. He was slightly sweaty from our activities. "Did you happen to look at the time? Now would be a bad time for Maggie to knock on that door."

"It's only eight." He palmed my ass with two hands and squeezed. "We still have time for me to finish you."

"No rush," I said. But my erection begged to differ.

Caleb chuckled, as his hand found my throbbing length, palming it. "You are going to get it so good." I groaned, and he laughed. "Let's have you on your side."

Obediently, I shifted my body into position. He grabbed my top knee, raising it into the air, planting my foot on the bed. I was sort of spread open for him, and it felt awfully dirty. I wasn't sure I liked it.

But then Caleb began to drop little kisses in my groin. He nosed through the hair above my cock, kissing me tenderly. Then he traveled down again, cupping my sac in one hand. Kissing me there. It was dirty and tender at the same time. And I began to float on the loveliness of it all.

Then he got down to business, taking me into his mouth. The first time he'd done this, it was shocking and fast and frantic. This time, I let myself drink in the sensation of his wet mouth all around me. He went slowly, too. As if he knew I wanted it to last a bit longer.

It was building, though. I began to shift my hips out of necessity.

"Mmm," Caleb said. Then he released me for a second, and I heard a wet sound, as if he'd sucked his own fingers. When he went back to work on me, one of his hands gently separated the cheeks of my ass. And then one wet finger teased my hole.

"Oh," I gasped. It was a revelation to me how good that felt.

"You like that?" he whispered. He made the wet sound on his finger again, and then that devilish, slippery finger began to tease me in earnest. I moaned, and he quickened his pace. He dove onto my cock, giving me a good, hard suck. And then another one.

I squeezed my ass around his naughty finger and came hard, making sounds I didn't know I was capable of making.

"Yeah," Caleb whispered, licking me clean. "So perfect." He climbed up to meet me. "I'm going to kiss you now," he warned. Then he dropped his mouth over mine, and tasted myself on his kiss.

"That was crazy," I said eventually.

"Crazy good? Or Crazy-and-now-you're-a-sinner?"

I turned my face away. "Both. But don't make fun."

"I'm sorry," he said, sounding worried. "But every time we touch each other, I feel more certain, not less."

"Certain of what?"

"Of this," he said immediately. "Of living my own life, the way I want to. It isn't just that it feels *good*." He squeezed my hand. "Although it sure the hell does. It also feels *right*."

"Really? Because I doubt Maggie is going to see it your way."

Caleb was silent, although his thumb stroked my knuckles. "I don't know what Maggie would think. But she's just one person."

"A pretty important one."

"She's doing us a big favor, to be sure. But that doesn't mean I have to take a wife someday to make her happy. Let's just see how things go at Maggie's house. The plan is to stay there a short time, anyway. Until we get on our feet."

"We need jobs," I said, stating the obvious.

"I'm hoping I can get work as a mechanic. But it's going to be harder for you."

"No kidding," I grumbled. "Nobody would set me loose on their car."

Caleb gave me a little squeeze. "That isn't what I meant. You don't have any I.D. Nobody can hire you legally without it."

I raised my head off the bed. "Really?"

He nodded. "Sometimes people get hired off the books, usually because they're illegal immigrants. But it's harder."

I flopped back again. "Well that stinks."

"A little," he said. "But there might be a way we can get you an ID. Maggie might know how. Come on, let's shower again." He gave my hand a little tug. "Then we can eat breakfast."

TO SAVE MONEY, we skipped the hotel restaurant. Caleb ran down the road to a place called McDonald's, because he said it would be the cheapest.

I tidied up our hotel room, and moped. Because I hadn't known that my lack of ID would be an issue. I never got a birth certificate, because my mother was not my father's first wife. The Compound couldn't tell the state about all the babies born there, probably because our Divine Pastor was trying to conceal all the polygamy. So only the children of the first wives got birth certificates. Like Caleb, who also had a driver's license.

Caleb came back with a tasty, salty egg sandwich for me. And a Coke, because I'd liked the one at the other restaurant. "Thank you," I said.

He touched my shoulder. "I'd give you anything. You know that, right?"

Maybe he would. But I didn't like being the person who always took. And if I couldn't get a job, that's exactly who I was going to be.

AT EXACTLY TEN O'CLOCK, our hotel room phone rang. Caleb gave me a nervous smile and answered it. "Hi," he said. "Room 112. I'll open the door."

He hung up, grinning. "Let's go! Just let me..." He grabbed his backpack off the floor, and I tossed my coat over my arm.

Caleb turned around slowly, eyeing the room, probably to make sure we hadn't left anything behind. Without comment, he went over to the other bed, the one we'd never used. And he yanked the covers down, leaving them in a tangle, just like they were on our bed. "Okay," he said, without meeting my eyes. "Let's find Maggie."

I opened the door and stepped out onto the sidewalk. And there she was! An older version of Miriam waddled toward us, a big smile on her face, and a giant belly protruding from between the halves of her wool coat.

"Hi!" she yelled, starting to run. When she reached us, she threw her arms around Caleb.

Behind her, a tall, grinning man with wavy brown hair jogged to catch up to us.

Maggie released Caleb, then lunged at me. I caught the hug, awkwardly. Because you don't hold another man's wife. It just wasn't done.

"Wow," I said, flustered. I took a big step back. "You're... wow. In a family way."

The man behind Maggie burst out laughing.

"I'm sorry," I said quickly. "I shouldn't..." My face was heating, and I didn't know what to say.

"Daniel," Maggie warned. "Don't laugh."

He held two hands up. "I didn't mean to. But I never heard anyone put it that way, except in *Little House on the Prairie*." Daniel looked to be about twenty-five, if I had to guess. The same age as Maggie.

Maggie put both hands on her belly and smiled at me. "You can just say 'pregnant.' Everyone else does. Josh, Caleb, this is my husband, Daniel."

"Nice to meet you, sir," Caleb said, extending a hand.

Daniel shook it, biting back a smile. "You definitely don't need to call me 'sir.' I'm just Daniel." He shook my hand, too. "Do you need anything before we go?"

"No s..." I stopped myself.

Daniel laughed again. "Our truck is over there."

They had a red pickup truck with a passenger cab. Daniel popped open the little door that led to the back seat, and I climbed inside, followed by Caleb. Daniel helped his wife into the passenger's seat, then went around to climb into the driver's.

"Give me another week and I won't even be able to get into this truck," Maggie complained. "It's getting ridiculous."

"When, um...?" I said, afraid of making Daniel laugh again.

"Another two weeks. And already I can't see my toes."

"Your first?" Caleb asked.

Maggie turned to see our faces over the seat back. "Our first! We've been married about two years, and we bought our farm at just about the same time. The farm isn't our full time work, though. Daniel is a carpenter and I help out a friend with her catering business."

"Carpentry," Caleb said as the truck turned onto a narrow

highway. "I always wanted that job on the Compound. But I'm a mechanic instead."

"Well, there's steady work for mechanics. And the pay is good," Daniel remarked.

"Is it? I have no idea. And I need a job, whether it pays well or not."

Maggie turned our way again. "I know you'll be eager to figure that out, but I don't want you to panic. I told you on the phone last night that we had a room ready, and I wasn't kidding. When we got married, I told Daniel that I was a package deal. If anyone came along from the Compound who needed a place to live, I wanted to be ready. I'm kind of stunned that nobody has turned up before. Has anyone else left, recently?"

"Yeah," Caleb said softly. "There've been plenty. But none from your family."

"Tell me about my family," she asked.

Caleb cleared his throat. "Your mother is still doing her embroidery. There's a new design from her on my mother's table-cloth. Your father does his thing in the smithy shop. Something's always breaking, so they keep him busy."

"And Miriam?"

My stomach dropped, and I watched Caleb lick his lips. "She's afraid. It sounds like they want her to marry soon."

"Damn it," Maggie swore under her breath. "I always hoped she'd find a way to marry *you*. I've been praying for that."

I couldn't even look at Caleb then.

"...I mean, I know they wouldn't allow it," she said quickly. "They don't give girls like Miriam to a twenty year old just starting out."

Daniel made an unhappy noise. "It kills me to hear you say 'give girls like Miriam.' You can't *give* somebody."

"But they do," I argued. It came out more forcefully than I would have liked. But I felt I needed to defend poor Caleb.

Daniel gave an exaggerated shudder. "I know. But *damn*."

"Do I want to know who is asking for her?" Maggie asked.

"Not really." Caleb said, his voice low. "It's Asher."

"Christ on a cracker," Maggie said. "We have to get her out of there."

"I want to try," Caleb agreed.

CHAPTER NINE

Josh

Maggie and Daniel's farm was on a low, round hill. The barn was red, and set back from the road. A second outbuilding rose up in the rear, and the sign on it read *Daniel Lacey's Furniture*. "Nice place," I said as the truck came to a halt beside a white farmhouse. "Wow."

"Oh, wait until a pipe bursts, or the wind starts blowing through the cracks in the walls," Maggie laughed. "It's cool and old, but it's also old and cold. But we love it. Every creaky inch. Come and see."

We stepped into a drafty little space that Maggie called the mud room, where all the shoes and jackets were hung. "We keep this door closed," she said, opening the way into the kitchen, "because it keeps the drafts out."

"Some of the drafts," Daniel corrected.

The kitchen had wide plank pine floors, and an ancient refrigerator. But the cabinets and countertops looked new, and the other appliances gleamed. "We're redoing this a little at a time," she explained. "Daniel built all of the cabinetry."

"Wow," I said again. I was saying that a lot.

"Now, our room and the new baby's room are upstairs. But

down here there's a living room," she pointed toward the front of the house. "And your room is this way." She turned toward the rear, and we followed.

"The laundry room is there," she pointed toward the right as she passed a doorway.

"We could, uh, stand to use that," I said.

She turned around, stopping our progress. "Any time, Josh. I'm not kidding. I mean for you to make yourselves at home. And I brought a couple of Daniel's things downstairs..." she stepped into the room at the end of the hallway, "and left them on the bed. I think Josh can fit these clothes, but I'm not sure about Caleb. We'll hit a Target store tomorrow or the next day."

We all came to a stop in a sunlit room with a queen-sized bed and a blue quilt. "This dresser is empty," she laid a hand on an antique piece of furniture, "for your things, when you have some. But there's no closet, so I put that armoire against the wall. And the bathroom is the nicest part. See?"

There was a narrow little door in the corner. When I peered inside, I saw a sunny bathroom with a big clawfoot tub. "Nice."

"We put that in ourselves. The laundry is on the other side of that wall, so the plumbing was easy." She clapped her hands together. "Obviously, the only real drawback here is that there's only one bed. For some reason it never occurred to me that the first people to show up would be two guys."

There was a beat of silence while I wondered what to say. I'd been practically sleeping *on* Caleb these past two nights. But I'd never admit it. "Maggie, we'll be *fine*. We shared a smaller room than this with four guys in it on the Compound. There's plenty of room here."

She tapped her chin. "I suppose one of you could sleep on the sofa if you weren't comfortable."

"There's no problem," Caleb said quickly. "We spent two nights in a truck, scared out of our minds. This is like heaven."

"Okay. Daniel built this bed just for this room, and his parents have stayed here before. They live in California. But maybe if his business slows down, he could make a couple of twin beds. He's pretty busy right now."

"Busy is good," I said, eager for the change of topic.

She lifted a pair of sweatpants off the bed and held them up to Caleb. "These will do, if only for laundry day."

"You have no idea," Caleb said, "how much this means to us."

She tilted her head sideways and took in the both of us. "Actually, I do. Someday I'll tell you about my runaway days. But right now, I have to make some lunch. Help yourselves to the washing machine."

Caleb and I closed the door to our room and changed into Daniel's clothes. I put on the jeans, which fit me well, as long as I turned up the cuffs once. It was great to pull on clean socks, even if poor Daniel's closet had been raided on our behalf.

I gathered up all our stale-smelling laundry in my arms, and Caleb put his hand on the doorknob. When I came close, he kissed my cheek. "We're going to be okay," he said. "You know that, right?"

"Yeah. Even if this is weird."

He opened the door, and then the two of us went into the laundry room to puzzle over the settings on Maggie's washing machine. "The choices are normal, casual, or delicate," Caleb said. "Which one, do you think?"

I dropped my voice. "We're definitely not normal."

Caleb snickered. "Casual?"

"Sure?"

"Fine. But now we need to pick hot, warm, or cold."

"Um...?"

Maggie poked her head in the room, grinning. "I just realized that you would have no idea how to operate a washer. Did you put in soap?"

Caleb shook his head. "Didn't get up to that part, yet."

"How funny are you two? I forget, honestly. It's been five

years. I *forget* that a man never touches a washer at the Compound, or sets foot in the kitchen. Now I get to teach you both to cook, right? It's a life skill. And it will amuse me." She giggled to herself, grabbing a bottle of detergent off the floor. "Fill it just to here," she showed me a line on the cap. "And let's see... those settings are fine. Pull that dial out to start it."

I gave the dial a tug, and felt the washer kick into motion. And it felt like the start of a whole new life.

CHAPTER TEN

Dear Washington,

Thank you for all your help!

We have arrived safely at Maggie and Daniel's place. Things are a little hectic because they are expecting their first baby in just a couple of weeks. But Maggie promises that we aren't underfoot, and we're welcome to stay as long as we need to.

Caleb is anxious to find a job right away. But all the garages in the area are a thirty minute drive in various directions, and he has to borrow Maggie's car or Daniel's truck if he wants to visit them. So it's taking him a while.

In the meantime, Caleb is learning how to use Daniel's computer, and I'm learning how to milk cows. Since I can't get a job yet (I have no ID, and no transportation,) I want to help Daniel and Maggie in the barn as much as I can.

I enjoy it, actually. Cows are good company. They look forward to seeing me at milking time, and they never get too ruffled about anything. Daniel sells his raw milk to an organic yogurt maker down the road, who picks it up every morning at ten.

When the baby comes, Daniel and Maggie are going to have their hands full, so I figure milking is the least I can do.

That's all our news, I guess. It might not sound like much, but we're ridiculously happy to be here. Thank you for all your help. I have no idea how we would have made it here without you. Caleb used Google to calculate that you drove us 1,750 miles.

We appreciate every one of them.

SINCERELY,
    Joshua Royce

CHAPTER ELEVEN

Dear Josh,

I am so happy to hear how well you're doing. When I got home, I told my wife Brenda all about you two. She said you sounded like nice boys.

That was tricky of Caleb to leave me his money. Would you thank him for me?

I never wanted money, though. But there is something you can do for me. When you run across someone who needs help, just do the same for *him*. Maybe it will take a while before you figure out who that will be. Just keep your eyes open, okay?

Don't be a stranger. Let me know how you're doing. I like hearing from you.

George Washington
(That's my real name. Don't laugh too hard.)

PART II

CHAPTER TWELVE

Caleb

Our first days with Maggie and Daniel were filled with small awkwardnesses, as Josh and I tried to figure out how to fit into their lives.

Daniel had his carpentry workshop out back, and he spent his working hours there. But in the evenings, he must have found his own house crowded.

After supper, we all watched television in the living room. "Think of it as cultural education," Maggie said. The first night, she had us all watching a show she liked about a bunch of rich, stuffy British people. But Josh and I had never had a television, so we were happy to watch anything.

The next night was Daniel's pick, and he put on a football game. "We have to teach you to be Patriots fans," he said during the commercial break.

But football had a million rules, and just when things got going, all the players would end up in a heap on the turf. Everything stopped while the camera focused on ornery looking coaches, with their earphones on, and gum in their mouths. The announcers would say a whole lot of nothing, and show the play seventeen more times, in slow motion.

The best part of football, as far as I could tell, was all those muscular athletes running around in very tight pants.

During a commercial, Maggie wandered in and sat down beside her husband, lowering her round body into the sofa with a deep sigh.

"Hey, babe. Can you get me a beer?" Daniel asked, giving her a nudge with his elbow.

Now, I thought it was pretty cold of him to wait until Maggie had gotten comfortable. But even so, what happened next surprised me. Maggie smacked Daniel in the chest and said, "you *asshole*."

Out of the corner of my eye, I saw Josh brace himself.

But Daniel just tipped his head back and laughed. Then he jumped off the sofa. "I'm going to get a drink, does anyone need anything?"

"I'm fine," Maggie said. "But you're scaring Josh and Caleb."

"Why? Because beer is a sin?"

She shook her head. "Because they expected you to backhand me for calling you an asshole."

It was true. In Paradise, the women waited on their husbands. Always. And backtalk resulted in punishment.

"Jeez." Daniel put a hand on his wife's head. "You can call me whatever you want, babe. Just don't call me late for supper." He disappeared into the kitchen, then reappeared a few minutes later with three bottles of beer and a glass of water for his pregnant wife.

Even though I was feeling bad about living off of Daniel, I accepted the beer. "This will be my first one," I said.

His eyes went wide. "*Ever?*"

"Ever."

He shook his head. "Wow. I'm honored."

Maggie put her hand on his knee. "A long time ago I said that I hoped you'd meet more of us. Because then you'd understand me better."

He took a deep gulp of his beer. "It does clear a few things up. It does."

"Do you two remember Isaac and Leah Abraham?" Maggie asked us. "You must have been pretty young when they ran away from Paradise."

"Sort of," I said. "I mean, I know the Abrahams family. But they don't talk about Isaac."

"Of course they don't. The Compound doesn't like to admit its failures." Maggie smiled. "Isaac and Leah are married, and they have the cutest toddler. They live in Vermont, about ninety miles from here. I talk to them a couple times a year. And guess who showed up on their doorstep one day? Zachariah Holtz."

"No way!" I said, laughing. "I love that guy. He talked me through my first oil change."

Josh snorted beside me. "Oh, the memories."

"Stop," I said, chuckling. "Zach's departure was the reason I got my cushy garage job. I always wondered what happened to him."

"He's working on a farm just down the road from Isaac and Leah," Maggie said. It's a big apple orchard."

"Glad to hear it."

"It took him a year to find his footing," Maggie said quietly. "It takes all of us a while to figure out where we're headed next. So don't panic, okay?"

"Okay," I said slowly. "Thank you."

I'd probably panic, though. A year was a long time to impose, even on someone as nice as Maggie.

LIFE GOT a little more comfortable as the four of us developed something of a household rhythm.

The cows were milked early in the morning and then again in the late afternoon. Although Josh had never shown much interest in the beef steers on the Compound, he took a shine to the dozen Jerseys that Daniel and Maggie kept. Each morning when I woke up, Josh was already outside, helping with the milking.

Sometimes I went out there with them, especially in the afternoon. But it wasn't for the sake of the cows. I loved watching Josh handle them. "Come here, pretty girl," he'd say, leading a big-eyed Jersey to the milking post. As his long, patient fingers nudged their flanks along, the cows blinked their long lashes at him.

After milking, Josh would come into the house smelling of a mix of sweet hay and clean sweat. I was aching for him, all the time. But every night we climbed into that bed together, Josh always kept to his own side of the mattress.

"Aren't you going to come over here and kiss me?" I asked the first night.

"Not in Maggie's house," he whispered. "They could hear."

"Hear a kiss?" I'd pressed.

But he didn't answer. He just turned his back to me.

This bothered me. A lot.

I didn't ask again, even though I wanted to. If that's how he needed things to be, I wasn't going to force the issue. So I stayed on my own pillow when we turned out the lights.

In the middle of the night, though, I would sometimes wake up to find Josh curled up to me, his long leg thrown over mine, his arm across my waist. I could bury my nose in his hair, and hold him. A sleeping Josh was an affectionate Josh. Since it was all I got from him, it would have to do for now.

But when morning came, I always woke up alone. And he did his level best not to undress me with his eyes anymore. (I never should have told him that I'd noticed.)

What kept me sane during these early days was my belief that our stay at Maggie and Daniel's was temporary. I knew I was employable as a mechanic. All I needed was a job — any job — and then we could make our way forward.

But finding work proved tricky. Since the Runaway Farm was

in a rural area, that meant a twenty minute drive to the nearest grocery, and a thirty minute drive to any of a few different automotive shops. And I didn't have a vehicle. So if I wanted to go anywhere, I had to borrow the truck, or Maggie's little Prius.

Then, when I managed to find the garage in question, they were always busy. "Come back in the early afternoon sometime," I was told by one shop. "Come back on a Thursday," another suggested.

Yet with Maggie expecting her baby soon, it was a busy time. She took us clothes shopping. Maggie put our new things on her credit card, which I hated.

"You can't get a job without clothes," she argued. "It isn't all that much money."

But that simply wasn't true. Every day that I couldn't work we were living off their cash. We ate their food, wore clothes they'd bought, and washed them with Maggie's supply of laundry soap. I felt as though I was digging a deep hole, with no way to fill it.

Josh seemed calmer than I felt. He milked cows, and he helped Maggie paint an old rocking chair she'd bought for the baby's room.

From late morning to early evening, Daniel worked by himself. "He's trying to finish a bunch of pieces before the baby comes," Maggie told us. "Because it's going to be hectic around here."

I asked Daniel if there was anything I could help him with in the shop, but he usually turned me down, unless there was sanding to do. "I would love to train you for more. But I'm on such a tear right now that I can't even stop to do that. Maybe after the baby comes."

Though I hoped I'd have a paying job by then. One garage I visited had asked me to fill out an application. So now I couldn't stop listening for the phone to ring, and it made me feel edgy.

Meanwhile, Maggie was making plans for childbirth. "I'm not going to do this at home, like the women at the Compound.

When the baby comes, I'll be away for two nights, at the hospital in North Adams," Maggie told us.

We'd already noticed the doctor's phone number on the refrigerator. The big note tacked up there read, IN CASE OF EMERGENCY: MAGGIE'S DOCTOR, with a phone number.

"... And Daniel's parents will fly out at some point. So you'll meet them."

"We can sleep on the couch," I said quickly.

Maggie shook her head. "See, you're not sleeping in the *guest* room. That's *your* room. His parents can stay at the Bed and Breakfast in town."

"But..." Josh tried.

"No," she said with some force. "You're not listening. I made that room for a reason. I had a really shitty time after I ran away from the Compound."

I realized with some horror that there were tears glittering in her eyes as she told us this.

"...If there had been somewhere safe for me to go, it would have made all the difference. That's why I asked Daniel to build that bed brand new. It isn't a cast-off. And that's why I sewed the quilt, and the curtains."

I hadn't even noticed the curtains, and now I felt like a jerk.

"I didn't know who I was making them for, but that person was *you*. And *you*," she added, touching Josh on the elbow.

"We're happy to be here," Josh whispered.

She smiled through her tears. "Good. Now let's go to the grocery store and buy one of everything. When this baby shows up, we need to be stocked."

THREE DAYS LATER, I still hadn't gotten any calls about jobs.

"Sometimes they take applications when they really don't need anyone," Daniel said.

"But they *told* me they did," I said, rubbing the back of my neck. It was so tight back there. How was I going to support Josh and I if I never got a call back?

"All right," Daniel said, his big calm eyes on me. "Then go back in there tomorrow and politely ask whether they need any more information from you. Call 'em 'sir' and everything, the way you do."

"Why? I filled the application out completely."

"Yeah. But some people want a guy who won't take no for an answer. They might want to see some initiative."

So I took his advice. Maggie let me borrow her car, and I went back to the garage, met different guys, and filled out a *second* application.

It had to work. Because I was running out of ideas.

That night, Maggie fed us lasagna. Afterward, I washed the dishes. Before coming to Massachusetts, I'd never washed a dish. But these days it was my big contribution to the family. Maggie wanted to teach me to cook a few things, but there hadn't been much time.

While I dried the plates, she came into the kitchen wearing a skirt and a sweater. "We're supposed to go to a cocktail party tonight," she said, taking a platter out of my hands and putting it away in the cabinet.

"You feel up to it?" Daniel asked, coming in from the mud room.

"I do," she said. "But I wish it wasn't thirty minutes to this place."

"That's what we get for living in the sticks."

She folded her hands. "We should go, though. It might be a long time before I make it to another party. So if Caleb and Josh don't mind..."

"Go!" I said. "We can watch some TV without you."

"I'll change my clothes," Daniel agreed.

After the truck drove down the drive, and the lights disappeared down the road, I went into the living room and sat on the couch. I held the clicker in my hand, but I didn't turn the TV on, yet. I waited to see if Josh would join me. I couldn't have even said why, but it was suddenly very important that he did. Even though I knew his reasons, more than a week of Josh practically shunning me had taken its toll.

From the back of the house, I heard a drawer open and close. Then the sound of bare feet crossing all those wood floors. "Caleb?" he called softly.

I'd been listening so hard that he did not know where I was. "In here," I said, my voice rough.

Josh appeared, circling the sofa. I expected to sit at the far end, keeping his distance. But that's not what happened. He sat down on the middle cushion.

Then, like two magnets suddenly aligned, he reached for me and I reached for him.

Josh's head landed on my chest with a welcome thud, and I pulled him close. "Where did you go?" I asked.

"Changing clothes," he said, his voice muffled.

But that's not what I'd meant. I wanted to know where he'd been the last eight or nine days, while I twisted in pain at the loss of his affection. But I didn't want to say that. So I ruffled my fingers through his hair, instead.

Josh had changed into Daniel's old sweatpants and a long sleeve T-shirt that read Cal Tech down the arm. I would have preferred that he changed into nakedness, but you can't have everything.

Pressing the button to turn on the television, I began to flip through the channels. But it was really just an excuse to sit there, with Josh cuddled up to me. I ended up leaving the channel on a cheery comedy, with a laugh track that rose and died whenever one of the characters said something funny.

Josh turned his face toward the screen, and we watched the various members of an extended family repeatedly offend one another. I wasn't paying attention, though. The weight of Josh's head on my chest was too distracting. His clean scent, and the feel of his hair sifting through my fingers was all the entertainment I really needed.

Beneath my hand, Josh went very still. I looked up to see what he was watching so intently. On the screen, two men were chatting about buying Christmas gifts. But their conversation wasn't the reason Josh was so captivated. These two men were cuddled up on a sofa, just like us!

The laugh track rose and died at one of their remarks. Then one grabbed the other's chin and said, "And that's why I love you, even though you have poor taste in tablewear."

And then *he kissed him.* Right on the lips. In front of God and everybody.

Josh stared and stared until the scene ended, and an ad for Audi cars started up.

Click. I shut the TV off.

Josh craned his neck to look up at me. "That was..."

"...Interesting," I supplied. "I wonder if Daniel and Maggie watch that show?"

"I was just wondering the same thing."

We sat with that thought for a moment. There were so many questions in our hearts right now. It could make a guy's head ache, from all the uncertainty. Where could I work? Where would we live?

What would Maggie and Daniel think if they knew?

And most importantly — would Josh and I get to be happy together? Or was that just a ridiculous dream?

"Sit up a little," I asked Josh, giving his shoulder a squeeze.

He lifted his head. "Am I hurting you?"

"No," I chucked. "But your face is kind of close to my dick, and I'm getting all horned up."

"Oh. Well then." Josh dropped down again and lifted the hem

of my T-shirt, kissing my stomach. Then, as I watched in disbelief, he put a hand over my crotch.

I made a noise of surprise. It was so unlike Josh to be aggressive. Yet now he was *rubbing me through my jeans*.

The moan I let out could probably be heard in Albany.

Josh popped the button on my jeans. But then he hesitated. "We should go into the bedroom."

Needing oxygen, I took a deep breath. "I thought you'd never ask. Literally."

Josh put his cheek on my stomach and looked up at me. "Well, it's hard."

"It is often *hard*," I teased.

"I'm being serious. I don't want to take advantage of Maggie's kindness."

Aw. Poor Josh was conflicted, and I didn't want to push him. Then again, his face was still a tantalizing few inches from my erection. "Do you suppose Maggie would regret helping us if she knew I was about to give you a blow job right now?"

Josh groaned, shifting his hips. "Wait. What was the question?"

Laughing, I bent down to kiss the top of his head. "Come on. You'll be able to think clearly again after I suck you off."

He closed his eyes and shivered. "The things you say."

"You *love* the things I say."

"Too much," Josh agreed.

There was a bolt on our door, thank the Lord. Once I'd closed it, Josh shed his clothes, a lusty gleam in his eye. He had a beautiful, blushing cock—long and lean, just like him. But with heavy balls that I wanted to cup in my hand.

I stripped off my shirt, and I saw Josh swallow, his Adam's apple bobbing. "You like anything you see?" I asked, moving slowly to tease him.

"Always," he whispered, pulling the covers down and lying on the bed.

I dropped the rest of my clothes and climbed up next to him. It was a high bed, and beautifully made. Daniel had done a fine job on it. And now it would make a comfortable place for me to suck cock. I reclined on my back, the pillows propping me up. "Come here. Straddle me," I demanded.

With bashful eyes, Josh threw a leg over me, sitting on my hips. What a view! His lean, muscular chest rose up above me. Josh had only a little hair trailing down the center of his abs, thickening as it approached his beautiful dick. I put my palms on his torso, rubbing him sweetly. "What are you thinking about right now?"

"Kissing you," he said immediately.

"Get to it, then."

He put his hands down onto the mattress and gave me his mouth. Lord, I'd missed this. His wet lips skimmed me first, and then his tongue came out to play with mine. We lost ourselves in those kisses. After only a few minutes, we were both moaning and fucking our hips against one another.

It was awesome. But I didn't want to come like this, though I was already close. "Sit up, baby," I begged.

Josh obeyed me immediately. I grabbed his dick in my hand and gave it a squeeze. "I want this in my mouth."

His breath stuttered. And then he tried to slide off me. But I caught his hip in my free hand. "No. Stay here. Slide forward on me. All the way up."

His eyes went wide, but he began to scoot up my body. I was hard as nails, too, with Josh spread wide for me, and right in my face. The musky scent of him made me desperate. And the bead of cum on the tip of his dick made me lick my lips. I craned my neck and licked it off.

Josh gasped.

"Come on, baby," I urged, lying back again. "Fuck my mouth."

He whimpered, then moved a bit closer. I reached under his legs and grabbed his ass, pulling him forward.

"I don't want to choke you," he worried.

"But what a way to go, right? Get in my mouth already."

On a moan, Josh pushed forward, the salty tip of him pressing between my lips, over my tongue.

"Mmm," I groaned. Perhaps Josh had been right to worry about making noise when Maggie and Daniel were home. I *loved* the sounds we made together. It would be a crime to silence them.

And I loved the taste of his skin. Opening wide, I sucked him down.

Above me, Josh grabbed the headboard and dropped his head back. I could see every ripple as his abs tightened in excitement. His lean, strong arms tensed when I gave him a good suck. He was in heaven, and it was me who had put him there.

He pulled back a bit, and I released him, kissing the tip, tonguing the sensitive place under the head. "Fuck my mouth, baby. I can take it."

Josh panted above me. "Don't know if I can last more than two minutes, anyway."

"Give it to me. I want to drink you down."

"Whew." He squeezed his eyes shut. "Make that one minute, if you're going to say things like that."

I yanked on his hips, pulling him into my mouth again. Breathing deeply, Josh began to ride my mouth in short, deliberate thrusts. I could feel how close he was, and just thinking about it made me want to come, too. I dropped one of Josh's hips so I could grab my own aching dick in one hand.

He began a keening moan, low in his chest. His hips became jerky, the movement unfocused. "Oh, Caleb," he sobbed.

The first spurt hit the back of my throat, and I swallowed. And it was more of the desperate, half-formed moans that Josh let loose which finally did me in. Thrusting through my own fist, I came hard, spraying my stomach, and probably Josh's ass.

He pulled out, sliding backward through the mess, landing on my chest in a shuddering pile. "Still coming," he gasped. I reached down between his legs, cupping those heavy balls. He groaned, writhing on my slicked stomach, and then collapsed.

"Jesus. I think you needed that," I said, rubbing his back, where the lean muscle was firm under my hand. I'd been yearning to touch him like this. Every time he passed through a room where I was, I had to hold myself back.

Josh answered me on a mumble that I could not understand. But it didn't matter. His fingers threaded into my hair while he kissed my neck.

We lay there, blissed out, until finally the dampness between us became uncomfortable. When Josh got up to start the shower, I joined him. Sleepily, we soaped each other and then rinsed.

"They'll be home soon," Josh worried.

"So? We're just getting clean, here. Like anyone would."

Sure enough, we were toweling off when the purr of the truck engine rolled past our window. Our lights were out, though, so nobody could have noticed the shadows of two naked men climbing into the bed.

Pulling up the covers, I wrapped myself around Josh, preventing him from exiling himself to the far edge of the mattress. "There's a damp spot here," he complained.

"Live with it," I growled, pulling him close to me. "I need you close. Good thing we've figured out the laundry, though."

"Good thing."

We lay there in the dark listening to two people entering the house, then climbing the stairs. I was just drifting off when I realized that the sounds up there never quite died away. There'd been a steady murmur, which now took on a peculiar rhythm. I grinned into the blackness as I realized what I was hearing.

After a couple minutes of rhythmic thumping, there were moans.

Josh picked his head up then. "Oh my."

I put my nose close to his ear, the way I used to have to do to share a secret. "Why shouldn't they?"

"Oh, they should. It's just that now we know this house has no soundproofing. And I'm going to have trouble looking both of them in the eye tomorrow."

"Then don't listen," I said, covering Josh's ears. I turned him toward me and kissed him slowly.

After a second, he got into it, climbing onto my chest, offering me his mouth. From above us, though, came a masculine shout, which made Josh laugh into my mouth. "*What* did I just hear?"

"Maybe his football team scored a touchdown."

"I think *he* scored a touchdown."

Josh curled up beside me, and we slept, only to awaken in the pitch dark some time later. "You hear that?" Josh asked me.

I did. It was the sound of the truck once again, its tires kicking up gravel in the driveway. "They're going somewhere?" That was odd. The clock read 4:03. "Maggie is having the baby," I guessed.

That seemed to wake Josh up all the way. "Wow. It's too early, isn't it?"

"A week doesn't even matter."

"I'm not ready," he said sleepily.

I laughed and pulled him close.

The next time I opened my eyes, it was eight, and I was in bed alone. Which meant that Josh was outside doing the milking by himself.

I dragged my sleepy ass out of bed and pulled on the sweatpants that Josh had dropped on the floor last night.

There was a note on the kitchen counter.

C & J,

It seems the baby decided to make an early appearance. If you could

handle the Jerseys we would be most grateful. Since anything could
happen, here's some grocery money, and we're leaving you the Prius.
Wish us luck, and we'll call with news!
Maggie & Daniel

THERE WAS an envelope with cash in it, and a set of car keys.

Whistling to myself, I made some coffee. Before leaving the Compound, I never had coffee. Our Divine Minister said that caffeine was a drug, and therefore an agent of corruption. But I'd always assumed that they just didn't want to pay for it. Water was the only beverage at the Compound.

There was nothing better than the smell of coffee brewing. Feeling cheerful (which was probably the result of sexual gratification) I took a carton of eggs out of the fridge, and melted a pat of butter in Maggie's omelet pan.

In Paradise, a man never cooked. Never *ever*. He'd chew off one of his own limbs before he'd go into the kitchen and rustle himself up a snack. Maggie knew this, so she'd already dragged me into the kitchen a couple of times to help her cook.

So far, I'd been entrusted with making toast, and buttering it. I could also make coffee.

But I'd watched Maggie scramble eggs a few times, and I thought I was ready for the challenge.

"I can crack eggs two at a time, because I once worked for a pastry chef." She'd had a bunch of short-term kitchen jobs in California. Her last one was at a hotel which Daniel's dad owned. That's how they met. "You should crack one egg at a time, though. And check for bits of shell."

I set out four eggs, and got down a bowl to crack them into. The first egg I hit too lightly against the bowl, barely cracking the shell. When I pulled it apart, I ended up fishing lots of bits of shell out. The second egg I hit too hard, making a bit of a mess on the side of the bowl.

Who knew this could be so hard?

By the time I'd broken all four successfully, the butter in my pan was smoking. So I cranked down the heat and turned on the overhead fan.

I scrambled the raw eggs with a fork, just like Maggie did. Then I poured them into the hot pan, remembering too late that she said to add a dollop of cream to the mixture.

Whoops.

The eggs sizzled, and I tossed them around with a rubber spatula. "Any idiot can cook an egg," Maggie had told me. "Heat them to a certain temperature, and the proteins harden. It's that simple. Many a bachelor has survived on eggs."

She wasn't wrong. Because this idiot's eggs began to look very nicely scrambled. They weren't as pretty as Maggie's, because the butter had darkened. But they smelled like the real thing.

Just as I took the pan off the heat, Josh came in the door. "Wow! Look at you!" he said, hanging his work jacket on a peg.

"I know," I said. "I'm awesome."

Josh kicked off his mucky boots and went into a cabinet for plates. "What else do we need?"

"Forks..." I grabbed a loaf of bread off the counter and opened the bag. "And butter?" I dropped two slices into the toaster and hit the button. My timing wasn't perfect, but this was the first meal I'd ever cooked.

By silent, mutual agreement, we ate breakfast standing hip to hip at the counter. It would have been weird to sit down at the table without Daniel and Maggie.

"This is great," Josh said, forking eggs into his mouth.

"They got a little brown," I hedged.

Josh winked. "No, they're perfect. And I like finding you half naked in the kitchen, making me breakfast." He touched a hand to my bare back before picking up his coffee mug.

I gave him a big, silly smile. Because right then? I had every-thing I needed in the world.

GOODBYE PARADISE

The outer door banged open in the mudroom. "Hey guys!" Daniel's voice called through to the kitchen.

By silent, mutual agreement, Josh and I leapt away from one another before Daniel made it into the kitchen.

"Hey! Josh called. "What's the news?"

Daniel stepped into the room, grinning. "Baby girl. Seven pounds, two ounces."

"Oh!" Josh's face lit up. "A girl! Do you have a name?"

"Chloe. Maggie was determined that it wouldn't be biblical."

That cracked me up. "That's awesome. She's sticking it to our Divine Pastor."

"Exactly," Daniel agreed. He looked exhausted, actually.

"I think it's pretty," Josh said loyally. "When do we meet her?"

"Probably tomorrow," Daniel said. "I just came home to shower and check on the animals."

Josh pointed his fork at Daniel. "I've been in that barn all morning, and the cows are in much better shape than you are."

Daniel snorted. "I'm pretty sure I got one hour of sleep last night. She woke me up with a sharp elbow and demanded to be taken to the hospital. But, dude. Thank you for milking. I don't know what I would have done if you weren't here for this."

Josh shrugged away the thanks, but I could tell that he appreciated it. "I'll cover you these next few days. You don't have to worry."

"The dairy truck comes in forty minutes..."

"I'll handle it," Josh said. "Let's get you some coffee."

Daniel dropped his head forward in gratitude. "Wow. I accept. And I knew you two were awesome." He took a mug of coffee and then went upstairs to shower.

When I turned to look at Josh, his eyes were glittering. "What's wrong?" I asked quickly. Was he freaking out because Daniel had startled us?

Josh gave a sigh, shaking his head. "Not a thing is wrong. I'm just so happy for Maggie. She gets her happy ending, you know? A

117

husband who loves her, and *only* her. She has a *job*, Caleb. She can wear jeans if she wants to. And now she has a baby, who will be called *Chloe*. Not something like Methuselah. And Chloe will go to school with her friends."

"And then to college," I added.

Josh nodded, his face solemn. He didn't mention Miriam. But she was heavy on his mind, I was sure. And mine, too.

CHAPTER THIRTEEN

Caleb

Now there were *five* people living in a house where only two had lived before. And the newest member occupied a great deal of attention.

Daniel's parents, a tanned, smiling couple came to dote on their newest grandchild. Mrs. Lacey took over the kitchen, making casseroles and soups. Mr. Lacey read the sports section in the living room and admired the cows in the barn.

Maggie all but disappeared. As far as Josh and I could tell, she spent much of her day in the rocking chair, nursing the baby. "Maggie," we heard Daniel call one morning from the stairs. "Why don't you come down for a bit?"

"The baby is fussy," she said. "And I'm just so tired."

He didn't argue, and instead took her a plate.

And Josh and I? We just tried our best to stay out of the way. I did the dishes whenever Mrs. Lacey left the kitchen. "Such helpful boys," she said a couple of times. But I didn't feel helpful. I felt restless.

In the evenings, when Daniel's parents retired to the B&B, the house got very still. From our room, we heard the low murmur of voices, and the occasional baby's cries at all hours.

The elder Laceys departed after four days, and Daniel headed back out to his workshop. "Can I help you with anything before I go to work?" he asked his wife.

"We'll be fine. I think she nursed every hour last night. We're both going to crash. I hope."

There was an uneasy pause. "All right. I'll come inside in a bit to see how you're doing."

On his way out to the barn, Josh stopped him. "Is she okay?"

"The baby is fine," Daniel muttered.

"I meant Maggie. She isn't herself."

"We were up all hours," Daniel said, stuffing his feet into his shoes. "It's just hard. She'll be okay."

UNFORTUNATELY, things didn't get easier for Maggie. Little Chloe became colicky, screaming her tiny lungs out whenever she was awake. The rare glimpses we got of her, she had a red, scrunched-up face.

Mornings, Daniel would stumble out to the barn, and then to the workshop. Josh and I would tiptoe around while Maggie and the baby slept. Inevitably, the screaming would begin before noon. And Maggie could be heard pacing upstairs, saying "shh shh shh," and sounding exhausted.

After a few days like that, Josh couldn't take it anymore. He threw down Daniel's newspaper and marched upstairs. "Let me try," I heard him say over the screaming.

"It's okay," Maggie protested.

"Please? Just give yourself a break, Maggie. Have some toast and juice."

Somehow, he must have pried the baby out of her arms, because they both appeared downstairs. Chloe looked ridiculously small against Josh's chest, her tiny fists balled up in rage as she cried.

Maggie sleep-walked into the kitchen, but Josh went into the living room instead. That's when the singing started.

"Amazing grace! How sweet the sound..."

I got a chill on my neck. When we were kids, Josh loved to sing. I hadn't heard his sweet voice in a long time. But it came back to me now—how wonderful he'd sounded. At some point before we were teenagers, Ezra had begun to tease him, and Josh had stopped singing out loud. During Sunday services, he mouthed the words like the rest of the boys.

"I once was lost..."

It took a couple of verses, and quite a few laps around the living room. But eventually Josh won. When he and Chloe passed me on their way into the kitchen, she was staring up at him with wide, newborn eyes, her tiny mouth making an "O" shape.

He was still humming, too. The deep, reedy sound of it stirred me so much that I had to stop myself from putting a hand on his arm as he passed by.

"Thank you," Maggie whispered. "I'm at the end of my rope. You have no idea..."

"Anyone would be," he said. "Besides, I like her. Nobody ever let me hold a baby before."

Maggie smiled the first smile I'd seen in days. "That's women's work."

"What other women's work can we do?" I asked. "I could drive to the grocery store."

"Oh, *would* you? I haven't been outside in days. But it's so cold out, and the pediatrician said to keep her out of public places for a couple of weeks."

I grabbed a pad of paper off the counter. "Let's make a list, and I'll go."

SO WE ALL ENDURED. Josh made many more trips around the house with Chloe, wearing out his repertoire of hymns. I did errands, and fretted about my lack of employment.

Daniel worked, and tried to keep tabs on the rest of us. I think it bothered him to come inside and find Josh holding the baby, which happened with some frequency. "I've got her," he'd say, and Josh would hand Chloe over. But half the time this caused the baby to start screaming again, probably because she'd been comfortable and did not appreciate being disturbed. Daniel did not know to sing hymns and walk past the windows. So she usually kept right on screaming. Daniel would declare that she was almost certainly hungry again, and pass her to Maggie, who felt obligated to keep her.

There was tension in the house, and it made me uneasy.

The only excitement I had during those stressful weeks was using Daniel's computer. He'd shown me how to use the internet browser to search for job openings, and I caught on quickly to the fact that I could search for information on *anything*. So I Googled "automotive jobs in Western Massachusetts" and "rules of football" and "polygamist cults."

Nothing came up about the Compound.

When Chloe was two weeks old, Maggie and Daniel took her to the pediatrician.

"Is something wrong?" Josh had asked when Maggie explained that they had an appointment.

"No. In the civilized world, the doctor keeps tabs on a baby's growth, to make sure that everything is going well."

That sounded like overkill to me. But I was happy about it anyway, because it gave me ideas.

Daniel and Maggie drove away at nine. And twenty minutes later, I heard Josh come in from the morning milking, which he'd completed alone after Daniel had to leave.

"Josh," I called out from the bedroom.

"Yeah?"

"In here."

A few seconds later, Josh appeared in the doorway, his cheeks red from the cold. I watched him take me in.

I'd pulled the covers down on the bed, and was lying buck naked on my back, and slowly teasing my own rather ambitious erection.

Josh licked his lips. "How long have they been gone?" he asked, his voice hoarse.

"Twenty minutes. We have at least an hour, probably longer."

He did not hesitate, thank the Lord.

Josh shut our door and bolted it. He yanked the curtains on the driveway side of the room closed. Then he began removing all his clothing in a big hurry. By the time he got down to his boxer shorts, he was tenting the front of them.

"Bring that over here, baby," I rasped. "I need you right now."

He let out a hot, happy breath and climbed onto my body. When our cocks met, he moaned.

I took his face in my hands and began to kiss him, just as I'd been hoping to. "I like you in the daylight," I said between kisses. "I want to watch your face when I make you come."

On another reedy moan, Josh dove deeper into my mouth. He was so responsive, so beautiful. I rolled him onto his side, so that we were facing each other. He slipped a hand between our bodies and palmed my cock, giving me one delicious squeeze. "Want you," he said.

"You have me. Now bend this leg," I coaxed, lifting his top knee toward the ceiling. I cupped his balls, which he loved. And I stroked his taint just behind them. Since he was spread so wide for me, I had good access to his ass. I eased a tentative finger back, just teasing him lightly.

Josh shivered against me.

"Do you like that?" I asked.

As an answer, he gave me a deep kiss.

"Hold on," I said, letting go.

123

He whimpered at the loss of contact, then watched me fish a little plastic bottle out of the bedside table where I'd stowed it. "What's that?" he breathed.

"Lube," I said, dripping some of it onto my fingers. "I've been doing some research online."

"What kind of research?"

"The kind that's going to make you come hard all over me."

He groaned. I loved that I could make him do that with just a little dirty talk.

I put my lubed fingers between Josh's legs, and worked that slickness into his crease. "What do you think?" I asked, teasing a slippery finger against his hole.

"Oh, Caleb," he moaned. "Don't stop."

Well then. I pressed the tip of my finger inside, and his breath hitched. "Okay?" I asked.

He let out a breath. "It's strange."

"Should I stop?"

He shook his head, then buried his face in the crook of my shoulder.

I took a moment to add more of the slippery liquid to my finger. "Relax, baby. Can you do that?"

He nodded into my neck.

Slowly, I pushed my finger into his body. With my other hand, I slowly stroked Josh's dick. I felt his chest rise and fall with a deep breath, and then he seemed to bear down on my finger. I stretched, reaching for the spot I hoped to find. And when my finger brushed his prostate, Josh shuddered in my arms.

"You like that?" I whispered.

He moaned so loudly that the cows probably looked up from their hay.

I stroked him again, loving the reaction. He fucked himself on my finger, and his breathing became shallow and quick. I kissed his face, his ear. Anything I could reach.

Pleasuring Josh was my favorite thing to do in the world.

There was nothing like it. Pausing for a little more of the magic liquid in the bottle, I tucked a second finger in with the first one, making Josh sigh and squirm against me. My own dick was throbbing, screaming for attention. *Later, buddy*, I promised. Hell. I might come from just listening to the impatient noises Josh made.

"Caleb," he panted. "Are you going to fuck me?"

I stilled my hands on him for a moment, so that he would be able to focus on what I was about to say. "I wasn't sure we should. Didn't know if you'd feel bad about it afterwards. I mean... it's more than just touching, you know?"

"The Bible says not to." His head lolled against my chest, and his tongue flicked out to lick my skin. "But I've always wanted it."

"Yeah? Do you think about it sometimes?"

He flexed his hips, as if trying to restart my hands on his body. "In my daydreams, you hold me down and fuck me from behind."

Just hearing the *words*, my balls tightened. "Whew, Joshy. I want to. *So* badly. But if we're trying this, I gotta see your face, okay? I have to know if I'm hurting you."

He began to suck on my nipple. His fingers closed around my dick, and he pumped me with his palm. "Caleb," he whispered against my skin. "Just make me yours."

"You," I said, kissing him on the forehead, "are already mine. You have *always* been mine. Now sit up with me." I hauled us upright, until I was seated on the bed, my legs together, my back angled against the pillows.

Josh looked drunk with lust. His face was flushed, and his eyes were heavy. But he knew what to do. I guess he *had* been thinking about this. He straddled me, knees on the bed, hands on the headboard.

I grabbed the lube and drizzled a sloppy amount on my dick. "Go *slow*," I cautioned.

But he was too eager to listen. Lining himself up over me, he sank down on my slippery dick.

I bellowed with pleasure. The sensation of entering Josh's

body was so overwhelming that I had to squeeze my eyes shut. Making love to Josh was all I'd ever wanted. And he felt every bit as good as I'd dreamed. I dropped my head until it collided with his chest, and took a deep breath of him. Wrapping my arms around him, I swam through a rush of emotion. Just being here with him was a gift that I didn't know if I deserved.

But Josh inhaled sharply, as if in pain.

Startled, I leaned back again. "Are you okay?"

"It burns," he confessed, his eyes red.

"We don't have to do this today," I whispered, rubbing his chest with my hand.

"Just give me a minute," he panted.

"Let me kiss you," I begged, wishing there was something else I could do to ease him. I reached up and took those gorgeous cheekbones in my hands, bringing his mouth down to mine. My kisses were tender, brushing his soft lips with mine, licking into his sweet mouth. With gentle hands, I rubbed his arms and chest. I let my fingers sift down through the light hair on his belly, until I brushed his cock.

"Oh," he said into my mouth as I began to stroke him lightly. "Oh," he said again as I grazed his nipple with my free hand, and tangled my tongue with his. I kissed him to say that everything was okay, no matter if we fucked or not. I kissed him to tell him how grateful I was that he loved me. *So* grateful.

Josh shifted carefully. He adjusted the angle of his hips, and the effect was a bit of friction on my cock, which was still buried inside him. I couldn't hold back my moan. It just felt so good.

That seemed to make Josh feel brave. He put some weight on the headboard and experimented with lifting himself up my shaft.

God in heaven, it was good. My kisses lost focus as Josh's firm body slid up and then down my shaft. He tipped his hips further, then did it again.

"Baby," I breathed. But that's all I said. Because speaking was beyond my capacity at the moment.

Slowly, he thrusted again. And *again*. Each time he moved, I felt everything. His body hugged my cock in the most beautiful way. And his sweet breath brushed my face, his tongue skimmed my mouth.

"It's so..." I struggled to tell him how I was feeling. "...*Hot* inside you. So... intense. Are you all right?"

He nodded, his nose brushing my face. "Feeling better," he breathed. "Good, even. Especially when I..." he broke off. Then he tilted his hips and bore down. "Right *there*," he panted. "There's nothing like it." Biting the corner of his lip, he picked up the pace.

It was magical.

Every thrust thrilled me. And the knowledge that Josh was riding me, taking pleasure from my body was just incredible. It was sensory overload of the very best kind. "Love you," I gasped.

Josh put more weight on the headboard, and moaned. He moved his hips faster now, fucking himself on me with more urgency. I slid a hand around to cup his ass. The muscle under my hand was contracting rhythmically. *Damn* that was sexy.

I wasn't going to last much longer. So I took Josh's cock in hand and started to stroke. I tipped my head back, trying to hold myself together. "Need you to come for me," I panted, skimming the pad of my thumb over his slit. "Shoot all over my chest," I begged.

Josh shivered. Dirty talk always made him hornier. I *loved* that. I loved to shock him a little.

"I'm going to come in your ass," I threatened. "You're going to feel my hot seed inside you. Probably for the rest of the day." His moans got louder, and I stroked him harder. But it was just all too good. The sights and sounds of our fucking were more than I could bear. "Gotta come," I growled. My hips began to shake, and then I was shooting, and shooting again. I gave a shout against Josh's pecs.

He whimpered, then froze, and I worried that something was

wrong. But then he drenched my hand with his seed. "Mmm," I crooned, milking him until he finally sagged against my chest.

For a long minute nobody said anything. We were pancaked together, both sweating and breathing hard. Josh's chin lay on my shoulder, and I flopped a hand onto his bare back.

We drifted on the most wonderful post-sex haze. Until Josh startled me by saying, "I'm going straight to hell."

My heart seized, because this was exactly what I'd been worried about. Josh's back shook under my hand, and I feared for the worst. "No!" I whispered. "That's..." I cut myself off, because I realized he was *laughing*.

"Caleb," Josh chuckled. "Thing is, I don't care that much." He lifted his body a little, and my exhausted dick slipped out. "We are *definitely* doing that again. But right now, we need a shower." Without another word, Josh climbed off of me.

Stunned, I followed him into the bathroom, where Josh was already testing the water's temperature with his hand.

I squeezed his shoulder. "You're really all right?"

He turned, rolling his eyes. "Don't ruin it, okay?" He stepped into the shower stall.

"Ruin it?"

"I hate that you think of me as *fragile*," he complained as I followed him under the spray.

"I don't think that," I said quickly. He'd always disliked it whenever he suspected me of babying him. "But it was you who said we were a *sin*."

Josh put soapy hands on my chest, rubbing me gently. His face was thoughtful. "I did say that. But that wasn't really the issue."

"What was it, then?" I closed my eyes as Josh began to shampoo my hair. His hands on my body were pretty much all I wanted out of life. When Josh was touching me, I was able to forget how fucking perilous our life was right now.

"I've always been the one they called *faggot*," Josh said quietly. "I didn't even know what it meant until after we'd lived in the bunkhouse for awhile. But I knew that it was a bad thing."

I hid my sigh under the shower's spray as I rinsed off the shampoo. "Come here," I said to Josh after I quit drowning myself. I pulled his slippery body to my chest. "That word isn't what we are. It's just a word for everything those idiots wanted to bash. It's just a putdown."

"Yeah, well," Josh grumbled, reaching for the shampoo bottle again. "You weren't the one getting put down."

I took the bottle from him and poured some shampoo in my hand. "Still don't know what that has to do with what we just did on the bed."

"Everything and nothing," Josh said. "I don't like thinking that Ezra was right."

"He," I said fiercely, unwilling to even repeat that fucker's name, "does not *exist* to us anymore, okay? If you let yourself think like that, then he wins."

Josh closed his eyes as I swirled sudsy hands through his soft hair. "I know you're right. But it's hard to forget."

Patience, I reminded myself. Josh only needed my patience. "Did you..." I cleared my throat, suddenly shy. "...Enjoy it, though?"

Josh didn't answer right away, because he was pushing water out of his face. When that was done, he shut off the shower. I could tell from his expression that he was listening—trying to figure out if Maggie and Daniel had come home while we were showering. But it was still quiet.

Meanwhile, I was dying just a few inches away, desperate to know whether Josh had found sex to be as life-changing as I had. As far as I was concerned, we should do that every day. Maybe twice.

Finally, his gaze made it back to mine. Then he smiled. "Next time, I want you to hold me down."

Next time!

129

I grinned, and grabbed his waist. "I'm free right now," I said, kissing him. Backing him up against the shower wall, I pinned his hips to the tiles.

"Mmm," he groaned.

Then we heard the sound of tires in the driveway.

Right.

Josh and I toweled off in a hurry, then got dressed. "I hope they don't notice that we both have wet hair," I whispered, jumping into my jeans.

"I don't think they've looked twice at us since the baby was born," Josh said in a low voice. Then he opened the door and went out.

After waiting a little while, just to make the timing seem random, I walked into the kitchen. Josh was holding the baby, and Daniel had already departed for his workshop.

"I really liked this doctor," Maggie was saying as she poured herself a cup of coffee. "She said no question was too dumb. And she gave me her cell phone number, and said I shouldn't be afraid to use it."

"That's nice," Josh murmured. He stood on the wide pine floors, bouncing his knees in a little maneuver that was part of his baby-soothing technique.

"I'll take her now," Maggie said. "No, wait. Let me pee first."

"Good call," Josh said, rocking his chest from side to side while little Chloe's eyes fluttered shut.

Maggie ran out of the room, and I just stared at Josh, fighting hard to keep my distance from him. He was so fucking cute.

"What?" he asked, his eyebrows arched in confusion.

I smiled. "You amaze me, that's all," I whispered. At the Compound, I only ever saw Josh doing the work that everyone else did, always careful to keep his head down. I didn't know that he would like babies, or cows. Or that he'd always choose the blue coffee mug, with the luminous glaze, but an unfortunate chip on the rim. Here in Massachusetts I got to see more of him, and not just his skin.

Now he was looking at me as with confusion. "Why?"

"Nothing." There wasn't time to explain. But there was time to move nearer to him, while listening closely to the sounds of the house. A toilet flushed somewhere, so there was an opportunity to sidle up to him and kiss his cheek. He gave me a startled look, and pink spots appeared on his cheeks. "Nobody saw," I argued.

"Chloe saw," he joked. We both looked down at the sleeping baby in his arms. "And it's true, by the way," he whispered.

"What is?"

"I *can* still feel you right now."

My stomach did a dip and a roll, and my neck heated. But Maggie's footsteps were coming closer, so I moved away from him, over to the counter.

She entered the room looking wearier than I'd ever seen her. Today she'd put on nicer clothes than usual, and they accentuated rather than hid her exhaustion. Without a word, she took the baby in one arm and her coffee cup in the other, then retreated upstairs.

THE NEXT MORNING, I heard Maggie answer the phone upstairs.

"Caleb?" she called. "You have a phone call."

My heart leapt into my mouth. *Could it be...?* I picked up the kitchen extension. "This is Caleb."

"This is Joe from The Perry Garage," a man's voice boomed into my ear. "I got an application with your name on it. Can you come back down here this afternoon and talk about the job?"

"I sure can, sir," I said, hoping that was true. "What time?"

"Wander by any time after one o'clock," he said. "See you then." He hung up.

Josh came trotting out of the laundry room, where he'd been folding towels for Maggie. He was sneaky like that — taking over tasks for her whenever he saw an opportunity. "Who was that?"

"The garage called. They want me to come in this afternoon."

His face lit up. "Awesome."

"What did I miss?" Maggie asked, making a rare appearance at the bottom of the stairs. Her arms were empty, so the baby must have agreed to take a nap.

"Caleb might get a job this afternoon!" Josh crowed.

"Can I, uh, use your car?" I asked, wishing I had my own wheels.

"Sure," she said. "All I need to do is hit the drugstore at some point. We're almost out of diapers and wipes."

"Is there one near the garage?" Josh asked. "Caleb could save you the trip."

"Oh, would you?" Maggie asked. "I'll make a list, with the brand names and everything." She went back upstairs.

"Is that okay?" Josh whispered. "I could go with you and do the shopping."

"No problem," I said.

A COUPLE OF HOURS LATER, I parked Maggie's car at the drugstore, which was about two hundred yards from the garage. "So..." I said.

Josh and I locked gazes for a moment. "I'll take my time here. Give me the keys, okay? I'll wait in the car when I'm done."

My eyes drifted out the window, toward the garage across the intersection. Yesterday I'd given Josh a speech which was meant to convince him that there wasn't a thing wrong with us. But the ugly truth was that I *did* need him to stay out of sight for the next hour. I needed this job, whether or not the garage was staffed by an entire team of Ezras. "I guess that's a good plan. I'm sorry that I can't say exactly how long I'll be."

"It's okay," he whispered. "I'll be fine." His clear eyes regarded me trustingly. It made me want to kiss him, but of course I didn't do it.

"Knock 'em dead." Josh grinned. "But not literally. Because they wouldn't like that."

I held up a fist, and Josh bumped it. We'd seen that little maneuver on television, our new favorite vault of cultural knowledge.

Then we got out of the car and went our separate ways.

I crossed two busy streets and walked into the front of the garage, where an older man with bushy eyebrows that I hadn't seen before was standing over the receptionist.

"Good afternoon," I said. "I'm Caleb Smith, and..."

"Caleb Smith!" the man boomed. "I'm Joe Perry. Glad you could come in, son. I got back from my vacation and the guys told me you'd come in twice to fill out an application."

"Yes sir."

Joe Perry snorted. "You hear that!" he hollered over his shoulder. "The new guy calls me *sir!* Y'all should show a little more respect, like he does." He chuckled. "Follow me, Caleb Smith."

The older man led the way into the service bays, where five or six mechanics in *Perry's Garage* jumpsuits had three cars up on lifts. "This is our operation. We're open six days a week. Can you work Saturdays?"

"I can work any day, sir."

Joe chuckled. "New rule, boys! The rest of y'all have to call me 'sir.'"

Great. Now they would all hate my guts.

A red-haired guy raised his head from the engine of an F-150. "Sir? You can kiss my ass, sir."

Joe Perry threw his head back and laughed. He jerked a thumb at the redhead. "That there is Danny. Stick with him, okay? He's smarter than he looks."

"Yes..." I caught myself before adding the "sir."

"Now let's get you some paperwork. Can you start tomorrow? I'll give you twenty hours a week to start, but it could go up. You'll have to do a lot of oil changes at first. Somebody's gotta be on the bottom of the heap, you know? You got a plan to get your certification? There's more jobs I can give you if you're certified." He stopped in front of a very messy desk and turned around.

"I want to get certified, but it's going to take me a little time. Been working on engines my whole life, but nobody cared about paperwork."

The old man's giant eyebrows lifted. "Why not?"

Self-conscious now, I rubbed the back of my neck. "Well, it was a kind of crazy religious place out west. Most people would call it a cult, I guess. I ran away from there last month."

"Jesus H.! That's a hell of a story, I bet."

Not one I'm sharing.

"You do have a place to live, though, right?" He looked worried, probably wondering if I was going to be a drifter.

"Absolutely," I said quickly. "I'm staying with a friend out in Cheshire. She ran away from the same place five years ago. Maggie is a real help to me. She's like family."

That seemed to appease him. He lifted a clipboard off the desk and handed it to me. "Fill out this W-9, and we'll see you tomorrow morning. Eight o'clock, sharp."

"Yessir," I said automatically. And he grinned.

CHAPTER FOURTEEN

Caleb

Working for Joe Perry was awesome. In spite of his messy desk, he ran a solid operation. I liked the guys there, too. They were relaxed in a way that was unfamiliar to me. On the Compound everyone was always jockeying for position. The garage was calmer, and it took me a week or two to figure out why. The guys there punched in, worked (reasonably) hard for eight hours, and then punched out again. For their trouble, they got a check every two weeks.

So even when the place was a little too busy or a customer got snippy, nobody minded too much. It was just a *job*. And when you clocked out, you could go home to whoever you wished, and say whatever you wanted.

To me, this was nothing short of revolutionary.

And Joe had been right about Danny. He noticed everything that went on at the garage, and had a kind word for everyone. Between Danny and his sidekick Jakobitz, there was always some-body telling a story, or making a joke.

I made sure to show up on time for all my shifts, and work hard each and every hour. Danny called me Caleb the Great, and said that I was the biggest ass-kisser the place had ever seen. "I'll bet you five bucks that Caleb the Great is managing this joint in five years. He's going to rule over us all," he told his friend Jakobitz.

At first, it bothered me. But pretty soon I realized that this was just Danny's brand of smack talk. He teased everyone, but not too much.

So I continued to do the work my own way. Because this job was everything to me, and I intended to do well at it.

The fact that had a job meant that I wasn't home with Josh and the family as often. And so I wasn't very focused on the fact that Maggie still wasn't doing well.

I'd never paid much attention to newborn babies or their mothers before. At the compound, men weren't encouraged to help or even notice them. And I hadn't lived in a house with women since I was sixteen.

So I didn't know what to expect for poor Maggie. All I could do was hope that things got easier for her. That she'd start smiling again.

She didn't.

Daniel was clearly worried, but he didn't say much. And they were both so tired. Josh and I would often roll over in bed to the sounds of a screaming baby, or the footsteps of someone pacing upstairs. Or both.

Sometimes we heard Maggie crying when she was upstairs with the baby. More than once, Josh had gone up there and taken Chloe from her, coming downstairs with worry in his eyes. He'd pace the floor, singing hymns for forty minutes until the baby slept.

I didn't think much of it, probably because I was preoccupied. My new job was exhausting. My twenty hours at the garage quickly became more, because Massachusetts got a nice heavy snowfall, and half the state showed up to get snow tires put on. I clocked thirty hours during my third week on the job, and was giddy at my own good fortune.

Commuting to work in Maggie's Prius was no problem, because she never went anywhere. That should have been a clue.

Things were tense at home, but I wasn't around much to notice. I had Mondays off, though, which left Josh and I standing around in the kitchen drinking coffee together after he finished the milking. That should have been relaxing, except that Daniel and Maggie were fighting upstairs.

"You're not eating, you barely shower," Daniel said. "And it's starting to freak me out."

"What do you care?" Maggie argued. "I'm feeding the baby all the time. When I'm not doing that, I sleep. You would too."

"Look, I know it's hard," he said. "But you have to buck up a little, okay?"

"*Buck up?* You don't know a thing," Maggie yelled.

There was a small crash, which froze Josh and I in place. Daniel must have kicked a shoe or a book or something, but where we come from, a fist to Maggie's face would not have been all that unusual. So we were both bracing for the worst.

"I know *plenty!*" Daniel yelled, "Not that you'll give me any credit! I'm tired, too, okay! But at least I'm *trying*." He stomped down the stairs so fast that Josh and I were still just standing there, mugs in hand, looking horrified when he appeared.

Daniel banged through the kitchen and into the mudroom. "And I have a fucking *audience* when I lose my shit and yell at my wife," he spat.

The door opened and shut as he fled for the workshop.

From upstairs came the sound of sobbing, followed shortly by the sound of a baby wailing.

Josh set down his chipped blue mug and marched upstairs, returning a moment later with the fussy baby on his shoulder. At three weeks old, her face was beginning to get round, and her eyes were open wide. Even screaming, she was really pretty cute. But who knew such a little person could be so much trouble?

Using his trademarked singing and walking past the windows,

he got her calmed down quickly enough. But the look on his face was troubled. "Something's not right," he said, pacing into the kitchen again. "Maggie isn't right."

"She's not sleeping," I argued. "That would make anyone crazy."

"I know," Josh sighed. "But even then, you'd smile sometimes, no? And make popcorn, and watch TV? She just *sits* up there, Caleb. It's weird."

"Shhh," I said. "She can hear you."

We were both quiet for a moment, and unfortunately the muffled sound of Maggie's crying was still audible.

Josh let out a big sigh. Then he marched over to the fridge and yanked the doctor's phone number out from under its magnets. He slapped the piece of paper onto the counter and then reached for the phone.

"What are you doing?"

"I'm telling her doctor that I think something's wrong," he said, dialing with the hand that wasn't needed to support the baby.

"She wouldn't want you to do that," I argued.

"Don't care," Josh said, lifting the phone to his ear. "If she's fine, the doctor will tell me to mind my own business, right?" He waited, a concerned frown on his face, until someone picked up. "Hi. I'm Maggie Beaufort's cousin. She had a baby three weeks ago, and I'm very worried about her. She cries all the time and she won't eat much. Sure, I'll hold."

I expected the doctor's office to laugh Josh off the phone. But that's not at all what happened. Someone came on the line and listened again to everything Josh had to say, and then asked a whole lot of questions. "Wait, I need to write that down," Josh said eventually. "Just a second..."

Grabbing the pad we used for grocery lists and a pencil, Josh began to scribble. "Okay. Got it. I'll make sure she gets there." On his shoulder, the baby began to fuss again. So I reached over and slid my hands under her little armpits.

Josh passed Chloe to me and went back to his call.

The baby was warm and heavier than I expected against my chest. But, God, how did people do this? I was terrified of dropping her. Not that she was slippery or anything. But I didn't like being the person responsible for that tiny body and that soft little head.

It took Josh maybe two more minutes to finish up his conversation, and they could not pass fast enough.

Finally, he hung up the phone, turning to me with victory on his face. "There's a thing called postpartum depression," he said. "And the doctor thinks that Maggie has it. Apparently, after you have a baby, a bunch of your hormones levels can crash. It kills your will to live. The doctor said it can be mild or serious. But it's a real thing."

"Oh." That sounded plausible. Because something about Maggie had surely crashed. "So... what do we do?"

Josh smacked the notepad with his hand, and then reached for Chloe. (Thankfully.) "The doctor wants to see Maggie at noon. That's in one hour. Will you drive her?"

"Well..." I cleared my throat. "Of course I'll do it. But we need to tell Daniel. He'll probably want to take her himself."

Josh bit his lip, clearly uncomfortable. Until that moment, I don't think I understood that Josh was afraid of Daniel. "Maybe I should ask Maggie what to do?"

I shook my head. "Maggie is the one who is sick, right? And she doesn't know why. Daniel needs to know. But I'll tell him," I said.

"Really?" Josh squeaked. "I'll go with you."

I held up a hand. "I got this." Without waiting for a response, I went into the mud room and stuffed my feet into my shoes.

Out in the workshop, I found Daniel hand-sanding a long rail, his arm working the sanding block with furious motion. When he saw me, his mouth made a grim line, but he did not stop working. After an awkward minute of this, he stood up straight and tossed the sanding block onto his work table. "Look, I'm sorry," he said. "I was just frustrated."

With a shrug, I just took him in. There were dark circles under his eyes. He looked almost worse than Maggie. There were half finished projects around the shop, including a rocking horse I'd never noticed before. It was probably for Chloe. Daniel was probably under a lot of pressure. His carpentry business was supposedly profitable, but not exactly easy. A few weeks ago it was just he and Maggie. And now he was essentially the head of a family of five.

That's how it must have felt, anyway.

"I didn't come out here for an apology," I said quietly. "But Maggie has a doctor's appointment at noon."

His chin snapped up. "Really? What for?"

"Well," I stuck my hands in my pockets. "We called her doctor — the one on the refrigerator. We were worried." I wasn't trying to take credit for Josh's good work. But it was a ballsy thing that Josh had done, and I knew there was some tension over how often Josh took care of the baby. "It turns out that there's a hormone problem that can make new mothers depressed. And the doctor thinks Maggie has it."

Daniel put both hands on the rail he'd been sanding, and dropped his head. "Shit. Did they use the words 'postpartum depression?'"

"Yeah. That's it."

"Shit. *Shit!*" He slammed his hands down. "I should have caught that." His eyes came up again, staring me down. "And *you* knew about that? I am such an idiot."

This made me laugh. "No, dude. It was all Josh. And he didn't know either. It's just that he was willing to call a doctor and freak out over the phone."

Even dropped his head again. "Fucking Josh. Obviously smarter than the rest of us."

"So true."

"I've even *read* about this before. It's in all those fucking pregnancy books Maggie made me read. God *damn* it." He kicked the foot of his sawhorse. "Sorry," he said quickly.

"Daniel, you can goddamn any goddamn thing you want. I don't care."

He gave me a weary grin. "Okay. I'm gonna go apologize to Josh, then explain to Maggie that I'm taking her to the doctor." He shut off his table lamp. "Hey. Do you think Josh would take the baby for a few hours? Ugh. I hate to ask him."

"I think he'd be happy to. He only wants to help."

Daniel grabbed his jacket off a chair and headed for the door. "He's really good with Chloe. Makes me feel like an idiot."

"I feel like an idiot pretty much all the time," I told him. "Why should you fare any better?"

Daniel shook his head, and we walked back to the house together.

TEN HOURS LATER, Josh and I sat at opposite ends of the sofa, our legs tangled together. We were watching a TV movie in a half-assed way. Josh was preoccupied with Chloe, who was drinking a bottle on his chest. And I was preoccupied with Josh.

"What?" he said, after the third time he caught me staring.

"Nothing. I just like you."

He rolled his eyes. "You're smirking."

"You're cute, okay? I can't help it."

He made a face. "She makes me useful. I really don't mind it."

"You *are* useful. You were a fucking *hero* today. If Maggie starts feeling better, she and Daniel are never going to forget this."

SARINA BOWEN

"Don't say fuck," he admonished me. "If it's Chloe's first word, I'm not taking the rap for that."

I poked his hip with my toe. "Why don't you want me watching you?"

He sighed. "It's not my most manly hour." He set the bottle on the coffee table and turned the baby onto his shoulder. With mild thumps, he patted her back.

You couldn't have paid me to look anywhere else. His long hands made the baby look tiny, and the arms he held her in were strong and sexy. "I think you have it all wrong," I said quietly. "A real man does what needs doing. He takes care of the people he loves. You know this instinctively, even though every man in your own life treated you like shit."

He looked up fast, and with so much surprise on his face that I felt a pang in my heart. "Except for you," he said.

"Except for me," I said. Taking good care of Josh was the only true achievement I could claim. That, and having good hands when it came to engine work.

Absently, he whacked Chloe on the back, until she gave a very unladylike belch. "Good girl," he sighed, turning her again until her eyes peeped at me from his chest.

"Is that something you think about?" I asked.

"What. Burps?"

I gave him another poke with my toe. "No. Manliness."

Josh groaned. "So what if I do? As you pointed out yourself, I spent years listening to a bunch of assholes question mine."

This was true. It's just that it was plain as day to me that the people who had put Josh down only did it to boost themselves up. Like the hens in my mother's chicken coop, they pecked at anyone ranked below them. As their favorite target, though, I guessed Josh couldn't see that as easily as I could.

"Josh?"

"Mmm?"

"If you *weren't* a man, I wouldn't want you so bad, like I do. That's the thing with me."

He gave me a funny little disbelieving smile.

"Do you know why I don't hold the baby very often? It's not because I think it's women's work."

"You don't want her to pee on you? It happens."

I laughed. "No, but thanks for the warning. It's because she scares me. Like I won't know what to do, and she'll start screaming and everybody will look at me and wonder what I did wrong."

His eyebrows lifted. "That's ridiculous. Any idiot with two hands can hold a baby. One hand is actually fine, too." He swung his feet off over mine and off the couch. "You can practice right now, because I really have to pee." He stood up and set the baby onto my chest, into my arms. Then he left.

I looked down at the little round face, which, besides her little starfish hands, was the only visible part. The rest of her was covered in pink fleece pajamas with yellow sheep on them. "Hi," I said quietly. "Please don't cry, okay?"

She gave me an appraising squint, as if thinking it over.

"I'll be your best friend," I offered. "When Josh and I have our own place, you can visit sometimes. I'll teach you how to change the oil on your car. It will save you forty bucks."

She wrinkled her nose, as if maybe she didn't like this idea.

"Okay, fine. I'll change the oil for you. You don't even have to get your hands dirty. Do we have a deal?"

Her mouth scrunched up. I was pretty sure she was about to let loose with a wail.

In the back of the house, a toilet flushed. That meant I was sixty seconds away from relief. "*Amazing grace*," I sang. Badly. "*How sweet the sound*."

She howled. I gave up singing and rocked her a little. Sort of. "Josh!" I yelled.

Josh came trotting back into the room. "What happened?" He

scooped the baby up and began bouncing his knees, saying "shh, shh."

"She doesn't like me. She can tell I'm afraid. The way a dog smells fear."

Josh rolled his eyes. "It's late. I think she's just tired." He made a lap around the room, and the crying tapered off. By the time it stopped, the baby was asleep on his shoulder.

Gingerly, he sat down again, and I put my feet in his lap. When Daniel and Maggie weren't home, I could be more affectionate. Someday, we'd have our own place. And I was going to touch him every chance I got. And, just as I was enjoying this thought, I heard a voice call out "I'm home!" from the mudroom.

I yanked my feet off Josh and put them on the floor. "We're in here," I said in a low voice, mindful of the sleeping baby.

Two minutes later, Daniel appeared in the doorway. He walked over to his favorite upholstered chair and sat heavily in it.

"Where's Maggie?" Josh asked quickly.

"They admitted her to the psych ward overnight." Daniel dropped his head into his hands. "She'll be okay, though. There's going to be medication. And if that doesn't work, there are other medicines they can try."

Josh and I were quiet for a minute, unsure what to say.

"I mean..." Daniel continued. "They *say* it's going to be okay. But she still looks like a mess. And she can't breastfeed the baby anymore, because of the meds. So she was crying about that."

"But there's always baby formula," I said quickly.

"Sure," Daniel said. "But she feels like a failure."

Josh sighed. "Poor Maggie. That's just not fair."

"I know," Daniel said. "And I still feel like a tool for yelling at her. I should have known it wasn't her fault. And here you sat all day with the baby. Can I take her?" he held out his hands.

Josh looked down at the sleeping pink person. "I think I should just put her in the crib. You'll get your chance in about three hours, I think?" He stood up.

"Thank you," Daniel said, as Josh headed for the stairs.

"I don't mind at all," he said, climbing the stairs slowly.

When he'd truly disappeared, I echoed Josh. "He doesn't mind, you know. It gives him a way to be useful."

Daniel rubbed the bridge of his nose. "Useful doesn't even begin to describe it. I was such a dick this morning. And you two have really saved our butts lately."

"But we eat a lot."

"I'm still coming out ahead," Daniel said, standing up. "I'd better go to bed. She'll wake up hungry before I know it. Is there baby milk in the freezer, or am I switching to that powdered formula...?"

"Ask Josh," I said. "He's the one who knows."

Daniel gave a sad little smile. "At least somebody does. Good night."

Half an hour later, I got into bed with Josh. He didn't shun me anymore these days. When I rolled toward him, he came into my arms willingly. "I bet you're beat," I said.

"Why?"

"You held that baby for, like, an entire day."

"She only weighs eight pounds. And I'm not the one who is going to wake up in the night to feed her." He was quiet for a minute. "I like Chloe. We understand each other."

Somehow, I avoided laughing. And even if I had chuckled, it wouldn't be because I thought what Josh said was ridiculous. It's just that he was so freaking cute. "She's lucky to have you," I said. "And so are Maggie and Daniel. You might have saved her, Josh. I'm not kidding."

"That's awfully dark."

I pushed a hand through his soft hair. "I don't mean to be dramatic. But you saw something wrong, and you got her help. Maybe Daniel would have done that eventually. But it was pretty amazing, and he was grateful."

"I hope the medicine works."

145

"It will. And they'll always remember it. You're in good, now."
I meant that last bit as a joke. But it was really quite true.

"I guess," he said.

I hugged him tighter. "You *guess?* Of course you are."

"They don't know about us."

"Oh." That was true. And, if I was honest, not a day went by
that I didn't worry about what it would mean if they knew. I
wavered between thinking that it might not matter and the
certainty that it totally would. "Maybe someday we can tell them.
After they've known us a long time."

"Don't do it," Josh said quickly.

I hugged him again. "I would never say a word without your
permission. Don't worry. I know you like it here."

"Yeah."

"Eventually they're gonna wonder, though. If it's ten years
from now, and we've been sharing a house, or whatever, and
neither of us has a wife."

"Ugh. They won't wonder for a long time, though. They won't
expect us to marry anyone for years."

"True." I rubbed Josh's stomach sleepily. The feel of his taut
body in my arms could make me horny in a hot second, if I let it.
But we didn't fool around when other people were home. Ever.
"Goodnight, baby."

He answered me with a tiny snore.

CHAPTER FIFTEEN

Josh

I woke up in Caleb's arms. After getting dressed, I stumbled to the kitchen alone. It was time for milking, but the house was quiet. The only sound I heard were little infant noises, coming from the portable baby monitor which had been abandoned on the counter.

Chloe was the first one awake.

The little sounds she made were one of my favorite things about her. Everything I knew about babies I'd learned in the past three weeks. But I found that I was drawn to Chloe's utter lack of self-consciousness. Chloe never thought twice before voicing her opinion. She never worried what we thought of her.

I envied her.

There were a couple of baby bottles discarded in the sink — the night's work of a sleep-deprived Daniel. Outside, the cows needed my attention. But upstairs, Chloe was going to burst into screams if someone didn't feed her fairly soon.

So I made a bottle, heating it in the microwave, then swirling the liquid around to even out the temperature. I tested it on my wrist just as Maggie had shown me a week ago.

Climbing the stairs, I could hear Chloe's breathy little sounds getting louder. They'd shifted from mere observations to complaints. But I made the deadline—she wasn't wailing yet. And when I leaned over her crib, her blue eyes opened wide, and her short arms began to windmill with excitement.

I loved that greeting. Nobody had ever been so happy to see me.

Scooping her up, I moved her to the changing table. It only took a minute to swap the wet diaper for a dry one. Then I snapped her back up and sat down in the rocker. Another thing I'd learned was that a hungry baby always attacked the bottle like she hasn't eaten for weeks. She sort of grabbed it in her jaw and shook it, before settling in to gulp at the nipple. It was fun to watch. She had so much life force already. So much *will*.

The milk disappeared at a steady clip, with the last couple of ounces going slowly, as Chloe sucked more lazily. When it was empty, I burped her, rocking us both in the chair. There was still nothing but silence coming from Daniel's bedroom. So I took Chloe with me downstairs.

Luckily, I found the baby carrier hanging from a hook in the mudroom. I put Chloe into it, facing my chest. Then I put my canvas work coat over that, partially zipping it around Chloe's back. The last thing I did was add a little hat for her fuzzy head.

It was December. Was it warm enough in the barn for a baby? It would have to be.

We went out into the barn, where the girls were eager to see me. The cows nudged each other to try to be first in line. All I had to do was wave Lady over to the milking stand. Holding Chloe's head with my palm, I crouched down to do a one-handed cleanse of the teat.

Chloe complained just a little bit when I jostled us both to hook up the milk line, but I apologized and began to sing to her. While the fresh milk ran through the milking tubes, Chloe looked up at me with big eyes.

We milked three cows before Daniel stumbled into the barn, sleep in his eyes. "Oh my God," he said. "I'm so groggy."

I laughed, because he really was. "Didn't mean to scare you, sneaking off with the baby."

He just shook his bed-messy head. "I knew who she'd be with. Just didn't know where. I woke up Caleb, looking for you."

"Yeah," I chuckled, nudging Clover's flank. "He's still finishing up his beauty sleep right around now."

"Let me..." Daniel said, stepping in to take over the milking. "You can take her inside, or whatever. I got this."

"All right. But I don't think she's too cold."

Daniel sighed. "It's not about that. But you're doing all the work right now, okay? I feel like a heel."

"Hey, I just got eight hours of sleep. I'm doing great. There's two bottles in the sink, which means you woke up at least twice."

"She woke me three times to eat, but at least she went back to sleep right away." Daniel unhooked Clover from the pump. "Nobody tells you it will be like this. And I wouldn't even mind, if Maggie was doing better."

"She will be," I said quickly.

"God, I hope so," he whispered.

"Well. Chloe and I are going inside for coffee. We'll save you some."

Daniel gave me a wave. "You're the best, Josh. Really."

I liked hearing it, even if I doubted his opinion would hold up if he knew the real me.

DANIEL BROUGHT Maggie home from the hospital that afternoon, still looking like hell.

"The drugs make her really sleepy," Daniel whispered after he'd gotten a zombie-like Maggie upstairs. "But it's supposed to even out soon."

He took the baby from me then, leaving my hands empty. And Caleb was at work. So I had nothing to do at all, except worry and wonder what would happen next.

There were practical things I might have worked on. I needed to write to the State of Wyoming and ask them to grant me a birth certificate. But I needed instructions from Maggie, who'd had to do the same thing. Or at least computer help from Caleb, who knew his way around Google.

With nothing better to do, I went in our bedroom and lay down on Caleb's pillow, because it smelled like him. And I had sexy thoughts about him as I drifted into a nap.

That night, after I ate macaroni and cheese that Daniel made from those blue boxes they sell at the store, I put the baby to bed again. This left Daniel in front of a football game with a beer, looking tired but content. And he didn't even fight me too badly on putting the baby to bed for him. I think he'd finally just given in and accepted my help.

I liked that. A lot. Because family is supposed to help family. Family is how Maggie viewed Caleb and I. Maybe Daniel could, too.

After Chloe was settled into her crib, I tiptoed into Maggie and Daniel's room, and perched on the bed.

Maggie opened a set of unfocused eyes, then seemed to locate me through her haze.

"I just came to say that I hope you feel better soon. And I'm sorry for your troubles."

"Thank you," she said, surprising me. "I'm embarrassed, though. That people have to fuss. That it couldn't just be easy."

I reached over to give her hand a squeeze. "You just described the first nineteen years of my life."

Maggie's eyes opened wide, and then she smiled. *Finally!* A smile from Maggie. So I smiled too. "I love you, Josh," she said.

My chest squeezed with happiness to hear it. So few people had ever said that to me. Caleb, and my mother. And my mother hadn't said it since I was seven. When I answered her, my voice was rough. "Love you too. I'll see you in the morning."

THAT NIGHT I got into bed before Caleb. And when he finally crawled between the sheets, and rolled to face me, I slid into his arms and kissed him. Hard. He opened for me, but not without making a surprised little noise in the back of his throat.

But Caleb was a smart man. He went for it, inviting my tongue to tangle with his. And his strong arms pulled me close, against that broad chest that I loved so much.

I'd been dying for this. While he was at work, I'd been yearning for it. Kiss after kiss, I lost myself in Caleb. Pushing my body into his, I could have stayed there all night.

"Baby," he whispered, dipping a hand into my underwear. "Let me make you feel good." His hand closed around my cock. But then he waited, asking permission to go on. His other hand stroked my back slowly. *Lovingly*.

"You can't fuck me, because I can't be quiet," I whispered.

In the dark, I watched him smile at me. "Can you be quiet if I blow you?"

Thinking that over for a second, I shook my head. "Stay right here with me." Tonight, I just wanted him close. I wanted to rub off on him, kissing him. Sucking on his tongue.

Caleb shoved his underwear off his body and tossed them on the floor. "Come here." He pulled me partway onto his chest, yanking my own boxers off of my ass.

I spread myself out on his hard body. He felt incredible underneath me. I could have happily stayed there forever.

Caleb produced his little bottle of lube and dripped some into his hand. When he gripped both our cocks in one slicked palm, I gasped.

"Shh, now," he reminded me.

I dropped my hungry mouth onto his, whimpering softly. Thrusting into his hand, my dick got as hard as a fencepost.

"You stay quiet now," Caleb whispered after breaking our kiss. "Can you do that?"

I kissed him again instead of answering.

He reached around me, spreading my ass with one slicked hand, teasing my hole with a finger.

Opening my mouth, I gave a silent shout.

"Next time," he whispered. "I'm gonna pound you from behind."

The beginning of a moan escaped my lips, and Caleb caught it in his mouth. I fucked my hips against him, while his naughty finger tortured my hole.

"Let yourself go. Kiss me, and come all over me. Right now."

My whole life, I'd always done exactly what Caleb asked of me. And right now was no different. My balls tightened up, and my breath hitched with expectation. Then I slanted my mouth over Caleb's and let it happen. All the tension of the last forty-eight hours just left my body as I shuddered and shuddered again.

Caleb let my tired dick slip out of his hand. But he took up his own, milking himself with my come all over his hand. We both looked down to see him erupt once... twice... I lifted my chin to watch his face. His head was thrown back into the pillow, mouth open in a silent gasp of pleasure.

Then it was just two sticky guys, breathing hard, listening to their hearts race together. I loved this part just as much as the sex. Because I never saw any regret in Caleb's eyes. He always looked so darned happy to lie there with me, painted with my seed, blissed out.

He never seemed to doubt himself. And that meant that he never seemed to doubt being with me.

I kissed his forehead. "Was I quiet?"

"Quiet enough," he sighed. "Don't really care at the moment, though. That was nice."

It really, really was. But you can always trust me to ruin the moment. "Do you think they'd notice if we ran the shower for a minute?"

Caleb pinched my ass. "We'd better make it a double shower. Less obvious that way." He grinned without opening his eyes.

"Good idea," I said.

And it was.

CHAPTER SIXTEEN

Josh

Winter

Maggie did get better. The rest of us breathed many, many sighs of relief as she seemed to slowly perk up over the next few weeks. She came out of her room more. Daniel brought the rocking chair into the living room, and she sat there with the baby, talking to whoever else was around. Which often meant me.

She started to cook again, too. I made it as easy as I could for her, by holding the baby when necessary. Standing in the kitchen, talking about flavors and recipes, she seemed more like herself.

Meanwhile, Chloe was growing fast. Every morning, when I got to hold her after the milking, she seemed bigger. And she learned so many new tricks. Like *smiling* at me. And pushing up off her tummy onto her little chubby arms to look around the room.

In February, when Chloe was twelve weeks old, she learned to roll over from her back to her front. So she basically did that all day long. But she couldn't figure out how to roll the other way, so when she got sick of lying on her stomach, she would screech until one of us came to rescue her, flipping her over like a pancake.

Another new trick she learned was sleeping through the night. I was not the beneficiary of this new maneuver, but Maggie and Daniel were over the moon. They stopped looking so haggard, and started joking more often.

As winter wore on, I worked with Daniel whenever I could. Sometimes he found jobs for me in the wood shop. But tools were not really my thing, and everything always took three times as long when I did it. I was better at sorting nails and screws, sweeping up sawdust and helping him move boards around.

There wasn't much of that to do, though.

Instead, I finally convinced him that I should do the morning milking alone. "Since Chloe sleeps past seven o'clock, so should you. Until I can get a full-time job, I don't mind spending a couple of hours with the cows every morning."

I gave Daniel this little speech one afternoon in the barn, when the two of us were shoveling cow shit into a wheelbarrow. I enjoyed the milking and the barn work, anyway. Taking care of cows didn't even feel like labor. They watched me with their big, liquid eyes, and their breath warmed the room, even on the coldest days.

Daniel leaned against his shovel, stroking his jaw thoughtfully. "All right. You know I appreciate the help. And Maggie and I need to get on top of your documentation. Sorry we haven't given that enough focus."

"You've been busy. But I don't want to just sponge off you guys forever."

Daniel shrugged and went back to shoveling. "I don't think you're a sponge. But I understand if you two need to make your own way."

We did, too.

Caleb was, as always, doing a pretty good job for himself already. The garage was pleased with his work, so his hours remained steady. He spent half his paycheck on gas and groceries for the house. That was the deal he'd made with Maggie. She'd insisted that he save up the other half. "I know you want a car. So bank your money, because one of these days you'll be able to afford one."

He'd saved almost two thousand dollars already. It sounded like a lot to me, but apparently cars cost plenty. Even old ones.

I needed to work. That much was obvious.

In January, Daniel and Maggie called the same lawyer in Wyoming who had helped to get her a birth certificate. There was some kind of petition you could file to ask the state to recognize your birth. I signed a form, and we sent it in.

"Mine took months, though," Maggie said. "So I wouldn't hold my breath waiting."

In the meantime, Maggie's friend with the catering business needed her back at work. And since a family of five needed cash, Maggie sat me down and asked me to babysit while she did some gigs with the caterer. "Obviously Daniel can take her after dinner-time. But sometimes I need to be at work in the afternoon."

"I'd love to do it," I said. "It doesn't make sense for you to work if Daniel has to *stop* working."

She grinned. "So true. Except that I'd probably *still* work, even then. Because I like this job, and I really need to get out of this house once in a while."

"Go on, then," I said. While we had this conversation, I was sitting in the rocking chair, holding Chloe, who was chewing on a plastic rattle. The poor thing was teething. And apparently, teething made you drool. Lately, she left little wet patches on the shoulders of all my shirts.

"I'll pay you," Maggie said. "It's only fair."

"Eh. If you're paying me, then I should pay you rent. And I can't afford it."

Maggie laughed. "But I'd feel guilty just skipping off to make strawberries dipped in chocolate while you watch Chloe."

I picked my head off the rocker. "Strawberries dipped in chocolate?"

Maggie grinned at me. "That's it! I'll pay you in desserts."

"Deal." I rocked the baby, feeling as calm and happy as I ever had in my life. Things weren't perfect, but for the first time in my life I didn't fear the future. Maggie wanted me here, in this chair, in this room, in this house. As did Caleb, and Chloe, and even Daniel. Hell, even the cows were happy to see me.

When dinnertime came, Daniel came into the house, lightly coated with sawdust. He changed his clothes and then found us in the living room. "My turn," he said, holding out his hands for Chloe.

"I don't see your name on the list," I said lazily. Chloe was a warm weight on my chest, and I didn't feel like giving her up.

"Pretty sure fathers are always on the list," he said.

"Well, if you want to get all technical about it." I handed Chloe up to him, and she started making excited noises. Chloe loved her daddy. When he took her, she put her little starfish hands on his face.

"Hi, baby girl," he whispered. "What have you been up to today?"

"Drooling on Josh and mommy," I answered for her. Daniel gave me a grin. Then I got up to go help Maggie set the table.

She'd lit the candles already, and their soft glow flickered on the wood of the table that Daniel had built. The warm lighting, and the sounds of a man saying sweet things to his baby daughter gave me an ache in my chest. The *good* kind of ache. The kind that means you're alive and well.

Any minute now, Caleb would drive up in Maggie's car. He'd shower off the smell of motor oil, then sit across from me at the dinner table. We'd be careful not to let our eyes linger too long on one another, and we'd never risk a touch beneath the table.

This was home, though. And for once in my life, I felt like I belonged.

CHAPTER SEVENTEEN

Dear Washington & Brenda,

Happy New Year (a couple weeks late!)

We got your Christmas card. Would you believe that it was the first one we ever got? (Actually, I'll bet you <u>do</u> believe it!) We never had Christmas at the Compound, because there's no mention of Christmas in the Bible, and our divine pastor decided that celebrating Christmas was gluttonous, and a sin. (Caleb says that it's just cheaper not to have holidays, though.)

Maggie prepared such a feast for Christmas that I'm wondering if the pastor was right about the gluttony. But I enjoyed myself anyway.

Caleb and I didn't have a lot of money to buy gifts, so I gave Maggie and Daniel coupons for babysitting, so that they could go out together. I really don't mind doing it, and she feels guilty asking me to do extra time with baby Chloe. So it's kind of perfect.

For Daniel, Caleb put a refurbished stereo in his truck, which didn't have one before. Caleb said he got it for almost nothing. He put it in one night after everyone else had gone to bed. Daniel was totally surprised when he found a bow on the dashboard in the morning.

Caleb's had a mechanic's job since Thanksgiving. They only gave him twenty hours to start, but then it crept up to thirty-five. So Caleb's savings account is looking pretty good these days.

His plan is to buy a car and then move out. I'll go with Caleb, even though I don't have a job yet. We just asked the state of Wyoming for a birth certificate for me. When they get around to giving me one, I'll be able to apply for a social security number, and get a driver's license.

Maggie has gone back to work part-time at her friend's catering company, and I'm her babysitter. It turns out that I'm good at taking care of things. Babies and cows seem to like me.

I'd never taken care of a baby before we moved here, but it's really fun. I spend a good portion of the afternoon on my hands and knees hanging out with Chloe. It doesn't seem like work, to be honest. But it helps Maggie, so it's all good.

So far we haven't had any contact with the Compound where we used to live. But tomorrow we're sending a package to Maggie's mother. All four of us worked on it, and we're hoping it gets through to her.

It was my idea how to do it, but Daniel is the one who really made it look right. Maggie's mom does a lot of needlework, so we're sending her a dozen little hanks of embroidery floss. The whole thing is designed to look like something she mail-ordered. Daniel printed out a mailing label with her name and the P.O. Box for the Compound. The return address says "Extra Special Needlework Products, Since 2010," which is the year that Maggie left. Daniel also printed "take care while opening, sewing needles within may be sharp."

We're hoping that nobody bothers to open the package before Mrs. Beaufort gets it.

But even if they open it, they still might not understand that it's a trick. There's no letter inside. But the packing list has a lot of information on it. There's a color listed as "Maggie's Magenta." And there's another one called "Massachusetts Maroon." And "Berkshire County Blue." There's a "Caleb Copper" and a "Joshua Jade" and "Cheshire, MA Red."

We replaced the little paper labels on every hank, and the new ones have Maggie's phone number on the inside, just in case the paper is lost. And the packing slip says "Visit our factory. Call anytime to make travel arrangements. Our doors are always open to you." The address and phone numbers listed are Maggie's, of course.

Isn't that sneaky? I was kind of nervous about sending them our exact location. I'm still worried that someone will try to get even with us. But Daniel tells me there's nothing to fear — that those in charge have more to fear from us. Apparently Caleb or Maggie or I could get them in a lot of hot water, and not the other way around.

We talk about this a lot, actually. Sometimes I just want to shut the whole place down. But the weird thing is there are people there who would be miserable if the Compound was broken up. They like it there, and they want things to stay the same.

This letter got very long. But I just wanted you to know that we're doing well. I like it here. I still need to figure out what I'm doing with my life, but Maggie says there are lots of guys my age in that situation.

We hope you're doing well, and we think of you often.

YOUR FRIEND,
Josh Royce

P.S. HERE IS a picture of Caleb and me with my favorite cow, Lady.

CHAPTER EIGHTEEN

February 3rd

Dear Josh & Caleb,

Good to hear from you! I showed my wife your picture, and she said you two were as cute as a button.

We both liked hearing about your sneaky package to Wyoming, too. I think it will work. Because what man is going to look too closely at a package of embroidering crap? You people are geniuses. You should work for the CIA.

I'm still driving that same route from Nevada to Albany. So if you ever get word that one of yours is stranded in Cheyenne again, call me. You never know. I might be nearby.

The wife and I are planning a little vacation to Florida next month. We are flying on a plane, because I tell her that driving is the last thing I want to do on vacation. If you're ever down toward Kentucky where we are, call us. It'd be fun to see you.

All my best,
Washington

PART III

CHAPTER NINETEEN

Josh

Summer

"Well..." Maggie said, turning slowly in a circle so that she could see each dingy wall of the little dumpy apartment. "A coat of paint would go a long way. The floors aren't bad. They look original."

I could read on her face, though, that she did not approve of the tiny little hovel in downtown Pittsfield that we'd brought her to see.

At this point, I was finding it hard to stay positive about our search for a new home. There were so few apartments for rent in our quiet region of Massachusetts. And when you factored in the budget that Caleb and I needed to stick to, the choices got squalid in a hurry.

"The kitchen is the worst part," Caleb admitted. "That stove looks a hundred years old."

Maggie cleared her throat, and I could feel her reaching for something positive to say. "A stove is a pretty simple machine. So that doesn't bother me so much. But this place is just so *small*. One tiny bedroom, and there's not even a closet. I suppose you could ask Daniel to make you a set of bunk beds instead of twin beds. Just like college kids have."

At this point, my shoes became suddenly fascinating. Because the size of the bedroom was not, of course, a problem for Caleb and I. We wanted to move out of Maggie's house so that we could frequently inhabit a very compact portion of our bed.

But of course I couldn't say that.

Maggie didn't notice my discomfort, though. Because she had more issues with the apartment than the bedroom. Thank the Lord.

"Then there's that *bathroom*. I've never seen a smaller shower stall. I just don't see how two men could live here and not kill each other. Why don't you just save up some more money, and try again in six months?"

Again, the truth was not a good option. *We need to have a lot of very loud sex.*

"We, uh..." Caleb started. "We can't lean on you guys forever. I thought that crappy first apartments were a rite of passage, anyway. That's what the guys at the garage tell me."

Maggie paced in a circle. (A very small circle. Because she wasn't wrong about the size of this tiny, dark, run-down place.) "Can I take you two out for coffee before you make your decision? I need to run something by you, anyway."

"All right," I said, heading for the door. I'd been excited to move out until we showed her the space. Truthfully, I couldn't picture Caleb and I here, either. What was I supposed to do all day? Caleb was still in the market for a used car, which he could drive to work at the garage. But that meant I'd be stuck in this neighborhood alone. Whatever job I found would have to be in walking distance.

Downtown, Pittsfield, Massachusetts was not a bustling commercial district. Finding a job would not be easy. As we walked into the dark-paneled coffee shop, I evaluated it as a potential employer. Would they need an inexperienced, slightly quiet, secret queer at the cash register?

Probably not.

Maggie ordered a latte and Caleb ordered plain coffee, black.

"I'm fine," I said when it was my turn. As the non-wage-earner among us, I didn't want them to pay for an overpriced coffee for me.

"He wants a chocolate chip cookie," Maggie said to the cashier, taking out her wallet.

"But..."

She held up a hand to silence me. "I'm celebrating something, okay? Don't kill my buzz. In fact," she said to the cashier, "add one more coffee, and a second cookie."

When our order was ready, we sat around one of the little tables together. Maggie broke off a piece of cookie and pushed the plate toward Caleb and I. "Guys, I have to run something by both of you. Hear me out, okay?"

I nodded, taking a chunk of cookie off the plate. I chased it with a sip of hot coffee, and the combination was, to be fair, exquisite.

"Cecilia has made me an offer that I'm having trouble refusing."

"What's that?" I asked. Cecilia was her caterer friend.

"She wants Cecilia's Catering to become Cecilia & Maggie's Catering."

Caleb grinned. "That's kind of a long title," he said. "I don't know if it will all fit on the side of the van."

I reached over and gave Caleb a playful shove on the shoulder. "Don't listen to him, Maggie. I think that's great. She wants you to be her partner?"

She beamed. "Yes! There will be more hours, but not *too* many more. And the pay will be so much better. But that's where you come in, Josh. I'll need more babysitting. And now I can actually pay you, because you're legal."

"Wow. Okay." Could Maggie solve my employment problem? Just like that? "But…" I swallowed another cup of coffee. "I'll have to commute to you if we're living in Pittsfield." And that meant a second car, which we couldn't afford.

She folded her hands together and looked and Caleb and I in turn. "See, that's the thing. I have a better idea. Have either of you seen the space above the workshop?"

"Sure," Caleb shrugged. "I went up there once to bring some tarps down for Daniel."

"Well, it's a big space. Daniel and I once talked about finishing it, but we haven't had the time. If you guys did a lot of the labor, then you could live up there for free."

"You'd still be supporting us," I argued.

Maggie shook her head. "You could pay the utilities, and you'd have your own kitchen. But refinishing a space is a lot of work. And someday, if you did move out, we'd be left with a finished apartment instead of an empty room. That adds value to our property."

"The materials will cost money, though," Caleb argued. "I suppose I could pay for them out of the rent deposit I've saved up. There's a lot of stuff to buy. Plumbing supplies. Flooring…"

"Daniel and I should pay for everything that's part of the building, since it stays there if you leave," Maggie pointed out. "But you'll need furnishings. Will you *please* consider it? Let's look at the space tonight. It would be so much easier to say yes to Cecilia on the partnership if I knew I had a babysitter on the property."

I eyed Caleb, trying not to feel too hopeful. Our own little place, yet still on the farm? Could we do that? Would it even work?

"I think…" Caleb snuck a glance at me, and then looked Maggie in the eye. "That just might work. If Daniel likes the idea, too."

Maggie tossed her head back and smiled at the ceiling. "Thank you for considering it. Because I really don't want you guys to move far away. And if you end up in that dump we just saw, I fear you'll be looking at jobs in some other state before you know it."

"Another *state?*" I yelped. "Nobody said *that* was on the table. I don't want to move away from you if I don't have to."

Under the table, Caleb's leg moved in close. He pressed his knee against mine, as if to tell me that he understood. "We'll see what Daniel thinks," he said.

THAT EVENING, after the milking, and after dinner, we all went out to clomp around the empty, dusty space over Daniel's workshop.

"Well," Daniel said appraisingly. "There's enough space up here, and the entrance is already separate. So that's something." He walked slowly around, carrying Chloe on his hip, studying the shape of the room. The roof was pitched in one direction, which meant that one end of the big space had a ridiculously high ceiling, which sloped down gradually toward the other end of the room.

Maggie spoke up next. "The way the windows are set, it makes the most sense to put the bedrooms at this end," she pointed to the shorter wall, "and the kitchen on that wall." She paced back into the center. "That doesn't leave much of a living room, but you could put a couch on the wall facing the kitchen."

Caleb cleared his throat. "I think the whole thing might work better if it was left as one open room. Maybe with a loft at the tall end."

"Oh!" Maggie whispered. "Good idea! That would look cool. There could be one bed up on the loft, and the other one underneath. Actually, the downstairs bed could be a futon. During the day, it could be your couch. But then one of you would have to make it up as a bed every night."

This time, when the subject of bedrooms came up, I hid my flaming face by staring out the window.

"Great point," Daniel said. "And this way, we wouldn't have to muck around with dropped ceilings. Except for in the bathroom, which I think you'd want to put in that corner." He pointed. "The workshop sink is on that same wall, which will keep the plumbing costs low."

"That's important," I said, happy that we weren't talking about bedrooms anymore.

"The bathroom and kitchen are the expensive parts," Caleb said. "Wall board is cheap."

"Yeah," Daniel agreed. "But I know a plumber we could hire to help us get through the tricky bits. This could be a fun project, as long as you feel you have the time."

"I can't wait to get started," I said, truthfully. But then I remembered that it really didn't matter what *I* thought. Because it wasn't me who was going to do most of this work. I was happy to sand the floors or paint the walls. But when it came to installing a toilet, I didn't have a clue.

Caleb rubbed his hands together. "This could be great. I just hope you really don't mind having tenants. I figure you'll want your house back to normal someday, and a renovation will take some time. And when we *do* leave, you still won't really be rid of us."

"But I don't *want* to be rid of you," Maggie said immediately. "You and Josh and Daniel and Chloe are my family. I'm trying to keep you close, not send you away."

"Well..." Caleb put a hand on the back of his neck, and looked at Daniel. "If you're *all* on board with it..."

Daniel switched Chloe from one hip to the other, and gave us both a quiet smile. "If you think there's enough privacy here, then don't think twice. Stay."

It was weird that he'd mention privacy. But I didn't dwell on it. I was too busy feeling happy. I wanted to move in here, and live within a two minute walk of Chloe and my adoptive family. And even the cows. I just hoped Caleb was as happy about it as I was.

CHAPTER TWENTY

DEAR WASHINGTON,

THANK YOU for the Halloween candy! You're right — we've never had any before. At the Compound, Halloween was considered a pagan ritual.

Caleb and I are busy converting the big room over Daniel's workshop into an apartment. It's a ton of work, but it will be nice when it's done. Daniel bought the fixtures, and Caleb and I are doing the work for free. (Caleb's labor is a lot more valuable than mine, but I'm pretty handy with the power sander these days.)

In other news, I now have a driver's license. Caleb taught me to drive, finally, using Maggie's car. Soon, Caleb is going to buy a used car. He says he's waiting for just the right one to turn up.

We are becoming more independent, but it's taking forever.

My love to Brenda,

Josh

CHAPTER TWENTY-ONE

Josh

Autumn

The apartment was *almost* ready. There was running water now — but only in the bathroom.

It was a Monday night, which meant that Caleb and I had been working on our renovation for ten hours. Monday was still Caleb's day off. And it wasn't a big catering day, either, so he and I always got a lot of renovation work done on Mondays.

The kitchen cabinets were in already, and the floor had been insulated from below. "You can't have an apartment over a workshop without good insulation," Daniel had said. "You'd hear power tools all day long."

"I wouldn't mind," I'd argued.

"We're going to do this right," Daniel had insisted, "because I don't want to redo it someday." He paid a man to come and blow foam between the apartment's floor and the workshop's ceiling.

There weren't too many other tasks we'd had to hire out, though. Daniel had built the kitchen cabinets, and Caleb and I were finishing them. As predicted, we'd needed some help with the plumbing, but it wasn't too bad. Caleb did the heating himself. "If I can fix a car's heater, I can put in baseboard units," he'd said.

And he had.

For my part, there was endless sanding and painting. But it wasn't fussy work, so I didn't mind it. When I finished the day with sawdust in my hair, I felt like one of the guys. It was a nice contrast to all the nursery rhymes and fairy books that Chloe and I spent the week looking at together.

At almost one year old, Chloe could say a couple of words. She wasn't a prolific talker, but she said "dada" and a variation with an "m" in it, which was supposed to be "mama," but wasn't quite. She said "more" and "bye-bye" and "no." (She said that last one a lot.)

She did not, however, say "Josh."

"I think the J sound is hard," Maggie had said more than once. Every morning I spent a few minutes trying to get Chloe to say "Josh." "You can do it," I urged her. "It doesn't have to be perfect, either. Say...*Josh*."

"No," she said instead.

"Fine," I sighed, as Maggie laughed. "But if you end up saying 'Caleb' first, heads are gonna roll."

Today I hadn't seen Chloe since lunch, though, because Caleb and I had sanded the baseboards, and then I put a coat of primer on the wall.

Working on our place with Caleb was fun — so much more fun than working at the Compound had ever been. Because we were working on something for *us*. That was just amazing. I didn't mind all the affection I received while we worked together, either. He touched my back when he asked me a question. And I got a nice kiss when we sat down in the middle of the bare floor for lunch.

Life was good. And now it was quitting time. "What color are we going to paint this wall, anyway?" I asked Caleb as I tapped the metal lid back onto the top of a can of primer.

"White, right?" he grunted.

"It doesn't have to be," I argued. "I like that yellow color in Maggie's dining room. It makes the place look sunny."

"Well..." Caleb chuckled. "If you want yellow, I got no problem with that. But you're the one that doesn't want to go public." He took off his tool belt.

"Why? What are you saying?"

Caleb grinned at me. "I'm saying that gay guys paint their walls bright colors. At least on TV."

"Really? Damn it."

Caleb came up behind me and wrapped his arms around my midsection. "I don't think a couple of yellow walls would really be all that revealing. I was just kidding."

I didn't know what to say, though. Lately Caleb had been making noises about telling Daniel and Maggie. He said that if our plan was to live here forever, then it should be addressed. "Because if they can't handle it, we ought to know that. So we can move on," he reasoned.

But if I had my way? We weren't *ever* having that conversation. Because I did not want to see Maggie's expression when she learned the truth about Caleb and me. I was too addicted to seeing admiration on her face, and the simple joy I found there when she came home from a long day to find Chloe and me cuddling on the couch.

It was just too risky. Maybe that made me a coward, but that was just the way I felt.

"Hey, guys?" We heard Daniel's feet on the stairs.

By silent, mutual agreement, Caleb moved away from me. He very casually picked up a broom in the corner of the room and leaned on it, as if he'd been there all along.

"Hey!" Daniel said, coming through our open door. "I'm heading inside for the night. Maggie said to tell you that she's making pot roast, but she started late. So dinner isn't until seven-thirty."

175

"Sounds great," Caleb said. "We'll be in soon, anyway. I think we've had just about all we can take."

"I'll bet. The lights are off in the workshop, okay? Just let the door lock behind you on the way out."

I gave Daniel a salute, and he disappeared down the stairs. A minute later, we heard the outside door slam as he went home for the night.

Silence descended on us, and I listened to it. This would soon be the sound of our nights here. Our new place was snug, and it really did feel quite private. Daniel never came back out to his workshop after dark, because he said daylight was imperative for doing quality joinery.

"I'm going to like living here," I said.

Across the room, Caleb set his broom into the corner and smiled at me. As I gathered up the tarp I'd used to protect the floor, I felt him arrive at my back. He put two hands on my ass and rubbed.

Since I was bent over, ass in the air, and wearing sweatpants, it could not have been more suggestive. Instinctively, I pushed backwards against him.

Caleb groaned. "Give me ten minutes of your time, and you can paint the walls any damned color you want."

I snickered, standing upright again. "Ten minutes, huh?"

He grabbed my hips in two hands, then leaned forward to speak directly into my ear. His voice was low and gravely. "I need you to walk over to that countertop and put your hands on it. Both of them."

My neck heated immediately. Because I loved that bossy tone that Caleb took on when he wanted sex. Before he even finished speaking, my dick began to feel plump and heavy.

He gave me a push on the bottom. "Right now," he said. "Hands on the counter."

I got moving. Crossing the room, I put both palms down flat on the new butcher block countertop.

"Good boy," Caleb said, following me over there. "Nice of you to wear sweats. I like the easy access."

Of course, I was only wearing those old sweats because I didn't want paint splatters on my jeans. But Caleb shoved them down, plunging his hand into the front of my boxers. I hissed at what he found there.

"You *are* a good boy. Getting hard for me already."

Truly, I was. We never got as much sex as we wanted. Though Caleb and I had both become masters of the silent orgasm, we didn't push our luck. So hearing his dirty talk out loud right now was so, so hot.

I reached a hand backward, trying for his fly.

Caleb batted it away. "Did I say you could touch me?"

Ooh! He was feeling bossy tonight. I felt another zing of heat steal through me, just from the tone of his voice. I planted my hands on the counter again, just waiting to see what he'd do.

He didn't make me wait long. Caleb stroked me once only, from base to tip. Then he shoved my sweats and boxers down all the way. "Off," he commanded.

I kicked out of my clothes, and Caleb whisked my T-shirt over my head, too. That left me standing naked before him, my bare back to his front.

"Nice," he whispered, running a rough hand down my spine. Then Caleb planted his hands on either side of mine on the counter, and pressed his firm chest to my back. "Lean over," he ordered. "Elbows on the counter."

I bent forward, like he asked me to. That put my ass in contact with his groin, where I could feel a nice, rigid dick inside his jeans. Slowly, he flexed his hips, pressing hard, letting me know exactly what was about to happen.

I was already looking forward to it.

Caleb rustled around for a second, removing something from his pocket. I swear, when I heard the telltale sound of the lube bottle opening, I got even harder. He must have been planning this. He must have been thinking about it all day.

He set the little bottle on the counter, and then two things happened at once. His lips landed on the back of my neck, and a warm, slicked palm came around my hip to slide up the underside of my dick.

"Mmm," I murmured. I'd never stood naked in the middle of a room before, getting sexed up by Caleb. Even though the risk of getting caught was nearly zero—Daniel would be holding his baby daughter right now, and having a beer with the wife he hadn't seen all day — it felt very, very naughty. I leaned into Caleb's hand, gently rubbing myself in his palm, and enjoying the hard press of his crotch behind me.

"That's right," he whispered in my ear. "We're going to break our new place in. I'm going to fuck you so good. Spread for me."

The words made me shiver with pleasure. Quickly, I worked my legs a bit wider, opening myself to him.

His hand retreated. When I next felt it again, that slicked hand was rubbing my crease, massaging my taint in the most wonderful way. One thick finger paused at my entrance, promising more than delivering penetration.

I held my breath.

A strong arm came around me, teasing my dick at the exact moment that finger pushed inside. The double assault made me gasp with pleasure. Tipping my head back, I pressed back against Caleb's hand, eager for more.

"Easy," he whispered. "It's been a while since we did this. We have to take it slow."

But slow wasn't good enough for me. The burn I was feeling was mild, and the excitement was not. Moaning, I forced myself backward, fucking myself on Caleb's finger.

"So eager," Caleb whispered. "All right." His hand disappeared for a second, and I heard him apply more lube. Then two fingers pushed inside me. *Yessss.* But still, Caleb teased me. He stretched me and kissed my neck, but he didn't deliver the erotic touch that I craved.

"Please," I whispered, trying to push back against him. "Please."

"There's something you want?" he chuckled.

"You," I panted. "Want you."

"Where do you want me?" he asked between kisses. "Here?" He slid his fist up and down my dick, and it felt so good. But that wasn't what I really craved, and he knew it. "How about... here," he suggested, finally stretching his fingers inside me, curving them to hit my spot.

I gave a shout of joy. It was so good. So good, yet not quite enough. "Fuck me," I hissed. "Please."

"Since you asked so nice," he whispered, "I think I will."

He worked me open for a few minutes longer. Then both his hands deserted me for a moment. The clink of his zipper unfurling was the best sound I'd heard in my lifetime. The fact that he was still clothed and I was standing there stark naked was strangely exciting. But there was only a faint rustle as he shoved his jeans down onto his hips. Then strong hands roughly positioned my hips.

Then he pushed inside.

It was, as always, weird and overwhelming. My breath caught in my throat. I tilted my head back, remembered to breathe again, and slowly let out my air.

Caleb's voice dropped low, and he said only one, soft word. "Okay?"

There it was. That one sweet moment of concern. The one that told me that no matter how bossy he was when we got naked, I was always safe with him. That he would always take care of me if I needed him to.

Knowing that, and the feel of his big body jammed against mine, into mine, all around mine — brought tears to my eyes. I took one more deep breath against the assault of emotion. Then I

SARINA BOWEN

pushed my ass backward. *Take me*, I begged with my hips. *I'm yours*.

With a happy growl, Caleb pressed his hands down over mine, where they lay on the counter, effectively holding me in place. He pulled back, then gave me a slow, purposeful thrust.

My knees practically buckled from the intensity of the experience. This forbidden thing we did together was so dear to me. The feeling of my lover's hard cock pushing inside me was all I wanted.

His hips set a demanding rhythm, and his hands curled over mine. It was possessive. I loved that. With a grunt, he canted me further over, which changed his angle. And, ohhhhh. There it was. Now each stroke hit my spot.

"Yeah," I began to pant. "Caleb."

"Louder," he demanded. "Tell me what you want."

"F...fuck me," I groaned.

"Like this?" He snapped his hips forward.

"Ahh!" *Yes.* It was perfect. I braced my arms against the counter and bore down on him. It was so naughty, and so good, too. I loved it.

Before long I was moaning and begging. "Please," I whispered. I wanted to come so bad. I dropped one hand to my own dick.

"Did I tell you to touch yourself?" Caleb asked.

I took the hand away. "Please?" I begged. But I loved it when he was bossy. He liked to draw things out, but it was always worth it in the end.

"I know what you need," Caleb panted. "And I'm going to give it to you." He slowed down his pace, his hips rolling forward. He hit my prostate even more squarely, and each stroke was like heaven.

"Aaahhh," I moaned.

"Yeah, okay," he agreed. "Let's go." His arms tightened around me. Then he took my dick in his hand. "Come for me, baby."

His hips began to piston, and I heard his breathing hitch. I was glad to have both hands on the counter, because my legs were shaking. As soon as Caleb moaned, I came, spurting all over the cabinet in front of me.

Good thing I'd painted that with polyurethane last week.

"Baby," Caleb gasped. "Yessss..."

AFTERWARD, we had to stand there for a few minutes to catch our breath.

"The kitchen counter?" I chuckled eventually. "That was hot."

He wrapped two arms around my chest and squeezed. I received another kiss on my neck. "It was. I'll be thinking about it all week. That's where my mind is gonna go every time I'm aligning somebody's tires."

I laughed. "Hope none of the guys you work with are mind-readers."

"Eh." Caleb shrugged against my back. "It's not like I feel like sharing. But I don't think they give a damn who I'm fucking. I assume that a couple of them have figured me out, anyway."

"Really?" I stood up then, forcing Caleb to take a step back.

"Really," he said, leaning down to fish my T-shirt off the floor. "I mean, they talk about pussy all day *long*. And I don't. It's just obvious that I'm not interested. It's not like I'm going to try and fake it."

"Wouldn't they just assume it's a religion thing?" I let Caleb drop the shirt over my head. I stuck my arms through the holes, and let him smooth the fabric down my ribcage. I loved the way he always tried to take care of me after sex. I don't even know if he realized that he did it.

"Well, it's just that I don't *sound* religious. I curse at least as much as they do."

This was true. Caleb had a potty mouth, and took the Lord's name in vain at every opportunity, which was just his way of sticking it to the Compound from afar. "Are you worried?" I asked.

"Nope," he said, handing me my boxers. Then he picked up a rag and began wiping off the poor cabinet door. "I don't get a bad vibe off these guys. I show up on time and do the work. And I'm easy to get along with. That's all they care about. If tomorrow I made a reference to watching some movie with my boyfriend, or whatever, I don't think they'd even stop chewing their gum."

Boyfriend. I liked hearing that word. I pulled my sweats on, trying not to smile. I needed a shower, because it was probably time to go back to the house for dinner.

But Caleb put his hands on my ribcage and backed me against the counter. "Can't wait to get a bed in here," he said, massaging my chest. "Kitchen sex is hot. But it's harder to get into that mouth of yours."

He reached up to palm my chin, and I just melted into him. Our lips came together in a sweet slide. This was all I wanted in my life, right here. In a month, maybe, we'd be standing here waiting for the coffee to finish brewing. There would be all the time in the world for slow, gratuitous kisses.

Caleb must have been feeling the same kind of romantic optimism, because he kept up the slow, sensual kisses. I let myself get lost in them. His tongue swept into my mouth, and he made a low noise of approval.

How far we'd come. A year ago, I'd never kissed anyone. Now I had my heart's desire, and a place to call our own. I took his head in both my hands and deepened the kiss. The world quieted down when I was in Caleb's arms. I sifted my fingers through his hair and sighed.

Big hands palmed my back. His tongue said *I love you*. And mine agreed.

"You'll never guess who just called!" someone hollered, crashing into the apartment from the stairs.

Later, I would wonder why we did not jump away from each

other. Maybe because it was already too late. Or maybe because the kiss was just *that* good.

For whatever reason, at the sound of Daniel's voice, Caleb did not let me go. Our kiss broke off gently, almost reverently. Strong arms remained wrapped around me. And I felt my body go absolutely quiet.

"Sorry," Daniel sputtered. "*Shit.* I always warn you. *Always.* But I just... forgot." He paused to take a deep breath.

"*Warn* us?" Caleb's eyes were only inches from mine, so I saw them widen. "My God, he *does.*"

As I stood there, retreating into shock, I realized Caleb was right. So many times, I'd heard Daniel call out, "hey, guys!" as he walked into the house, or down the stairs.

Why did he do that? I was slow to realize what it might mean. Because I just didn't trust it. Daniel *knew?*

"Look," he said quietly. "I could just walk out of here again, and keep on pretending that I don't know how things are with you two. But it's getting kind of old."

At that point, my heart stuttered. The rational response — fear — was just kicking in. And even though it made me look even guiltier, I ducked my head, burying my face in Caleb's shirt, where I felt safe.

Caleb put a hand to the back of my neck and cleared his throat. "How long have you..."

"Eh," Daniel said. He sounded winded, like he'd just run from the house. "It's not important. But you should probably know that every time you search for something on Google, that search term stays in there. Unless you clear it out."

I felt Caleb's chest contract with a bark of sudden laughter. "Oh, my fucking god."

"Yeah," Daniel said, his voice full of restrained humor. "Google thinks I'm interested in Star Wars, used carburetors, and anal sex."

My groan was muffled by Caleb's shirt. "Does Maggie know?"

Daniel hesitated. "I don't think so. I never asked her."

I heaved a sigh of relief. Until I realized that it was weird that Daniel had never discussed this with his wife. He must think that Maggie wouldn't be okay with it.

"Listen," Daniel prompted. "We definitely need to finish this discussion. But there's some news that can't wait. Are you ready for this? Miriam called."

Both our heads whipped toward Daniel. "What?"

"Yeah," he grinned. "She's at a hospital in Casper. But she's fine, okay? She's going to be fine. And we're going to bring her here."

"Oh my God," Caleb said. "Why the hospital?"

"She has a black eye, apparently. The police brought her there when they found her walking on the road in the middle of the night. I guess it's pretty cold there right now, and she didn't have a coat. So they brought her to the hospital, and she said, 'I want to call my sister.'"

"That's..." Caleb swallowed. "I'm so glad she called."

"Yeah. Maggie is over the moon. In fact, she's going to wonder why we're still standing here. I ran out here to get you."

Caleb took a step back from me, but he put both his hands under my jaw. "Try not to freak out, okay?"

"Okay," I whispered. But I *was* freaked out. My life was *unraveling*. I could feel the end of my happiness approaching. And that terrified me.

"I'm going to go and talk to Maggie," Caleb said. "You take a minute if you need it."

"Okay."

The two of them went out the door, leaving me alone. I stumbled into our mostly-finished bathroom and turned on the shower. I couldn't go into the house until I washed Caleb off of me. So I stripped and quickly scrubbed myself down.

My guilt wasn't easy to rinse off as cum and soap.

I dried myself on a hand towel and stepped into the jeans I'd dropped in a corner that morning when I put on my painting clothes.

But even then, I didn't feel ready. So I sat down in the middle of the room and admired our work. It was starting to look like someone's home, now. And I'd hoped it would be *my* home. It was selfish, really. Lying to Maggie just so that she'd love me.

It was selfish, but I wanted to keep doing it, anyway.

I sat there awhile, afraid to go into the house and pretend that everything was normal. I had no idea what excuses Caleb made for me.

Eventually I heard footsteps on the stairs, and I looked up at the doorway. But it wasn't Caleb who came in. It was Daniel. "Hey," he said.

"Hey." I looked at my hands.

"Come downstairs to the workshop for a second. There's something I want to show you." He turned around then.

It was tempting to just sit here forever, and not face him. But I was a well-behaved person to the core. So I followed Daniel downstairs and into the workshop.

"Months ago," Daniel said, flipping on the overhead lights. "Maggie asked me to build you two some twin beds."

My stomach clenched even as Daniel pointed to a bed in the corner. Twin sized.

"I built the pieces right away. That one is finished, as you can see."

It was beautiful, too, with a sturdy maple headboard in an unfussy design.

"...I started the second one," he continued, pointing at some rails in another corner. "But I didn't think you'd want twin beds. And I didn't want to out the two of you. So I've just been changing the subject every time she asks me how long it takes to build two freaking beds."

"I'm sorry," I said quickly. He was lying to his wife for me.

Daniel shook his head. "You don't have to apologize to me. I grew up outside of San Francisco, Josh. There is nothing that scares me about a couple of gay guys. My best friend from high school is married to a dude. There are pictures of them in the dining room. From that fishing trip?"

I knew those pictures. But I'd never understood who I was looking at in them. "But Maggie..." I let the sentence die.

"Well. Maggie *didn't* grow up outside of San Francisco. You know exactly where she grew up. And you know exactly what kind of bullshit they fed her."

"She'd hate me."

Daniel shrugged. "I don't think so. See, Maggie is a great girl. And she loves you with all her heart. It might be a little bit of a surprise to her. She's got no experience with this. But that doesn't mean she can't get used to the idea."

I shivered. Even if I thought there was an eighty percent chance she'd be okay with it, that still wasn't enough. Because if Maggie ever told me that she regretted asking me to care for her child...

That's the sort of thing I didn't know if I could get over.

"I don't want to tell her," I said.

Daniel's face fell. "But how does this end?" he asked.

I had no earthly idea.

"It's your secret to tell," Daniel promised me. "But I think you'd feel better if you got it out in the open."

Maybe he was right. But I was too scared.

CHAPTER TWENTY-TWO

Josh

The next few days were crazy.

Maggie and Daniel bought Miriam a Greyhound bus ticket. "I would have flown her out here," Maggie said, "but she has no ID, so she can't get on a plane." Instead, they put her on a bus and wired her money for food. She was set to arrive three days after she'd phoned.

Meanwhile, Operation Apartment Renovation kicked into high gear.

"We can sleep out there even if there's no plumbing in the kitchen," Caleb pointed out the morning after Miriam's fateful call.

"True. But we might as well just push through and finish it," Daniel argued. "What if we both took the afternoon off to install the appliances?"

Caleb arranged that with his boss, and so the two of them went for it.

Maggie, though eager to help plan for her sister's arrival, had to work. The preparation of a wedding reception for two hundred and fifty people could not be put off. It was a big wedding for a small catering company, and they'd been planning it for weeks.

That meant Chloe and I spent some quality time together while Maggie and Cecilia prepped for the wedding. "Thank the Lord this event happens before Miriam comes. I can't wait to take care of her," she said.

"I'll bet," I agreed.

"Hey, Josh? I want you to work this wedding with me tomorrow night."

"What? You mean babysit?"

Maggie shook her head. "Cecilia and I need an extra set of hands. And I choose you."

"But what about Chloe?" I asked.

"She's too young to carry passed hors d'hoeuvres," Maggie quipped. "Daniel can take her for the evening. He and Caleb can't work *all* night long on the apartment."

"Okay," I said. Once in a while I helped Maggie with a catering gig, usually when she was short-staffed.

"Wear those black pants I got you and a white shirt, okay? Be ready at six."

"Sure," I promised. "Now, Chloe. Are you ready to say 'Josh' this morning?"

"Dada" she said.

Right.

~

AT SIX O'CLOCK, I was waiting for Maggie in black trousers and a white shirt. I was wearing a pair of Daniel's shoes, because I didn't own anything more formal than work boots. Caleb and I still lived incredibly frugally, owning almost nothing. We were just so *used* to owning nothing. Shopping wasn't a habit of ours. I had everything I needed, anyway. Being with people who loved me were all that I really cared about.

After a long day of food prep, Maggie came home to change. Then we sped off together in her Prius. I was happy to be buzzing along with Maggie in her car, watching the quiet country roads pass us by. Maybe she'd chosen me to help tonight because I didn't get out much. If that was the reason, then I appreciated it.

"Here's the schedule," she said. "We're doing passed appetizers from seven until seven-thirty. You'll carry a tray, okay? After that, we'll move the guests into the dining room for dinner, which is served buffet style. At that point, I'll need you to fill water glasses and then pass out flutes of champagne for the toast."

"Got it," I said. Weddings were strangely fancy in the outside world. They went on for hours, and everybody wore what I thought was outlandish finery. The girls from the Compound would die of shock to see the wedding dresses at these affairs. At least the big white puffy thing made the bride easy to spot in a crowd.

This wedding reception was held in a converted barn, and I loved the place immediately. It had high ceilings with thick, pine beams and giant old doors. In the roomy kitchen, I helped set up the trays for cocktail hour.

"Josh? This is Trey," Maggie said, grabbing my arm and introducing me to another man. "Trey, this is my cousin, Josh."

I shook his hand, trying hard not to notice his giant green eyes. "Wow," he said in a sing-song voice. "Aren't *you* pretty."

"Trey," Maggie chided. "Save it for the bar tonight, okay?"

"I just call 'em like I see 'em," Trey said, giving me a wink.

"Ignore him," Maggie said. "Trey is a huge flirt. Sometimes the guests want to chat him up. But when he's not distracted, he's one of our best servers."

"*One* of?" Trey yelped.

Maggie flashed him a smile and walked away.

All the while, my chest squeezed in discomfort. It wasn't because I didn't find Trey fascinating. In fact, I had to make a big effort to turn back to the tiny quiches I was loading onto a tray. But men weren't supposed to call each other pretty. Not that I had even a lick of experience guessing these things, but my gut said that Trey was gay.

Did Maggie know?

Gay Trey. My stomach spasmed with the urge to laugh at my own joke. *Easy*, I cautioned myself. It was going to be a lot of work to ignore him tonight, when what I wanted to do was study him. But if I paid too much attention, Maggie would notice.

Not worth it.

I became an appetizer machine, loading trays like there would be an inspection any minute.

"Guests arriving!" Trey called out in a high voice.

"Battle stations!" Cecilia called from the stove.

Trey and I and two other servers all took platters of food and carried them into the cocktail area. Hungry guests swarmed, of course. My plate of quiches was empty almost immediately, and I headed back to the kitchen.

"Here, hon," Trey said, passing me a platter of tuna tartare. "These are always popular."

"Thank you," I said, my voice strangled. When he was close by, it was like I didn't know where to put my eyes.

Luckily, the next hour was an exhausting whirlwind of food and beverage service. There wasn't time to be preoccupied with gay Trey. I kept my head down and served round after round of appetizers, and then about a hundred champagne flutes.

That's when we got a breather. It was rude to have servers walking around during the toast, so I stood at the back of the room like my coworkers.

A woman got up from the head table to make the toast. Usually men did this job, so that was the first thing that got my attention. My eye fell to the head table, taking a casual inventory of the wedding party. *Uh oh*. The bride was missing. Why would they start a toast without the bride?

Nobody else seemed bothered by it, though, which was odd.

"Family and friends," the woman said with a smile on her face, and a flute of bubbly in her hand. "I have helped to plan weddings before. But never have I had so much fun as helping Joe and Evan plan their special day."

Something went a little wrong in my stomach when I heard these words. *Did she just say what I think she said?* My eye fell on the table again, where two men in tuxedos were smiling at one another.

I leaned back against the wall behind me, because I felt a little lightheaded all of a sudden.

"...When my baby brother said the following words five years ago, I was stunned beyond belief."

I'll bet.

" 'I met someone,' he said." The audience chuckled. "Maybe that doesn't sound unusual to you. But my brother spent his high school and college years dating every man on the Eastern seaboard."

There was loud laughter then, and I actually wondered if I might be having a dream.

"After only a few months, Joey told me, 'Evan is the man I'm going to marry.' And I actually laughed. Because it was wayyyy too romantic a thing for my silly little brother to say. And I didn't take him seriously. I laughed him off, even though he sounded serious. But I wish I hadn't."

The mood in the room dimmed a little bit, then. A current of worry washed through the place, and I didn't know why.

"...That fall, Joey told us that there was something a doctor had found on his lung, and that he had to have a little procedure. We were all really upbeat. I mean, Joey was only thirty-three. Why worry, right?"

At the front of the room, the woman's eyes had begun to sparkle.

"Joey, it was a long three years, baby brother. There were scary, scary days."

I didn't know these people. I'd never seen them before in my

SARINA BOWEN

life. But it was as if I had been just sucked into their little reality. I was hanging on every word, wondering how this story ended.

"...Through every minute of this awful time, Evan was there. When he shaved his head in sympathy during your chemo..." The woman stopped to brush the tears from her eyes. "I've never laughed and cried so much in a single day. I'm *so* impressed with your love for each other, and the way you dealt with the dark times. You're both so strong and amazing." She had to stop again, this time to take a deep breath. "Nothing makes me happier than to stand up here and toast your beautiful marriage. I could not be happier for you both. To Joey and Evan." She raised her glass, the tears running freely down her cheeks.

The room erupted into applause, and glasses began clinking together all around me.

That's when I kind of lost it.

My eyes began to pour forth, which in turn triggered my instinct to flee. Since Maggie was somewhere to my left, I went right, ducking out of the room and ending up in a hallway. I was on the wrong end of the building for the men's room, so I dropped onto a bench and tried to look invisible.

That's hard to do when you're sobbing.

"Hey!" someone said, sitting beside me. "What's the matter, hon?"

It was gay Trey. Of course.

"I just..." Gulping, I tried to find a logical answer. "Um..."

"Got a run in your pantyhose?"

"Uh..." I sobbed. Even if I felt like leveling with him, I probably couldn't have managed it. Because it wasn't clear at all to me why I was crying. But my heart had just been ripped from my chest at the idea that two men could survive so much together. And that a sister would stand up in front of hundreds and be so proud to support them.

It was as if the world had suddenly grown into a bigger, brighter place than I'd thought it was.

192

Not that I was going to try to explain it to a stranger.

Trey put a hand on my back and rubbed, just like Caleb would have done if he was there. "That speech made more than a few people cry, you know. Not every Joey finds his Evan."

I'd already found mine. I was just terrified of having to choose between him and my home. "You should h...help Maggie," I stammered. "She's sh...short staffed."

Trey stood up. "I'll tell her that you're feeling a little ill."

"Thank you." I took several deep breaths, finally getting myself under control.

About sixty seconds later, Maggie came skidding around the corner. "Josh! There you are. Oh God, honey. I didn't mean to wreck you."

"You... what?" I wiped furiously at my cheeks, but my damned eyes just wouldn't stop leaking.

"I wanted you to meet Trey. And I knew this wedding was really special, so I wanted you to see it. But maybe I overshot a little."

Pinching the corners of my eyes, I tried to figure out what she was trying to say.

Maggie sat down beside me just where Trey had been, and put a hand on my back. "You know I love you, right?"

Oh boy. More flooding was imminent. "I love you, too. And Chloe. And Daniel."

"That's never going to change. And I feel terrible that you've worried about what I'll think of you."

"D...did Daniel..." *tell you?* I couldn't finish the sentence. Even now, I couldn't bring myself to do it. I was too afraid to take the last step.

She cleared her throat. "Well. With Miriam coming, I started badgering him about the beds again. I wanted to call the mattress company and order a set of twin mattress sets for your apartment."

"Oh," I said. My eyes were still leaking, but somehow I got my breathing under control.

"Yeah. Daniel said, 'just don't worry about the freaking beds, okay?' He just sounded so exasperated. Somehow, that's what it took. I just understood all of a sudden." She kept rubbing my back. "I'm sorry I didn't catch on before."

Now she was apologizing to me? That made no sense. "No, Maggie. You don't have to... It's not your..." I shoved my face in my hands. "*I'm* sorry. *I* am."

Maggie looped her arm around my shoulders. "It's only been a year, honey. You spent a long time listening to all the hateful things they say at the Compound. I can only imagine what you'd hear there..." she cleared her throat. "It's still echoing in your head, I'll bet. I forget sometimes how recent that was. One of the reasons I loved Daniel pretty much immediately was because he is so free of that kind of thinking. I got raped, Josh."

What? I stopped hiding my face and turned to Maggie. "You... when?"

"Right after I ran away from Asher. I left the compound, and I was homeless. And a man offered to drive me to California, so I got in his car and..." Now Maggie's eyes were leaking. "It was bad, and I was such a mess afterward. I felt really guilty and used up. First a teenage bride to a mean old man, then a stupid girl who got into a stranger's car." She shook her head. "I felt dirty and horrible. But that's not what Daniel sees when he looks at me."

"Of course it's not," I said, grabbing her into a hug.

She smiled at me through her tears. "See? I know you went through hell, too."

"Not like that," I said quickly.

She shook her head. "The hell in *here*." She tapped my forehead with one soft finger. "But we don't think like that, Daniel and I. We love you and Caleb. And if you love each other, that's really great, Josh. It makes you *lucky*."

Oh, boy. I was probably going to float away on my tears. "I *am* lucky."

"I know. And I want you to be able to feel that way without worrying, okay? That's why I brought you here tonight. I've known Trey a while now. He doesn't apologize for himself. And the men who got married tonight — they sure don't."

"It's hard for me to get used to," I said.

She gave me one more squeeze. "Yes, it is. It won't happen overnight. And, I'm so sorry, but we have to serve dinner now. Two hundred people aren't going to understand if we're..."

"...Sobbing in the hallway?" I supplied.

Maggie pulled me to my feet. "You get to load the trays this time. Because your face is a mess. And I'll man the buffet with Trey."

The kitchen was mayhem. "About time you two turned up," Cecilia complained from the stove. "Take that tray of salad, and let me know what needs refilling."

Maggie grabbed the salad and high-tailed it out of the kitchen.

Cecilia turned to me with a frown. "As for you..." she stopped. "Are you all right?"

"I'm fine," I said, getting embarrassed. "Just give me a job."

Cecilia squeezed my shoulder. "Okay, honey. Find some more pats of butter in the walk-in."

WE WERE all exhausted by the time the cake was cut. But at least I'd pulled myself together well enough to help serve coffee. We all cleaned the kitchen, and then it was finally time to go.

"Nice meeting you," Trey said as he shrugged on his coat at the end of the night. "I hope your week turns around."

"It already has," I said quietly.

To my surprise, he leaned in and kissed me on the cheekbone. "You are *so* cute, so I need to ask. Would I be making anyone angry if I did that again?"

My face heated, probably turning the color of a strawberry.

"Yeah," I said.

"Bummer." He brought his car keys out of his pocket. "It is a guy, though, right? I'm not totally losing my mind?"

Now I was sweating. Because I couldn't believe what I was about to say. "Yes. It is."

Trey held up a hand, and luckily it took me only a half a beat to realize that he was waiting for a high-five, which I delivered. "He's a lucky guy. Night, Josh."

"Night, Trey."

THE CAR RIDE home was quiet. Maggie probably understood that I was too exhausted to talk much. But as we approached the final turn toward Runaway Farm, she cleared her throat. "I hate to bring it up one more time, but there's still the matter of... furniture."

Oh. *The beds.* We still had to talk about the stupid beds. "We're okay with whatever," I choked out.

"Well, we could move the queen-sized that's in your room up to the apartment. And Miriam could have the twin that's finished."

"Okay," I said quickly.

"But... if we have to call the mattress company either way, I was thinking we should get a king-sized for you two, and leave the other bed for Miriam."

"Either way," I said quickly.

"I'll call them tomorrow," she said. "You and Chloe can take delivery, because I have to go out and buy my sister some real clothes! And nice shampoo. And a hair dryer. All the things that she hasn't had before. Fuzzy slippers. Nightgowns that don't look like Laura Ingalls made them." From the passenger seat, I could see her grinning in the dark.

"She'll be so happy, Maggie."

"I know." She was practically bouncing in her seat. "Right now, she's on a bus somewhere, having no idea what happens next. But we are going to just *wrap her up* and hug her until she isn't worried anymore."

That sounded just about right. "Maggie, moving in with you guys was the best day of my life. I thought... *finally!* This is what a house is supposed to be like. And not because of the shampoo or the clothes."

Turning up the driveway, Maggie smiled at me. "Oh, Josh. I love you to death. Don't ever move far away, okay? Or if you guys do, I need you to visit all the time. I need all my people near me."

"Okay," I promised. And, damn it, my eyes watered *again*.

CALEB WAS asleep in our bed when I got there. I peeled off my clothes and brushed my teeth. Then I climbed into the bed and fit my body up against his.

Maggie *knew*. And nothing had changed for me. Except that I didn't have to leap away from Caleb anymore if we were standing close to one another when someone else arrived at home.

His warm, solid body felt so good against mine. I tucked a hand around his waist and squeezed.

"Hi," he said sleepily. "You okay?"

I buried my nose in the back of his neck. "Yes. Except I had a total meltdown at this wedding. That was a little embarrassing. But I'm over it now."

He struggled to roll over to face me. "Really?"

I nodded in the dark. "Maggie knows now."

His eyes closed. "That's good?" He seemed too sleepy to keep talking.

"Yeah," I whispered. "It really is."

Caleb slept. And after I lay there admiring him for a while, so did I.

CHAPTER TWENTY-THREE

Josh

Miriam's bus wasn't due into Pittsfield until the next afternoon. So Maggie went out for hours to shop, while I took delivery of a king-sized mattress and box spring. When the truck rolled up the gravel drive, I directed the deliverymen to bring it up to the apartment.

But there was a problem with making the turn up the stairs, so Daniel came out to help by taking the apartment door off its hinges, buying a crucial couple of inches of extra room to negotiate.

Meanwhile, I stood around holding Chloe and blushing furiously as Daniel helped the men set up a bed for Caleb and I in the sleeping loft we'd built.

"Do you want to try the mattress before we drive away?" one of the men asked.

"I'm sure it's fine," I said quickly, turning a darker shade of red.

"Me," Chloe demanded, reaching for the cushioned surface with both arms.

"Okay," I said, happy for the distraction. "You try it." I let her gently fall to the bed, chubby arms first.

"Big," she pronounced, sitting up, looking around.

"Yup," I said, wondering if it was possible to burst into flames from embarrassment.

"Sign here," the delivery guy said. I scribbled my name, and that mortifying little chapter of my day came to an end.

Whistling, Daniel went back to his workshop, and I followed him down the stairs.

"Dada," Chloe said, watching him disappear.

"Dada has to work for another hour. You and I are going to eat lunch."

"Nums," she said as I carried her at a trot toward the house.

"That's right."

Inside, I made her a bowl of Maggie's barley soup. Setting her into the high chair, I picked up the spoon and offered her a bite with a bright orange cube of carrot on it.

She ate some soup, humming to herself between bites. The "mm-mm" sound she made when she was hungry was priceless. It was hard to believe that I actually got paid for this. Caleb was under a car somewhere in a frigid garage, and Daniel was out in his workshop trying not to saw off his fingers. But my work day would include a mandatory nap, and snuggling on the couch with a book.

Eventually, Chloe lost interest in the soup and began pointing at a square of cornbread I'd tried to conceal behind the napkin holder. It was awesome cornbread, but I'd been saving it until after the soup was gone. "Nums," Chloe demanded.

"This is what you want?" I said, pulling it into view.

At the sight of it, she got all excited, reaching one thick little arm toward the plate.

"You can have it," I teased, "if you say *Josh*."

Chloe looked up at me and smiled an open-mouthed smile. We played this game a lot.

"Go on. Say, *Josh*." This was the part where she said "dada" instead, and then I gave her the cornbread anyway. As it turns out, the J sound was one of the last that most babies learned. It was harder to say than many of the other consonant sounds. Go figure.

"Bosh," Chloe said, her voice tentative.

My heart stuttered. "What did you say?"

"BOSH!" she reached for the plate.

Laughing, I passed it to her. "Close enough, babycakes. Close enough."

MAGGIE RETURNED A BIT LATER, her little car overflowing with purchases. "These are for you," she said, handing me a bag with king-sized sheets in it.

"I would have..." Our finances were hopelessly tangled at this point. I would probably die owing Maggie and Daniel money.

She held up a hand. "My treat. And I know how much you enjoy the topic of beds and bedding. So just roll with it, my little blushing cousin."

I turned away, hearing her snicker.

"Mama," Chloe said, toddling into the room.

"That's right. Mama is home." Maggie scooped her daughter off the floor. "Did you have your nap?"

"That would be no," I said. "Somebody wouldn't even consider it. I think it's just a little crazy around here today." Chloe might not know what was going on, but she could sense the excitement. "Maybe she'll pass out in the car when you go to meet the bus in Pittsfield."

Maggie chewed on her lip. "Actually, Josh? Could you stay here with Chloe? I mean, I haven't seen Miriam since she was twelve. I'm not sure I can pick her up and keep myself together. I'm weeping all over the place, Chloe might get freaked out."

"No problem," I said immediately. "I'll stay with her."

WHEN THE TIME came for Maggie and Daniel to drive off, Chloe was not happy with this arrangement. They left, and she *howled*. Not only did she want to go with Mama and Dada, she was exhausted from skipping her nap.

"Let's go read a book," I suggested. I tucked her crabby self under one arm and *The Very Hungry Caterpillar* under the other. And I carried both upstairs to Maggie and Daniel's bed. If she fell asleep on me (and I hoped she would) it would be a short trip to the crib.

Whimpering a little, Chloe let me settle her on my chest. Yawning myself, I opened the first page of the book, and began to read in my most sedate voice.

It worked on both of us...

There were voices coming up the stairs. Excited voices. But my head was heavy on the pillow. What's more, there was a warm, heavy weight on my chest which even in my sleep I recognized as Chloe.

When you're napping underneath a toddler, there is no guilt. Even asleep, you are performing an essential function: making a small, volatile human less irritable. So even though I had a vague awareness that there might be some important reason to wake up, I ignored it in favor of more time peering at the inside of my eyelids.

I was just slipping back under the sleep waves when the voices came closer.

"Oh my! She's... oh, Maggie! She's beautiful!"

Reluctantly, I opened my eyes. And there stood Miriam, right over me. She still had the same beautiful smile, and glossy brown hair. But she also had two black eyes, a cut on her cheekbone...

And a giant pregnant belly.

I just barely held off my gasp of surprise.

Sitting up a little, I shook off my sleep. It killed me to see evidence that someone had hurt Miriam. So I grasped at the good news. "Lord. More babies? I'm not ready."

Miriam pressed her hands over her smile, and her eyes watered. "God, Josh. It's so good to see you. You have no idea. Just look at you two..." she flicked tears away from those bruised cheeks.

"Come here." I pulled her down into a hug. She smelled like the stale air of a three day bus trip, the poor thing. "Maggie has lots of plans to spoil you," I said.

"So I hear."

Maggie was standing in the doorway, with Daniel too, looking fit to burst. I could see on her face that there had already been many tears.

Chloe chose that moment to wake up, her blues eyes popping open to see a black-and-blue stranger leaning over us. She opened her mouth and shrieked.

"Oh sweetie," Miriam crooned. "I'm sorry."

Tears began to pour out of Chloe's eyes like two fountains. That's what happened when a toddler woke from her nap at just the wrong moment. It meant nothing, but I worried that Miriam would take it personally, unless I worked a little magic.

I scooped Chloe up, facing her into the shoulder of my shirt.

"Bosh!" she wailed.

"Shh, shh," I said, rocking her. "Some naps have a rough landing. Nothing we can't fix with a bottle of milk."

"Baba," she agreed.

"Okay, missy." I scrambled off the bed.

"Oh, you two are killing me," Miriam said. "That's the cutest thing I've ever seen."

"Isn't it?" Maggie said, stepping out of my way. Because she knew better than to get between a hungry one-year-old and her baba. "Those two have a special relationship. *Bosh* is indispensable."

My face began to heat, of course. "Where's Caleb?" I asked to change the subject.

"Still at work. It's only five."

"Ah," I said, holding the railing to walk down the stairs carefully. I had precious cargo on my other arm. I was still waking up, too. By the time I made it to the kitchen, my brain was functioning again.

And I realized that Caleb was going to walk in here in less than an hour, see those bruises on Miriam's face, and flip *right* out.

WHEN I HEARD his tires in the driveway, I was standing in the kitchen, peeling a cucumber for Maggie. Chloe was in her father's arms in the living room, where he was chatting with Miriam.

I set down my salad prep, shoved my feet in my boots, and went outside to meet Caleb.

It was dark already, and his headlights nearly blinded me before he shut them off. So I couldn't see his face after he jumped out of the car, slammed the door, and approached me.

"Hi baby," he said under his breath. He leaned in and kissed me on the lips, right in front of God and everyone. Well, we were alone out here. But it wasn't something that I would have let him do a week ago.

But today? The kiss made me deliriously happy.

"Hi," I said, putting my hands on his shoulders.

"Hi yourself. Why are you outside?"

"Ah," I said, giving his shoulder muscles one quick squeeze. "I wanted to warn you before you come in. Miriam is fine, okay?"

His chin snapped upward by a couple of degrees. "Okay."

"But, Caleb, somebody hit her. There are bruises and a cut."

Under my hands, he took a slow breath. "All right."

"And Miriam is very, very pregnant."

His body jerked backward, and my hands slipped off of him. Later, I'd remember that as the moment when everything went bad. Although, there in the driveway, I still couldn't quite read his face. "She's... pregnant?"

"Yeah."

"Someone *hit* a pregnant eighteen-year-old girl?"

"I don't, uh, know the story. I don't know if Maggie knows it yet, either. But I just wanted to tell you so you could keep your cool."

"Jesus fucking Christ." Caleb put the heels of both hands to his forehead. Then he walked around me and into the house.

In the kitchen, Maggie stopped me with an update on the meal we were making together. (Teaching Caleb to cook hadn't gotten any further than scrambled eggs and toast. So she'd turned her attentions to me, probably so that her child would not starve during the work day.) So I actually missed the moment when Caleb greeted Miriam. I heard her give a little shriek when he walked into the room. But I didn't see his reaction. I only heard the rumble of his voice, low and reassuring.

It's going to be fine, I told myself.

But when dinnertime came, Caleb seemed withdrawn, barely speaking. After the meal, he sat in a chair in the living room with Maggie and Miriam.

When Chloe was asked who she wanted to read her a bedtime story, she said "Bosh." So I spent an hour getting her ready for bed, and down for the night. Putting Chloe to bed was always Maggie or Daniel's job, but today was weird in every possible way.

When I came back downstairs, I couldn't find anyone in the living room. But there were female voices coming from Miriam's new room (which was my old one.) Daniel and Caleb were missing. I decided that they'd gone over to discuss something in the apartment. So I headed for the back hall and my shoes.

I nearly tripped over Caleb, who was standing outside our old room, eavesdropping.

My mouth flew open to say something, but Caleb raised an angry finger to his lips.

I didn't know what to make of that. But I didn't want to spy. (Knowing me, I'd probably be caught, anyway.) So I continued to the mud room, put on my shoes, and let myself out the door.

The workshop and apartment were completely dark. I flipped on the entryway lights and went up to our new space. The sheets Maggie had bought were sitting just inside the door.

Alone, I put the new mattress pad on the new mattress, then made the bed. Maggie had provided us with an old quilt that was large enough for a king-sized bed, and Caleb had bought a blanket.

The bed was ready, but I was still alone.

I brushed my teeth and got ready for bed, with Caleb still missing. I was reading my library book when the door finally opened. But Caleb did not call out a greeting.

Moments later, heavy footsteps thudded on the loft stairs we'd built. Caleb walked around the bed to his side and got in, his back to me.

King-sized beds are large. There were three feet of space between us.

I shut off the light. "Caleb," I asked. "Are you okay?"

"No," he said.

"Can we talk about it?"

"No."

There was really nowhere I could go with that. So I didn't push.

It took me a long time to fall asleep, though. This really wasn't how I pictured our first night together in the apartment. I rolled to face his back, eying his strong shoulders, willing him to turn to me.

But he never did.

CHAPTER TWENTY-FOUR

Josh

The next morning should have felt ordinary. I milked cows. I joined Maggie and Chloe in the kitchen for breakfast.

Caleb left for work while I was still in the barn. That wasn't unusual. It's just that he hadn't spoken to me at all since yesterday.

"I'm taking Miriam to the doctor later this morning," Maggie said, stirring her coffee.

"Is something wrong?"

She shook her head. "Not a thing, Josh. But pregnant women are supposed to get a lot of checkups. She hasn't had a single one. So they'll scan her belly and try to figure out when that baby is going to drop. She thinks it could be as soon as Christmas."

"Wow."

"Yeah," Maggie grinned. "Would this be a terrible time to mention that I'm also pregnant?"

I choked on my coffee.

Maggie laughed. "Sorry! I should have timed that better. I mean the statement. Not the baby."

"Oh my God."

"Wow, now I have Josh swearing."

"Congratulations! I just didn't expect it."

"Apparently Daniel and I are very fertile. It was a 'first try' situation."

That was more information than I really needed. "So when...?"

"May. And the doctor told me right away that I wouldn't necessarily have postpartum depression again. It's not a given."

I reached across and squeezed her hand. "Even if you do we'll make it through."

She squeezed back. "Damn straight."

"Hi," a shy voice said.

We turned to see Miriam in a nightgown and bathrobe, peering at us.

"Sweetie, come here!" Maggie leapt up. "Let's get you some breakfast."

"I slept and slept. And you have no idea," Miriam said, hugging her sister, "how amazing it was to wake up here."

"Actually," Maggie said, releasing her, "both Josh and I know *exactly* how amazing it is. We do it every day."

Miriam laughed. "I'm just so happy I might spend the day crying."

"I think we're going to spend it digging my maternity clothes out of the attic instead." She pointed at the loaf of bread on the counter. "We have toast and juice. And I can scramble you an egg..."

"Don't forget the coffee," I put in. "Coffee is one of the pleasures of leaving the Compound."

"Where's Caleb?" Miriam asked.

"At work," Maggie said, dropping a slice of bread into the toaster.

"Did he seem okay to you last night?" Miriam asked. "I thought he was... off."

Maggie turned to look at me, which meant that Miriam also turned to look at me.

"Um..." I said, blushing. "He was kind of quiet, right? I couldn't get a word out of him last night."

Leaning a hip against the counter, Maggie frowned. "He didn't talk to you?"

"Well..." I rubbed the whiskers on my chin. "I think he's freaked out that Miriam had a rough time."

"I'm going to be fine," Miriam protested. "I just slept for eleven hours."

"I know you are," Maggie said gently. "You don't have anything to prove."

THAT AFTERNOON, Chloe had just gone down for a nap and the house was quiet when I saw an unfamiliar car pull up the driveway. It went past the house and toward the workshop.

Feeling nosy, I peeked out the mudroom door, and was surprised to see Caleb get out of the car and go into the workshop.

Today was Friday, when he only worked a half day. But I'd forgotten that.

A couple of minutes later, he emerged again, this time with Daniel. The two of them got into the strange car and then drove away again.

It was hardly the oddest thing that had ever happened. But I still felt a quiver of uncertainty. Would someone please just tell me what was going on?

Forty minutes later, the strange car and the pickup truck both returned. Caleb and Daniel got out. But then they spent a couple minutes talking in the driveway. Strangely, they seemed to be having an argument. It ended when Daniel threw his hands in the air then stomped off toward the workshop.

Caleb turned to look at the house. I held my breath, wondering if he could see the crack in the curtains where I peered through. He seemed to gather himself. Then he began walking toward the house.

By hurrying, I managed to be back in the kitchen, casually pouring myself a cup of coffee in the chipped blue mug when he came in the door. "Hi," I said when he poked his head in from the mudroom.

"Anyone else here?" he asked by way of a greeting.

My stomach dropped. "Chloe, but she's napping."

He nodded, face deathly serious. "We need to talk."

For a moment, those words just bounced around in my chest. The words weren't necessarily ominous. But in my gut, I knew that something was wrong. "What about?"

Caleb looked down at his hands. "I'm going to marry Miriam."

"What?" I could have sworn that he'd just said he wanted to *marry* Miriam.

"She needs someone to take care of her," he said. "And her child needs a father."

The words settled into my stomach like lead. My first thought was a selfish one. *But* I *need you.* And wasn't that just a sissy way to think? Miriam was eighteen years old. She was pregnant and probably unemployable.

She had, however, a family who would care for her.

"You don't have to do that," I said carefully. "She isn't going to starve in the street."

His eyes were flat. "I get that. But this is better for her. She'll have someone to lean on. She asked me to marry her once before, and I said no. This time, I'm not going to let her down."

Oh, no. I realized that I was probably going to cry. I could feel the telltale scratch at the back of my throat, and a burning in my eyes. "I think I hear Chloe," I said. As casually as I could, I lifted my chin and left the room, expecting Caleb to try to stop me.

He didn't.

$\sim$

209

UPSTAIRS, I did not cry. I couldn't afford to. Chloe could wake up any minute, and she wouldn't know what to do with a sobbing babysitter.

I tiptoed into her room and lay down on the twin bed that Daniel had put in here just yesterday. It was the bed that had sat in the corner of his shop, the one that he thought nobody needed.

Well I needed it. Probably tonight. Because if Caleb was serious about leaving me, I was not going to spend another night beside him. Not ever again.

I lay there, shocked, trying to wrap my head around Caleb's so-called decision. It didn't even seem real. I half expected him to pop his head into the room and say that he'd been kidding.

But he'd never kid me like that.

So if it *wasn't* just a sick joke, I had to sort myself out. And how would that arrangement look? If he actually married her, Caleb and I would need some distance from each other.

Maybe he and Miriam would move out to the apartment.

Our apartment.

I'd worked so hard on that place. I'd wanted to live there with Caleb so badly. And I'd spent exactly one night there. One!

And if I was traded in for Miriam? The hundred yards between the house and the apartment weren't going to be enough distance. Not even close. So I would have to make some big changes.

Staying here to watch Caleb and Miriam become a family was not something I could stomach.

And — holy God — I used to lie in my twin bunk in Paradise and think these *exact same thoughts*. It was the freakiest damn thing. A year had passed. One glorious year. And here I was trying to imagine a future for myself without Caleb. *Again.*

There *had* to be somewhere else I could go. Babysitting for another family, maybe. Or carrying appetizers for another catering company. Maybe Trey would have some ideas for me.

Why did he pop into my head? *Right*. Because I had no friends that did not live on this property, or work for C & M Catering.

My mind spun in twisted circles. Everything I thought I'd known about my life was suddenly up for grabs.

"Bosh?"

I sat up fast. I'd never been so happy to see Chloe, and to think of someone else's troubles for a change. "Hi, sweetie." I got up off the bed and stood over the crib. She lifted her chubby arms up, waiting to be held.

She was heavy against my chest, and sweet-smelling.

I felt the sting of tears threaten once more, but I blinked them back. "Let's get you a fresh diaper, and then a bottle."

"Baba," she agreed.

Caleb was not in the house when I went downstairs, which was a blessing. And when Maggie and Miriam came home a little later, they were brimming over with happiness. Miriam had a strip of sonogram pictures of her baby, which the doctor had decided was healthy and on track for a late December birth.

"It's a girl!" Miriam said. "The doctor is fairly sure."

"We have so many girl clothes, too!" Maggie gushed. "I'm glad I saved everything."

Nobody noticed that I was practically mute, luckily.

I made hamburger patties while Maggie played with Chloe. My hands were still covered in goo when I heard the mudroom door open and shut again.

I braced myself to see Caleb's face, but it was only Daniel who came into the kitchen. And when he saw me, he frowned. "What the fuck?" he whispered.

As if I had an answer.

"What the ever-loving fuck?" Daniel pointed outside, toward the apartment. "Did you tell him he's insane?"

I hadn't, actually. So I shook my head.

Daniel kept his voice low, but his anger on my behalf was obvious. "Seriously?" he hissed. "*You* have to open up a big can of righteous indignation. Because that's a huge mistake that he cannot easily undo."

Blowing out a breath, I realized that Daniel spoke the truth. Caleb had stood right in this kitchen and dealt me a blow. And what had I done? Run from the room.

Sure, I'd been shocked. But I realized now that my initial reaction wasn't good enough. Ducking conflict was something I'd done at the Compound, because my survival depended on it.

But it didn't anymore.

"Josh? Daniel?" Maggie came into the room. "Have you seen Caleb?"

Daniel just stared at me. I stuck my hands under the sink and started washing them off. "Actually, Maggie, I'm going to go find him. He and I need to talk."

Her eyes widened. "Okay. Aren't we having dinner in a half hour?"

"I don't know," I said truthfully. "I can't worry about that right now. I'm sorry."

At that, I walked out of the room.

Caleb wasn't difficult to find. He was in the apartment, sitting on the bed. My side of the bed.

I'd marched up the stairs like a warrior. But seeing him there, head in his hands, it took a little of the fight out of me. "Caleb."

He didn't look up.

"Caleb, you need to listen to me."

Still, nothing.

With my heart pounding, I walked over and grabbed his chin in my hand, yanking his head up to look into my eyes. "You do not get to ignore me. Not now."

"Josh..." He hesitated. And I waited, because I was a polite person to the core, whether that was logical or not. "I'm sorry," he continued, "but there's no more to say."

My slap rang out a second later, and I could barely believe I'd done it. But my hand was stinging, and there was a bright red mark on Caleb's cheek. And so much shock on his face.

"You are a coward," I spat.

"*What* did you say?" His voice sounded dangerously angry.

In my whole life, I'd never been afraid of Caleb. And the tremor I felt now was definitely fear. But I was more afraid of myself at that moment than I was of him. In spite of the fact that he looked murderously angry, and I'd just hit him in the face. "You might as well run back to Wyoming and join up again," I told him.

His face reddened, and a vein bulged in his forehead. "That's bullshit, Josh. I'm just trying to take responsibility for once."

"*That's* bullshit," I threw back. "You made a promise to me. But now you're panicking. Because you made a choice and a couple of the details got messy."

He jumped up off the bed, and we were suddenly nose to nose. "Messy? *Messy?* Broken dishes are messy, Josh. Miriam was given to a man who *beat her*."

My heart squeezed with misery. "I can see that. But she's here now. And you didn't hurt her."

"Yeah I did. I *let* that shit happen. That's my fault. And now I've only got one way to make it up to her."

At that point, my vision was *red*. I'd never felt so much stress in my body as I did at that moment. My fingertips began to tingle, and I could hear my pulse in my head. Because you can't throw one person overboard to save the other one. And I could either take this lying down, or argue against the welfare of a pregnant teenager.

It was an impossible situation. And Caleb was the one who put me there.

Yet, if I was ever going to speak up, this was my only chance. Before things got even more twisted.

"You are *not* doing the right thing," I spat. "It's terrible what happened to Miriam. But marrying her isn't going to undo it."

"It will ease the burden," he said, his chest rising and falling as if he'd just run a marathon. "It's all I can do for her, so I'll *do* it."

"In other words," my voice was somehow almost level, even though I was dying inside, "you'd wreck me so that you can *not quite* save her? Does that sound like a solid plan?"

"You won't be *wrecked*," Caleb sighed. "You'll just hate me for a while."

"Not true," I whispered. "Because when I said I love you, I meant it. And I would do anything to make you happy. And if you throw that away, I will not get over it."

The hard lines in his expression finally softened, if only a little. "Yeah, you will."

I shook my head. "No, I really won't, and I'll be homeless too. If you marry her, I'm going to leave here. Because I *will not watch*." I whirled around, as if to walk away, but stopped short. Turning again, I squared my shoulders. "Okay. Since you're so smart, I have an even better idea. *I'll* marry Miriam."

"What?" his face was pale now.

"Sure!" I said, sounding manic. But honestly, I was onto something. If Caleb wanted to understand what this scenario really meant, I was going to show him. "*I'll* marry her. Because, what's the difference, right? *Any* two people who don't love each other can sleep together every night." I snapped my fingers. "Let's not forget that *I'm* the one who's good with babies. And this way, if one of us has to be homeless, it can be *you*. In fact, I'm betting that you'll feel very selfless and useful when you bed down in that car you just bought, but didn't bother to show me first."

His mouth opened and closed like a fish in a bowl.

My crazy brain just kept offering up more details. "Before you go, though, I think you should attend our wedding. No—you should be *in* the wedding. You can stand up there and smile while I promise to love and cherish someone else. But that won't bother you too much, obviously. Since it's really no big deal! And I think Miriam and I should live here in the apartment, where there's a little more space. And *privacy*. So that when we get around to consummating the marriage, nobody will hear us. *You* can keep the bedroom in the house. I'll help you move your things back in. Let's do that now."

I was on such a roll. Turning around, I found the dresser that I'd refinished. It wasn't fancy, it was just something Maggie and I had found at the second-hand store in town. I ripped open the top drawer and took out Caleb's shirts, tossing them on the bed. "Here you go. And the underwear..." I opened the next drawer down and tossed those onto the pile. Then his jeans.

It took about sixty seconds to stack up all his belongings. In a year, we hadn't accumulated much.

"There," I said, straightening up. "We can get your toothbrush out of the bathroom, and move Miriam's things in here. Won't take but ten minutes." I turned around to face him again.

Tears. There were tears running down his face. "Josh, never meant to hurt you."

My blood pressure was still off the charts. I could feel it throbbing in my neck. But somehow my voice was still steady. "You said that already. But it didn't mean *shit*. So pardon me if I don't need to hear it again. Now pick up your clothes and get out."

"Josh," he swallowed and his throat worked. "I can't think straight. Ever since last night, when I heard her tell Maggie..."

"OUT!" I screamed. I stomped over to the window, the only one on the loft level. There was no screen in it yet, which only made my job easier. With shaking hands I pressed the latches and flung it upwards. Then I marched over to the bed and grabbed an armful of Caleb's stuff. Three seconds later, I'd flung it out into the bitter night. "That," I spat. "...Is what you just did to me. Threw me away like garbage. Did you see that? Should I show you again?" My voice was shaking now, and my legs were unsteady beneath me. But I staggered over to the bed and bent over, gathering up the rest of Caleb's clothes.

"Stop," he whispered. He put two big hands on my forearms, and held me in place. "Just stop."

"Why should I?" I cried, my voice finally breaking. "I'm the only one making sense."

"Just..." he took a big, sobbing breath, and military-crawled toward me. He stretched his arms onto my back and tried to gather me up.

"Get *off* me," I whispered.

"I don't *want* to leave you," he bit out.

"You don't get to say that now." I tried to hold myself together. "*Nobody* gets to throw me away, you *shit*."

"I'm *panicked* here!"

"I DON'T FUCKING CARE!" I bucked, shoving him off my body. "At least when Ezra got out the duct tape for my hands and feet, he didn't try to pretend he was doing the world a favor!"

"Josh...!"

"GET OUT! Right now. Go find your jeans outside." I was still lying on the bed, my arms half on top of a pile of T-shirts. It was a ridiculous pose. But I turned my head to the side where I couldn't see him at all.

There was a long silence. I found myself holding my breath. I'd just ordered him repeatedly to leave. And now I was terrified that he would.

And then he did.

The sound of the outer door downstairs broke me in half.

CHAPTER TWENTY-FIVE

Josh

I must have slept. Because I woke up in a panic, sitting up in the dark, my heart pounding.

"Josh?" A female voice was calling my name.

"Yeah?" My voice was rough, almost unrecognizable.

"Can I come up?"

If only my heart rate would decline. I reached over and switched on a lamp, which was sitting on a little table that Maggie had found in her attic. So many little details had gone into making this place habitable. But it was all so foreign to me. Like I'd fallen into this unfamiliar world, and all I wanted was to go back to the old one. Crawling into our old bed with Caleb in the house together — that's all I needed.

Things had been so simple for a while. And now they... weren't.

Maggie appeared at the top of the loft steps. "Are you okay? You haven't eaten."

"What time is it?" I rasped.

"Ten. I brought you barley soup." She sat down on the end of the bed and took a piece of foil off of my favorite mug. The blue one with the chip in the rim.

SARINA BOWEN

She passed it to me, along with a spoon.

I took a sip, because it was easier than talking. Maggie's barley soup was divine, too.

"That was my favorite mug, too," she said suddenly.

"Mmm?"

"That whole set of mugs came from Daniel's grandmother's house. When they moved her into a condo, he took some things for his first apartment. I don't know when the blue one got chipped. But that was my favorite. Still is."

I looked up in surprise. "Sorry..." I'd been using her mug for a year now, and she never said anything.

Maggie grinned at me. "The thing is, I saw Miriam choose that one this morning, too. There's something special about it."

"Mmm," I said around a spoonful of soup.

"The glaze has so many other colors hiding in it. Little flecks of red and yellow. It's unexpected," Maggie said. "But it's also the chip. That ugly gash of white, right where it shouldn't be. No matter how the mug is turned, you can always see it."

This was true.

Maggie reached over and put a finger over the rough spot where the chip met the glaze. "It took me a long time to trust that Daniel really loved me. I had no confidence, Josh. That place took it all out of me."

I found myself holding my breath, and I didn't even know why. Maggie's words probed the ache in my heart, the way you finger an injury, finding it tender.

"...I always chose this mug because it was just like me. I had a rough spot that could never be made smooth again."

Looking down at the chip, I realized she was right. I'd selected this mug from Maggie's collection the first time I drank coffee with her. There were three or four more perfect mugs I could have taken. But I thought this was the one I deserved. The broken, left-over thing.

"Miriam's chip is even bigger than ours, I think," she whispered.

I took a big bite of soup so that I didn't have to meet her eyes.

"Caleb thinks it's his fault." Maggie laid a hand on my arm. "It isn't, though."

"He..." my voice was scratchy. "He left her there. I got tossed, and he left." Talking about Caleb made me *ache*. I was so angry at him, and so hurt. But I ached *for* him too. Even when someone you love is being an asshole, it's hard not to empathize. "Caleb was always the responsible one. Always. It kills him that he couldn't save us both. His words." And it killed *me* that I needed to be saved at all. I did, though. Caleb saved me a year ago. Without him, I'd be in a homeless shelter in Cheyenne. Alone.

Maggie cringed. "Tonight, he came into the house with an armload of his clothes," her eyes smiled at me. "He couldn't even speak, he was so upset."

"Oh," I said, my voice flat.

"Do you want to tell me what happened?"

"What did he say about it?"

"Nothing, honey. He put the clothes down, and he said he was going out. Then he got in his car and drove away."

My neck began to prickle. "He's not here?"

She shook her head.

"Where could he be?" Fear settled into my chest.

"Out?" Maggie suggested. "With a friend from the garage? Just because he isn't home at ten o'clock doesn't mean anything bad has happened to him."

I blew out a breath, uneasy. "We had the most awful fight."

"That happens," Maggie whispered, her face gentle.

"It doesn't, though." Caleb and I *never* fought. "I slapped him, and I threw his clothes out the window."

She clapped a hand over her mouth, and a nervous chuckle escaped. "Oh, Josh, I'm sorry to laugh. But that's just not like you."

Hot tears sprang into my eyes. "I *know*, but..." It wasn't like me. I'd finally stood up for myself. And doing that wasn't like me, either. "I went too far. I *snapped*, Maggie. Because Caleb was trying to throw me away."

Her eyes bugged out. "He would *never* do that."

"Yes he would. He *did*. I don't even know what's going to happen now."

"God, why? That makes no sense."

"Because..." I looked into her patient brown eyes, and I got it. I understood why Caleb would want to pay back all the wrongs he felt he'd caused. There were flecks of gold in Maggie's caring eyes. She was beautiful and Miriam was beautiful and they deserved everything. "Miriam," I choked out. "He said he should marry her."

Maggie gave a long, slow blink. "Oh." Her shoulders sagged. "Oh, Caleb, you idiot."

"What?"

"He's trying to undo one disaster with another one."

"Well..." I swallowed hard. "It's only a disaster for *me*."

She shook her head. "Not true. What if there's a man out there for Miriam. Someone good and true, who she deserves to meet?"

"But what if there isn't?"

Maggie shook her head. "It's not easy to be Miriam. An eighteen-year-old single mother with no education. She's going to have a tough road. But we're all here to help her. And she deserves to figure some of it out for herself. Not to have some guy she was half in love with throw his life away so they can be unhappy together. That's a recipe for heartbreak."

Just hearing her say it eased me. Even if I didn't know if Caleb would ever believe it. "She always wanted to marry him."

"And so do you!" Maggie cried. "I love my sister, Josh, and so does Caleb. But he doesn't love her like *that*. It's not fair to anyone."

"Except the baby," I pointed out.

Maggie threw her hands out wide. "This baby is getting *five* parents and a cousin. No baby ever had it so good."

A fair point.

Maggie sighed. "Oh, *honey*. I hope he comes to his senses soon. I think he may have shared this plan with Daniel, actually. He's all grumpy, too. And he won't tell me why."

"*Men*," I said.

Maggie giggled. "Did you really throw his clothes out the window?"

"I really did."

"I'm sorry I missed it. And maybe Mr. Stupid got the message that you are not to be trifled with."

Did he? Obviously not. Because if he had, he wouldn't be gone right now.

CHAPTER TWENTY-SIX

Caleb

I'd driven to Ralph's Tavern for two reasons. The first was that I couldn't face any of my family. And the second was that I only knew of one bar in the county. The guys from the shop often came here, and spoke of it frequently.

Parking my new (to me) Toyota in the lot, I'd heard the sound of music and laughter before I even opened the door. Inside, I liked the look of the place. There was dark wood paneling and soft lighting. Two pool tables lined the back wall.

My next thought was just a reflex. *I should bring Josh here*. It took me a second to realize how fucked up my brain really was. I'd just wrecked things with Josh. I'd made him *cry*, for God's sake, and slap me. The look on his face was going to be with me a long time. And even if I made it up to him somehow, he'd still know.

Nobody gets to throw me away, he'd said. But that's exactly what I'd tried to do, without realizing how he'd take it. And then! Even if Josh could forgive me, there was still poor Miriam to consider.

All I had was impossible choices.

"Hey! Look who it is!"

I turned my head to see Danny and Jakobitz sitting at a high table on bar stools. "Hi," I said, realizing that this had been a mistake. When I first started working at the garage, they'd asked me several times to join them here. But I never did.

It's not that I didn't want to go out with them. It's just that I couldn't justify spending money on beer. And what's more, I couldn't justify hanging out at the bar with these guys while Josh waited at home. And bringing Josh with me... I didn't know how that would go.

So I'd always begged off.

But now here I was, finally accepting their invitation, on the night when I was a giant fucking wreck. *Nicely done, Caleb. You idiot*.

"You meeting someone?" Jackbitz asked.

I went closer to them. "No. Just needed to get out."

Danny cocked his head toward an empty bar stool. "Get over here, then."

I sat down, and a waitress appeared immediately, temporarily saving me from further conversation. "What'll it be?" she asked.

"Uh," I didn't know much about beers. "Let me buy a round," I said, taking out my credit card. "I'll have one of whatever they're drinking."

She took the card and walked off.

"Don't take this the wrong way," Jakobitz said, pausing to drain his glass, "but you don't look so good."

I must look almost as bad as I felt, then. Because Jakobitz wasn't the most perceptive guy I'd ever met. "Yeah," I sighed, tucking my wallet back into my jeans. "I fucked up tonight."

"Bad?"" Danny asked.

"Bad," I confirmed.

"We're talking, like, life-changing fuck up?" Jakobitz asked.

I nodded, miserable.

He whistled. "Did you cheat?"

"No," I said immediately. But then my heart seized. Because I might as well have said yes. I'd told Josh that I meant to marry

Miriam, and to me, that was nothing but a giant sacrifice. But from where he sat, it wouldn't look like that.

"Does she *think* you cheated? Women can't ever get over that shit. They *tell* you they will, but they don't."

My heart dipped. The waitress set a beer down in front of me, and I took a sip of it before I looked up at Danny and Jakobitz. "Well. Is the same true for guys?"

Jakobitz's beer halted on the way to his mouth. "You're with a guy?"

I sighed, setting my beer on the table. "I was until about an hour ago. You got a problem with that?"

Danny let out a hoot and smacked the table with an open hand. "He *does* got a problem! His problem is that he owes me twenty bucks. Pay up."

"Christ," Jakobitz swore, opening up his wallet. He took out a twenty and threw it at Danny.

"You had a *bet?*"

"Don't be mad," Danny said, tucking the money away. "We bet on everything. Jako once won ten bucks off of me because the boss took a piss break before noon, not after."

It took me a minute to relax, though. I had exactly zero practice telling people I was gay. The only person I ever told was Josh. Everyone else just guessed. "Where we're from, they would have jumped us for being together."

"Cuz you're from... Iran?" Jakobitz quipped.

Danny thumped him on the chest. "There are assholes everywhere, moron."

Wasn't that the truth? And now Danny and Jakobitz were both staring at me. "I don't say much about my life. Pretty much all of it is freaky."

"I don't know, man," Danny said, shaking his head. "Lotta people I know could say the same thing. The bar is set pretty high around here."

At that, I smiled for the first time all night.

Our waitress was passing by, and Jakobitz reached out and touched her arm. "Can we get six shots of Jack? Seems like we need it."

"Sure, hon." She moved on.

I didn't know what Jack was, but I bet it was going to be strong. "You know I have zero tolerance, right?"

Jakobitz grinned. "Could be fun, then. You eat dinner?"

I shook my head.

He got up and went to the bar, where I heard him order some fries.

TWO HOURS LATER, the room was swimming, and I clutched the edge of the table with both hands, just so it didn't get away from me.

"That is fucked up, my man," Danny was saying. "If this girl knows you really want your boy, not her, she won't marry you. A woman don't work that way."

The whole story had come pouring out after that first shot of Jack. All of it. Stealing the gun. Getting Josh kicked out. Finding him in the dirt behind the bus station. Washington. Maggie. Daniel. Chloe.

Miriam. Miriam's *rape*.

"I don't know what to do for her," I slurred. "She's eighteen."

"You're twenty-one, right? Just a baby yourself. It's not your fault what those assholes did to her."

"Yeah, it is. She needed my protection and I ran away instead, so I could finally get laid."

"Can't believe you were a twenty-year-old virgin," Jakobitz muttered. "That's the weirdest part of this story."

Danny ignored him. "You need to go home to your guy and apologize. Plead innocent, by reason of insanity. You gotta stay with the guy, because faking it with the girl sounds like a bad plan. You can still help her, though. Just not with a wedding and a ring."

They made it sound so easy. "When I think of what those fuckers did to her, I just want to hurt somebody."

"No kidding. But if you do this, you're only hurting your guy, yourself, and that girl."

"Why do people keep saying that?" I asked.

"'Cause you're in need of hearing it," Jakobitz said. "Listen to Danny. He's smarter than me. Just ask him."

Danny gave Jako another thump in the chest.

"I need to go home," I said.

"Yeah, you do. But none of us are driving. It's taxi time. One for us, because we live close to each other. And one to drive you out to the sticks."

"Shit." That would cost a fortune.

"Or you could call home and ask for a ride." Jakobitz pulled a phone out of his pocket.

I took it.

HALF AN HOUR LATER, I was holding up the exterior wall of the bar with my ass. My hands were slowly turning to ice. But the cool air on my face was helpful. It made me feel a little less drunk, although the war between whiskey and greasy fries in my stomach was not going well.

Beside me, Danny and Jako were betting on whether or not I was going to puke before my ride showed up. There was five bucks riding on it.

Finally, Daniel's truck pulled into the lot. But the passenger door opened, not the driver's. Josh jumped down, slamming the door. When he turned to me, I saw a look on his face that I never thought I'd see.

Disgust.

"Is that your guy?" Jako asked. "He looks pissed. I don't think you're getting any make-up nookie tonight."

"Shut it, moron," Danny muttered under his breath. Then he put a hand on my shoulder and called out. "You Josh? I got good news and bad news. The good news is that Caleb is really sorry, and he knows he's been an asshole. The bad news is that he's drunk off his ass, and probably going to puke in the next ten minutes."

Josh took three steps closer, then stopped. He folded his arms and just stared me down. As if he was trying to decide something.

"I'm sorry," I said.

"See?" Jako piped up. "He's sorry."

"We're both sorry about a lot of things," Josh said. "It's what you *do* about it that matters."

Ah. So true. If only I wasn't so drunk, this would be easier. "I shouldn't have freaked out like that. I wouldn't last a day without you."

"Aw!" Jakobitz crowed. "Keep going, dude. You're on the right track."

"I want to come home," I said. "To the apartment," I added, in case that wasn't clear. There could be no more fuck-ups. I couldn't afford them.

Josh kicked a pebble in the gravel at his feet. Then he glanced at my car where it was parked against the fence. "Is your new toy a manual or an automatic?"

"Auto..." I burped in the middle of the word. "...Matic."

"Oh, man. You didn't show him the car yet?" Danny yelped. "Jesus, Caleb. You are kind of an asshole."

I sighed. "That's nothing I don't already know."

Josh may have hidden a tiny little smile at that point. But then he buried it, and held out a hand. "Keys."

"Wha? You're driving?"

"You're sure as hell not," he said.

I pulled them out of my pocket just as another car pulled up to the bar.

Jakobitz held his hand up to his eyes to shield them from the headlights. "Can you, like, kiss and make up, now? Because our taxi is here."

Josh rolled his eyes as he took the keys from me, which he managed to do without even brushing my hand.

"Uh, guys," I said. "Thanks for everything tonight, but you can go on home."

"We don't get to know how this ends? What a rip!"

Danny gave his arm a tug. "Come on. You can talk to Caleb next week."

The two of them stumbled into the taxi together, and it drove away. So did Daniel's truck, after Josh went over to the window and waved him off.

That left just the two of us. "Can I take you out to dinner?" I slurred.

"Now?" He squinted at me as if I'd lost my mind.

I hadn't, I just wasn't expressing myself very well. "Not now, but soon. Some night. Just you and me. We never do that."

Josh sighed. "Ask me tomorrow. I really just need this day to end."

That was probably a good call. "Okay. Let's go." I let go of the tavern wall, and began walking to the Toyota. But it wasn't easy. And my stomach rebelled just as Josh bleeped the locks. "Just a sec..." I said, but then had to double over and vomit on the gravel beside the car. My stomach heaved, and then heaved again. The sour heat of whiskey permeated my senses, and tears of discomfort flushed my eyes.

Fuck. Why did people drink?

I spit a couple of times, then opened the door. Josh thrust a water bottle in my direction, the one I'd put on the console earlier in the day. "Thanks." I rinsed and spit, and then got into the car with him.

"That was really sexy," Josh deadpanned.

"You're..." I stopped a second, trying to figure out if what I had to say would be taken well. "You should fight back more often," I said quietly. "It looks good on you."

Josh gave me a long, exasperated look out of the corner of his eye, and I wondered how much time would pass before his anger wore off. I'd brought him low tonight. I got that now. And it would probably take a while before he trusted me again.

I would wait. Forever, if necessary.

He put the key in the ignition and turned her on. Putting my new baby in reverse, he slowly backed out of the parking space.

"Josh?"

"What?"

"It's easier to drive at night if you turn on the headlights."

With his foot on the brake, he dropped his head onto the steering wheel. "I'm sorry."

"Don't be sorry. The lever is here." The smooth skin at back of his neck was visible in the moonlight, and I yearned to put my hand there to sooth him. Instead, I reached over to flip on the lights.

With a sigh, he sat up again. "I can do this. It's only eight miles on a lonely road," he said.

"You can do anything, baby," I whispered. "I only hope I'm allowed to stick around and watch."

Without comment, Josh put the car in drive and rolled toward the road.

SEVERAL UNEVENTFUL MINUTES LATER, we pulled up in front of the workshop. Josh got out and shut the door, then waited for me to haul my drunk self out and into the building.

My toothbrush was still in the bathroom. So at least I knew that he hadn't finished evicting me.

SARINA BOWEN

I made my way carefully up into the loft, then I stripped off every stitch of clothing and climbed into bed. The bedside lamp was still on, blinding me, so I rolled to the side to escape its glare.

A few minutes later, Josh padded softly up to join me. He shut the lamp off and slipped into bed.

Three feet of empty space lay between us, and I was afraid to breech it. Who wanted a drunk asshole like me, anyway?

Nobody, that's who. And to think I'd begun the night imagining myself the savior of not one, but two people.

What a crock.

CHAPTER TWENTY-SEVEN

Caleb

When I opened my eyes in the morning, I was disoriented. The new king-sized bed felt different under my body. And the sunlight on the slanted ceiling above me was unfamiliar. A dull pain thumped in my head, and my mouth tasted of whiskey and sadness.

I turned my head, and was comforted by the sight of a sleeping Josh. His eyes lay peacefully closed, and his tousled hair fanned out over his ear.

He hadn't gotten up to do the milking. My achy brain worried over this for a moment, until I realized it was Saturday, the day that Daniel milked by himself. Several months ago he'd told Josh to sleep in on the weekends. Those were the same days that I could sleep in, too. Looking back on this, it was clear to me now that Daniel had arranged this on purpose—given us two days a week to wake up slowly together.

Another gift from Daniel, and I hadn't even realized it.

Looking over at Josh again, my heart gave a squeeze. It was a privilege to wake up beside him. And yesterday I'd somehow told him that it was something I could do without.

Not only was I an ungrateful asshole, I was an idiot, too.

As much as I wanted to hold Josh right now, I didn't know where we stood. And the poor guy was sleeping. So, to escape the temptation, I slipped out of bed. On the main level, I took a long shower, cleansing myself of sweat and whiskey and yesterday's mistakes. Then, wrapped in a towel, I made myself a piece of buttered toast and then ate it standing at the sink. I put the coffee on, too, but left it to drip. In our bathroom, I drank two tall glasses of water and brushed my teeth aggressively.

It was almost ten o'clock now, and I was lonely for Josh. So I went back up to the loft and dropped my towel, lying down again in the bed.

Josh was just as I'd left him, the sheets half-way down his back, exposing the honey-colored skin of his shoulders. If I went any longer without touching him, I would die.

Scooting toward him, I palmed his lower back. My hand met warm skin and firm muscle. He was beautiful and alive, and I don't know how I thought, even for a few hours, that I could give him up.

Sleepy eyes flickered open, and he studied me from under the fringe of his soft hair.

"Good morning," I whispered. He didn't say anything, but neither did he turn away. So I scooted closer, then reached for him, pulling his upper body onto my chest.

With a sigh, Josh settled into me, throwing one knee over mine, burying his face in my neck. We just lay there quietly, while I wondered how things would go between us now. I put my arms around him, my palms flat on his lower back. The more of him that I could hold and touch at once, the less awful I'd feel.

I ran my hands up his back slowly, pressing firmly on all the muscle I felt there. And then I ran them down again, my fingertips digging in just the way he liked.

I didn't get a moan or an appreciative wiggle, though. Josh was silent.

Sticking my nose in his hair, I inhaled. The clean scent of him was almost enough to make me feel better. I palmed the back of his neck and held him close. Then I let my hands dance all the way down his back, onto his waist. With strong fingers, I massaged the muscles of his lower back. Then I slid my hands down into his boxers, rubbing gentle circles into his ass. Just touching him. *Loving* him.

If he shifted against me, I would find a way. If he pushed closer, or spread himself for me, I would know that it was okay to ask for more. But that didn't happen. He remained still, his sadness rising like mist around us.

"I love you," I whispered, even though it was too little too late. "I'm sorry I freaked out yesterday. It wasn't your fault. And it wasn't right."

Josh let out a slow sigh against me. But if I wasn't mistaken, he melted into my chest just a little bit.

"You feel so good, baby," I whispered. "Let me love you."

He didn't say yes. But he also didn't say no.

By now, I was feeling all kinds of arousal. My cock was hard, and laying against my belly. And everywhere we were connected, my skin was on fire.

I would never stop wanting Josh. No matter how big an idiot I was, he would always have this effect on me. Always.

Taking his hand, the one that he'd flung over my chest, I kissed his knuckles. Then I put that hand on my belly, where my hair thickened as it approached my groin. It was a place that I knew he loved to touch me.

Sure enough, his fingers sifted through that fine hair. As I stroked the skin over his taut ass, I felt his breath hitch.

I turned my head and spoke right into his ear. "I'm so hard for you right now. That's never going to change. Whether I'm stupid or smart, and whether you still love me anymore, or not. I never could help loving you. It's just the way that I'm wired."

Josh became very, very still. I could feel him resisting the pull of me, and I didn't really blame him. It couldn't be easy to just roll over and let the man who broke your heart yesterday fuck you.

I thought about this for a second. But only for a second. Because I knew what I needed to do.

Hiking up a knee on the bed, I spread myself a little bit. Then I took Josh's hand off my belly, and I draped it across my balls, until his fingertips hung down between my legs. "Josh," I whispered. "Will you fuck me?"

First, he made a small noise of surprise. Then he turned his head away from me, as if to think. But his hand, with those beautiful long fingers, reached down, skimming my taint.

Damn, that felt good. "Yeah," I encouraged him. "I want you right there. Do this for me."

With a sigh, he raised himself up on an elbow, finally looking me in the eye. "Why?" he whispered. "Why now? You never asked for that before."

I pulled his head down, right on my chest. "Sometimes I fantasize about getting fucked by you. But I never told you. It's because I always needed to maintain this illusion that I could be in *charge* of everything. Like, if I let go of the reins for a second, everything would fall apart."

For this explanation, I received a very gentle kiss to my left nipple. It was the first kiss I'd gotten from Josh for forty-eight hours. So that was something.

"I get it now. I can't always be in charge," I continued. "There is so much out of my control. And I hate that. But I need to get over myself."

Josh kissed my chest again. "You think if I fuck you, you can get over yourself?"

My stomach contracted with a huff of laughter. "I like you sassy," I chuckled. "Seriously."

He sighed. "You didn't answer the question."

"It's a start. Besides, you always make it look like fun. I *love* taking you. But I would like to try being taken."

Again with the thoughtful silence. "I always assumed you wouldn't want to... submit to me."

Submit. It wasn't a bad word for what I wanted to do. "It's true that I have trouble giving up control. But it isn't about equality."

Josh grunted. "You don't think of me as your equal."

"That is *not* true," I said immediately. "And I hate that you think so. At the Compound, I got the good jobs and the driver's license. But none of it made me feel superior, because I could see how shallow it all was. But that shit followed us here, too. I'm the one with the job, and with friends that don't live here on this twenty acre lot. But you can have all that, too. You're almost there. It'll only take a little longer." I pushed my fingers into his beautiful hair and rubbed his head. "What we do in bed isn't related to any of that crap in our past. I just hope you know that."

"Sometimes I hate being the one who stays at home and waits for you. And some days I think it's the best scam ever."

I ruffled his hair. "How do you feel about always being the bottom?"

"Mmm," he said. "I get all boned up just thinking about it. But fucking you would be really hot. Mostly because I want you to know how it feels."

I was pretty boned up myself at that point. "How *does* it feel?" I dropped a hand to my hard dick and squeezed. "Does it hurt?"

Josh shook his head against my chest. "Only that first time, when we didn't know what we were doing."

"You didn't know," I corrected him. "I'd searched it six ways 'til Sunday already. Apparently I gave Daniel's computer a gay hard-on."

Josh smiled against my ribcage. "Fine. If you go too fast before you're opened up, it's going to burn. And there's always this moment at the beginning when it just feels awkward. But if you get through that, and there's a nice, thick dick hitting your spot over and over again..." He shifted his body against mine, and I

235

could sense his arousal. "...There's nothing like it. And when you finally come, it's spectacular."

I let out a hot breath. "Please fuck me, Josh. Please?"

He moaned, and I loved the sound. "Right now?"

"You got a bus to catch?"

I'd meant it as a light joke, of course. But as soon as I said those words, I felt last night's troubles creep back in under the door.

Josh pulled himself up into a crouch, looking down at me on the pillow. "If you *ever* try to tell me again that marrying a woman is going to solve anyone's problems, I *will* catch a bus."

Jesus. That was the last thing I wanted. Reaching up, I tugged his face down near mine. "I know. I'm sorry. Temporary insanity."

He quirked an eyebrow.

"That's what my drunk friends told me to say."

He smiled all of a sudden. "Do I get to meet them sometime? When you're not all wasted?"

I craned my neck and kissed him. "Absolutely. Now get down here and loosen me up. Make me a member of the club, already."

"Jeez," his cheeks pinked up. "Roll over." He scrambled to the side of the bed to get the lube that he must have put in there when we moved in. We'd spent two nights in this bed already, with no action.

Nice, Caleb. Way to ruin everything.

"Ass in the air," Josh ordered. His voice was bossier than I'd ever heard it. I knew he was still mad at me, which gave this morning's decision to bottom some interesting timing. That was the point, though. Josh would never hurt me, no matter how mad he was. I knew I couldn't take back the awful thing I'd done yesterday. This was the only way I could think of to hand myself over to him in a way that felt real.

Leaving my forehead on the bed, I lifted my naked ass in the air, as he'd asked me to. It wasn't the sexiest position, either. "I feel so exposed," I said.

A beat went by before he replied. "It *is* so exposed," he said quietly. "There's no getting around it. You have to trust the one you're exposing yourself to."

Of course. Josh gave me that trust all the time. Now I knew I'd never be careless with it again.

I felt him move into position between my legs, and I clenched, as if waiting for the invasion. But it didn't come. He leaned over and kissed my lower back. Then he did it a few more times. Finally, a smooth hand began gently tracing the crease of my ass, slowly spreading me wider.

Blowing out a breath, I tried to relax.

Soft kisses rained down on my back, my hip... even my ass. And a smooth hand stole around my hip and cupped my balls. "That's it," he whispered. "Spread yourself for me."

I widened my stance even further, and Josh rewarded me by moving his hand onto the column of my dick. I rocked into his palm, gently fucking his hand. That felt good, and it made me relax.

"Good boy." The sound of Josh's praise soothed me, and I relaxed even further. His fingertips teased the entrance to my hole, and I let myself enjoy it. I was so sensitive to his touch. It was unfamiliar, yet utterly arousing. "Good boy," he said again, and the low tone of his praise made me even harder.

I wanted very much to be a good boy, if this was how that felt.

It was all going well so far. "I can take more," I told him, "should I grab the lube?"

"No," he breathed. "We don't need it yet."

I was about to argue the point when I realized why he'd said that. Josh's lips landed at my crease, and at the same unbelievable moment, his wet, hot tongue swept over my hole.

The moan I let out could have been heard down at Ralph's Tavern.

"Mmm," Josh said, kissing me. *Licking* me. He was pressing his tongue *everywhere*, and it was crazy.

"God in heaven," I panted. "That is...unnng." I couldn't finish the sentence. All that wet warmth made me push my face into the pillow and moan. And this while he stroked my dick with one hand and my inner thighs with another.

"You're so beautiful," Josh said behind me. The timbre of his voice was the sweetest thing I'd ever heard. "I can't wait to fuck you."

"Do it," I panted.

"Not just yet." He moved around for a moment, and then the lube bottle popped open and then shut again. A slippery finger took over where his tongue had been. With a gentle firmness, he pushed inside me.

"Okay," I said to the pillow. The feeling was... odd. It neither hurt nor felt good.

"Relax, baby," Josh said. "You can do this. Ease yourself back on me."

It did not hurt. But it *was* weird. Gingerly, I rocked back onto his finger.

"There you go." He moved inside me, while I focused on relaxing for him.

That got easier a minute later when he stretched that naughty finger and brushed something that made me hiss. "Oh," I panted.

Behind me, Josh chuckled. "Now you'll understand."

Did I ever. I pushed back, fucking myself on his finger, hoping for a little more of that glory. His hand disappeared, though. I heard the sound of the lube again, and then he pressed forth, this time with two fingers.

Again, I needed a minute to adjust. But this time I understood what pleasures were to be had. So I breathed deeply while my body adjusted. Josh worked his fingers apart and then together again, just like I'd done for him so many times. It was so odd to be on the receiving end of this treatment.

Before, I'd *thought* I understood what it meant to bottom. Josh seemed to do it effortlessly. But even though I'd warmed him up countless times before, I never really knew what was required. This was an activity full of will and intention. Letting someone else into your body required patience and a lot more trust than I'd ever known.

Before long, those two fingers were making me crazy. Every stroke began to feel like a gift. I fell face first onto the bed again. "Please," I begged the mattress. "I'm ready."

He kissed a sensitive place at the bottom of my spine. "I'm going to take you now."

"Do it," I gasped.

Trembling, I waited a few seconds for him to lube up one more time. My ass was in the air, and I no longer cared. I had no room for worry, only breathless anticipation.

Then I felt it — the broad head of his cock seeking entrance. With a groan, I eased back. There was a moment there when I thought it wouldn't work. But then I gave way, and the first part of him slid inside.

"Oh," I sighed. He was bigger than I expected. Again, my body needed to adjust.

Josh did not thrust. I heard him taking, long, deep breaths. Gently, he worked his way forward, until he was seated inside. "Caleb," he panted. "You feel unbelievable."

I took a big lungful of air and made myself relax. "Do it," I whispered. "Fuck me."

Josh's hands gripped my hips. Slowly, he experimented with rocking.

"Aah," I gasped. I felt so *full* of him. It was overwhelming.

He drew back, and then immediately pushed forward. It was good, and I could tell that it was about to get better. "More," I begged.

Josh provided. He began to thrust — gently at first. The sway of his balls against mine was exquisite. Every sound he made lit me up—from the huff of each little breath, to the soft moans he made in between. The sound of his arousal stoked my fire. And then he did something so sexy. He reached forward and wrapped his long hands loosely around my neck. I felt *claimed* when he did that. Owned. *Taken*. And all the while he fucked me from behind, his pace picking up speed as he went.

I began to meet him with each thrust, and that's when it got really crazy. When I moved my hips, he hit my spot just right. "Oh, shit," I gasped. "That's..." I blew out a happy breath.

"You like that?" he whispered. He shifted the angle of his pelvis and really pounded forward.

My breath caught in my throat. "Baby..." He was riding me, and together we were headed somewhere beautiful.

"Getting close," he grunted. "You're so tight." One hand left my neck and slipped around my hip. Then his hand was on my dick, and every time I moved my hips, he stroked me.

"Yeah," I encouraged him. "Do it."

Josh began to moan. His thrusts got short and choppy. I loved that. When we had sex he always lost himself in it. "Oh, Caleb," he gasped. "I need to..." That's when it happened. I could even feel the heat of his seed filling me up, while Josh groaned with pleasure.

And that's all it took to get me there, too. My spine hitched, and the most wonderfully deep orgasm began to sweep me under. "Oh, *fuck*." I was shuddering and shooting all over our new bed. Collapsing forward, I brought Josh down on top of me.

"Jesus," I gasped into the pillow.

Josh grunted his agreement. He was quiet again, but it was okay now. Tired arms grabbed my hips as Josh slid off me. I rolled to pull him into my embrace.

We lay there, breathing together, our breath mingling the way it was supposed to.

We're going to be okay, I promised myself.

Time passed. The sun rose higher in our new windows. "Baby?" I asked Josh after a while.

"Mmm?" He sounded so happy and calm, I didn't want to ruin

it. But there was one more thing I needed to tell him. "I want to explain why I freaked out so bad yesterday. Not to *excuse* myself," I added in a hurry. "But there's something you should know. How Miriam got those bruises on her face."

He turned his sweaty face to me, listening.

"She wouldn't go to Asher willingly. They were married, but she wouldn't..." I sighed.

"Oh," Josh breathed. He tucked his feet closer to mine in the bed.

"So, Asher taught her a lesson. He let a couple of his pals come over one night. He tied her down, and they all took turns."

Josh's eyes squeezed shut. "Oh, hell."

"I know." I took Josh's hand and kissed it. "I want to just fly there and shoot him."

"Poor thing," Josh said, his eyes flicking toward the house. "That's what you overheard the other night?"

"Yeah." I kissed his hand again. "So when this baby is born, we can't breathe a word about who she looks like. Because Miriam doesn't *know* who the father is."

I watched Josh take a deep, shaky breath. "Okay. But why did she have two black eyes? Because what you're describing would have happened months ago."

"Yeah. From what I could gather, Asher wanted to make an example of her. He stopped treating her like a proper wife. Since she got pregnant the way she did, he called a whore and slapped her around in front of the other wives."

Josh squeezed his eyes shut again. "Too bad you pawned that gun."

I kissed him on the forehead. "I know. The good news is that Miriam might get a chance to send him to jail. I looked it up on the internet. You can prosecute a rape in Wyoming no matter how long ago it was. So she can settle in here for years before she decides whether to tell the police what happened."

Josh groaned. "That poor girl. She'll probably be too afraid to ever set foot there again."

"Mmm," I pulled him closer to me. "I didn't tell you this to make you feel bad. But it *is* bad."

"Yeah," he sighed. "At least I understand now why you flipped." He wiggled closer to me. "I'm glad Miriam got away from him."

"Me too."

"You're a gentle soul, Caleb."

"Not as gentle as you," I whispered. And that was the truth.

ANOTHER HALF HOUR WENT BY, both of us lost in our thoughts.

"I could just lie here all day." Josh's words were muffled by the pillow.

It made my heart swell to hear that. He hadn't kicked me out of bed. "That works for me. But eventually, we'll need groceries."

Josh flopped onto his back. "Yeah. We have to feed ourselves now."

"Not totally. Maggie said we should still have dinner with them every night." I reached over a put a hand on his belly. Today I planned to touch Josh any chance I got. I wasn't even going to let him out of my sight.

I cuddled closer to him, while we both listened to the silence. "Please forgive me," I whispered eventually.

The short pause before he spoke almost gutted me. "I need you to love me, even when things get hard." he said.

"I do, though. Always. I'm going to prove it to you."

The only question was how.

EVENTUALLY, we got up and showered together.

"Let's go to the store," I said afterward. "We'll get food for our new fridge."

Josh smiled, grabbing his coat. "Okay. We should ask Maggie if there's anything she needs, though."

"Good idea."

A few minutes later, though, I felt a little nervous walking into the house. Surely my reputation had suffered since last night. When I'd told Daniel my plan to marry Miriam, he'd told me I was crazy. And that was *before* he'd had to drive Josh out at midnight to pick up my drunk ass.

And then there was Miriam. We used to be close. But in the forty-eight hours she'd been here, I'd barely spoken ten words to her, because I was busy freaking out.

Today was Saturday, and well after the milking, so the whole family was sitting in the living room, drinking coffee. Maggie had some classical guitar music playing on the stereo. She and Daniel sat on the couch, each with a section of the newspaper. And Miriam sat in the rocking chair, with Chloe on her lap.

Josh stopped in the doorway, and I drew up beside him. In a maneuver that I would have never considered before, I put an affectionate hand on the back of Josh's neck. In front of God and everyone. "Hi," I said softly, as they all looked up.

"Hi," Daniel said carefully, letting his newspaper fall into his lap. "How are you this morning?"

I cleared my throat. "Saner, I think."

Daniel grinned, as did Miriam. She looked up to the place where I'd rested my hand on Josh's skin, and her smile grew.

For a moment I just stared at Miriam. The bruises on her face had faded almost to nothing. She was beautiful, and so, so young. Impossibly young.

"I need to..." the words got stuck in my throat. Because I'd just spent two days trying to figure out what it was that I really did need to do. Marrying Miriam was not the answer. But it left

243

me with little else than a few words. "I need to apologize to Miriam. Can I do that?"

Miriam's smile faded. "Don't, Caleb. What happened to me isn't your fault."

"It is, though." My voice was rough, and I wondered if I could do this without it breaking. "The day I left, I should have taken you with me. The three of us..."

She shook her head. "You tried, sweetie. You told me I could put on my coat and go."

Everyone looked at me then, their faces inquisitive.

Had I really said that to her? I thought back to our frantic conversation in the pantry of Miriam's family house. At any moment, we might have been discovered. There was barely any time to say goodbye, let alone plot another escape.

I *had* told her she could come, though. I'd said those words. But there had been a catch. "I didn't... I didn't *push*, Miriam. Because I was worried about Josh, and I knew I was running out of time. It was almost meaner to throw it out there that way. I didn't give you even an hour to think about it."

She shook her head. "Doesn't matter. You said to put on my coat and meet you at the main gate. And for a second, I was ready to do it. But then I made a different decision. My father was ill, and I was worried about my mother. I stood there and *chose*, Caleb. I didn't want to leave them."

"He was ill?" She hadn't told me that.

She nodded. "He died a little while after you left. Mom is remarried to Elder Michael. But Michael is out of favor now. So Mom and I both ended up in unfortunate situations. She's the one who told me to run away last week. She gave me Maggie's phone number, and all her kitchen money. And she sent me away."

"I'm still sorry," I said, my voice rough.

Her eyes were filling, but she smiled anyway. "I know, Caleb.

Me too. But it's going to be okay. You don't have to worry about me anymore."

"I want to help, though." My voice finally broke on the last word, and so Josh slipped an arm onto my back.

"You will," she said, a single tear rolling down her cheek. "You can help me in so many ways. I'm just across the yard."

Blowing out a breath, I felt my shoulders relax for the first time in two days.

I needed a minute to compose myself, which Josh seemed to sense. So he changed the subject. "We were heading to the grocery store, actually. Our new fridge is empty. Do you guys need anything?"

Maggie stood up. "Go after lunch. I have two quiches in the oven. I'll make you a shopping list while they cool."

"Someday you'll have to stop feeding us, Maggie," I said.

"I don't see why," she returned. "It's a few eggs and some flour, big guy. Get over yourself."

I was trying. Really I was.

"We'll need more coffee," Daniel said, following Maggie out of the room. "I'm putting it on the grocery list. If you're really willing to make a trip to that zoo on a Saturday, I'll take you up on it."

"Deal," I promised.

"Down," Chloe said suddenly.

Miriam helped the little girl slide off the chair. She toddled over to us. "Bosh," she said, raising her arms. "Up."

My partner bent over immediately and lifted her into his arms. "Hi there," he whispered. "You miss me?"

"Baba."

"Yeah?" He lifted her a little higher and smelled her backside. I recognized that as one of those childcare maneuvers that separated the naturals from those who were just phoning it in. "Let's take care of this diaper first. And then we'll find you some milk." He headed up the stairs with Chloe in his arms.

I watched him go, admiring him until the backs of his long legs disappeared upstairs.

When I turned around again, Miriam was smiling at me. "Cute."

My cheeks heated. "Yeah, he is."

She giggled. "I meant you, silly. Come and talk to me." She got up and took her sister's place on the couch.

I sat down beside her, and she kicked her stocking feet into my lap. Sitting here like this was forbidden on the Compound. Because the path to hell was paved with friends touching each other's feet.

"I can't get over the hospital Maggie took me to. I thought all babies were born at home."

"Yeah," I said, squeezing her instep. "I'll bet that seems pretty strange. But if anything goes wrong, they can help."

"I have to stay two nights." She made a face. "Maggie said she'll stay with me. But I don't want to take her from Chloe."

"I'll stay a night," I suggested. "And Maggie can stay the other one. We'll split it."

Miriam turned her smile on me. "You know I love you, right? But I was thinking of asking Josh if he'd take a shift."

I tipped my head back against the sofa and laughed. "That just figures."

"Don't be mad. But I'm a little scared of babies. And he..."

"...Isn't," I supplied.

"Yeah." Her voice was soft. "I'm happy that you have him, Caleb. I truly am."

There wasn't a thing I could say to that, except the obvious. "Thank you."

"I thought we were doomed, you know that? Both of us. And I won't pretend that the last year was easy. But I'm so optimistic now."

"I'm glad," I ground out, because my throat had seized up completely. And suddenly I was losing a battle with tears that I didn't even know I'd been fighting. My chin sagged onto my chest, and a sob came heaving from my throat.

"Oh, noooo!" Miriam crooned. She scrambled into a kneeling position, grabbing my head against her giant curvy body.

I *hated* breaking down. But that was the thing about tears— they didn't care. It had been so long since I let any out that now they poured out of me like a river. Another sob burst forth. "I'm sorry," I said for the thousandth time.

"Shh," she said. The sound of her voice was precious to me. Miriam was one of my oldest friends. I'd been looking out for her for as long as I could remember. I thought it was my duty. The part I didn't understand, though, was that I didn't have to do it alone.

I cried anyway, though. I shed tears for those who wouldn't wake up here with us tomorrow: for whichever girl Asher targeted next, and for my own mother, who used to knit me new socks every year. I shed tears for the kids who wouldn't go to a real school, and for the boys who liked boys and were terrified to admit it.

I'd come so far, and yet there was no way I'd ever be able to fix all the things that were wrong.

A few minutes into my crying jag, Josh appeared at my other side, his hands free of Chloe. He must have pawned her off on someone else, because he shoved me over a few inches and took a seat on my other side.

Now *both* my oldest friends were holding me while I struggled to breathe normally again.

Breathe in. Breathe out. Repeat. That was my only job this morning. But it was so hard to set my burdens down, that even this seemed impossible.

When my sadness finally lifted, I found my head on Josh's shoulder. He stroked my hair slowly, patiently.

"Josh?"

"Mmm?" he said.

"Can we get married?"

His breath caught, and then I felt his smile against my forehead. "You do mean to each other, right?"

I squeezed his knee. "Yes. Would you do that for me?"

"I would like that very much," he said in a small voice.

"Oh, man," Miriam said, raising a hand to her face. "Now you're going to make *me* cry."

"So?" I gave her knee a little pinch, the way I would have done when we were kids. "Why should I have all the fun?" Sitting here together, a warmth spread through my chest. I took a deep breath through my sniffly nose and felt calmer again. "We'll hold off on the wedding until after you have the baby," I said. "So you can fit into one of Maggie's dresses."

"I know a good catering company," Josh said.

"We won't even need them," I said. "We don't have very many people to invite."

Miriam sat up a little straighter. "Let's send invitations to everyone on the Compound. Asher will probably have a heart attack reading it. If we're lucky, he'll go face down in the mashed potatoes."

Yesterday, the sound of the word "Asher" had made me furious enough to boil my blood. But now I actually laughed. "Wouldn't you just *love* to see the looks on the Elders' faces?"

The three of us sat there in a row on a couch, chuckling over this bit of humor. We used to sit like this on the school bus in second grade, when Miriam was in kindergarten. "Like bumps on a log," my mother had always said.

Josh held my hand, his thumb stroking my knuckles. Miriam made wedding jokes. And we were happy for once, just sitting and talking and having nowhere we needed to go, until Maggie called us in for quiche.

CHAPTER TWENTY-EIGHT

DEAR WASHINGTON,

THANK YOU for the Christmas card. Our second one! It's hard to believe that it's been more than a year since I sat in your truck, wondering how Caleb and I were going to survive the next week.

I have news.

And I started writing this letter a hundred times, and couldn't figure out how to tell you. So I'm just enclosing this invitation instead. Sorry if I'm giving you one heck of a surprise.

There isn't a whole lot else to say, I guess, except I hope we can still be friends. If we can't, that will make me sad, but I'll still think of you as someone who changed my life.

My love to Brenda.

Josh

YOU ARE INVITED

Joshua

Caleb

A VALENTINE'S DAY WEDDING
4 O'CLOCK IN THE AFTERNOON

RALPH'S TAVERN
2900 SOUTH BOULEVARD
HINTENVILLE, MA

RECEPTION TO FOLLOW

CHAPTER TWENTY-NINE

Caleb

THE NIGHT BEFORE OUR wedding, Josh and I spent a quiet evening on Maggie and Daniel's sofa.

We'd been very busy that week. My fiancé was now taking GED courses at a community center in Pittsfield, in between babysitting gigs and the occasional catering job.

In fact, we had a marked-up calendar hanging in our new kitchen helping us map out who needed the car and for how many hours. Sometimes I had to borrow Daniel's truck in a pinch, though Josh wouldn't drive it. "I can't park that boat," he complained. Although by now he was a very good driver.

In addition to our busy work schedules, we tried to get out together sometimes, too. Once a week, we ate dinner at a restaurant, just the two of us. "Date night," is what Maggie called it. Money wasn't quite so tight now, so we spent a little cash on things like movie tickets and the occasional bar tab.

We'd met Jakobitz and Danny a couple of times at the Tavern for a bite and a beer. Josh was just so-so on all their betting talk, but he did like the burgers and fries. And once, Danny decided to teach Josh to shoot pool, which I thought was sure to be a disaster.

How wrong I was. Ladies and gentlemen, allow me to introduce my fiancé, the pool shark. There was just something about all those angles which spoke to Josh. By our second trip back, he was beating strangers in the bar.

"Damn," Jako complained after Josh won his five dollars. "You should study engineering, or some shit. After you get that high school equivalency."

"Agricultural engineering," Josh muttered, lining up a shot.

"What?" I asked.

He sunk a combination shot before answering me. "It turns out you can get a degree in how stuff should work on a farm."

"Cool. Really?"

"Really. I've been reading up."

So I made a mental note to figure out how to pay for some college classes for Josh. I wanted that for him. In fact, the best revenge I could think of against the Compound was for Josh to earn a college degree and make a better living than any of the assholes who used to rule over us.

The night before our wedding, I wasn't thinking about revenge, though. It was quiet in the living room, after Maggie, Daniel and Miriam had gone to bed. We sat at opposite ends of the sofa, our legs tangled up in the middle. I was trying to wrap my head around what was happening tomorrow.

We were having a *wedding*, of all things. Back when we still lived on the Compound, even in my wildest fantasies there was no wedding for Josh and I. At best, I'd imagined us living together somewhere as closeted "roommates." But even that had seemed like a pipe dream most of the time.

It's really quite shocking to get what your heart desires.

At the other end of the sofa, Josh adjusted Miriam's nine-week-old baby girl, who wiggled against his chest.

Wilhelmina (or "Willy" for short) was a bit of a night owl. She hadn't learned to sleep through the night, yet. So Josh was doing a favor for Miriam by sitting up with her. In a half hour or so he would give Willy a final bottle, then sneak her into the crib in Miriam's room. This afforded the new mommy an extra two hours sleep that she would not otherwise get.

Naturally, I kept sneaking looks at Josh. The TV movie we were watching simply could not compete. My gaze lingered over his square shoulders, and the little V of skin above the buttons of his flannel shirt. I wanted to unbutton it a little further, and then put my lips right there.

"What?" he asked me finally, after he'd caught me staring for the third time.

"Nothing. I just like you."

He grunted, giving Willy a pacifier to chew on. The baby took it, her big eyes trained upward on his face. The babies of Runaway Dairy saw a lot of that view — Josh's strong jaw, and peaceful blue eyes.

"Josh?" I asked suddenly.

"Yeah?"

"Are you going to want kids someday?"

He looked at me with genuine surprise. "What do you mean? I'm up to my ears in kids."

It was true, too. Maggie's belly got bigger each and every day. One day I'd heard Josh and Maggie doing the math on how many continuous months of diaper-wearing the family would tally up before it was through. It was not a small number.

"I mean kids of our own." I'd been wondering if that would be important to Josh. And after seeing how much diapers cost, I'd tried to imagine how we could swing it.

"Um, Caleb? You know we can't impregnate each other, right?"

I chuckled. "It would have happened already, I suppose." Since moving into our apartment, we'd had *so* much sex. It was like we were trying to make up for years of abstinence these last three months. "People adopt, though. I just want to know if that's something I should be ready for."

He looked down at the top of Willy's fuzzy little head and

frowned. "But I *have* kids. Two of them, and one on the way." He looked up again. "Do *you* want kids?"

I wasn't sure how to answer that. "It's not on the top of my list. But if you wanted them, I'd listen."

Across the sofa, he smiled at me. "Actually, I'm happy renting. I don't need to hold title, Caleb."

Aw. I reached over and squeezed his knee. "Good. That works for me."

"It's nice of you to ask, though. I like to hear your wheels turning."

My hand was still on his knee, and I liked it there. "My wheels are always turning, baby. I try to stay a step ahead of you. But it isn't easy."

He yawned. "It gets easier this time of night."

"You're tired? That's a shame, because I had some plans for you later."

Josh glanced at me out of the corner of his eye. "I could rally. We get to sleep in tomorrow, you know. Nobody will bother us on our wedding day."

"I'm counting on it."

"Me too." I slid my hand further up his leg, my fingers brushing his inner thigh.

"Are you nervous about tomorrow?" he asked suddenly.

"No," I said right away. "But I don't like being the center of attention."

Josh nudged me with his knee. "This was your idea."

"I know," I chuckled. "But I love *you* so much more than I love reciting vows in front of people."

"There will only be, like, ten people," Josh said.

"True."

He looked down at the baby in his arms. "Willy," he said quietly. "Let's get you that bottle. I could swear you were looking sleepy."

"That's the spirit."

He got up off the couch and then leaned over me, depositing Willy in my lap. Then he quickly left the room.

"Wait!" I protested. But it was too late. I could hear him opening the refrigerator, looking for the bottle.

Willy looked up at me, a question in her eyes. *You don't have a clue about babies, do you, buddy?*

"Sorry," I whispered. "You're just going to have to put up with me for a minute." I picked her up a little higher, and she rubbed one of her drooly little hands on my wrist. "You won't have Josh to kick around for a few days, you know," I whispered. "Be good to your mommy while we're gone."

In reply, Willy made a gassy smile.

I'd booked three nights at a hotel in Miami Beach, Florida. It would be our first vacation ever, and I couldn't wait. The pictures on the hotel's website showed couples lazing in hammocks, or sipping cocktails beside the pool.

Also? Miami Beach was supposed to be one of the gayest vacation spots in America. And Caleb and I had never seen the ocean yet. There was just so much to look forward to.

Josh came back into the room, scooping Willy up again and settling in to feed her. It made my heart swell to see him calmly tuck her into the crook of his arm, and slip the nipple between her tiny lips.

How did I end up with someone so caring and beautiful? It boggled the mind.

"I love you, Josh."

"That's just the horny talking," he said, without looking up.

"Not true," I promised, and he grinned.

CHAPTER THIRTY

Caleb

AS WEDDING DAYS GO, ours was pretty relaxed.

Josh and I slept in on Saturday, and then made ourselves scrambled eggs and bacon for brunch. We took turns showering and shaving.

Then it was time to suit up. We both had new clothes for the wedding — matching navy blue suits and white dress shirts. Maggie had bought us each a red silk tie with tiny white hearts. "You're getting married on Valentine's day," she said. "There *have* to be hearts."

I hoped the guys from the garage wouldn't give me a hard time. Much.

I'd never owned anything as fine as these clothes, and since they weren't overly fancy, I could wear the suit again sometime.

At three-thirty, we got into our car and drove together to the tavern, where an Episcopal priest was waiting to marry us. Maggie took care of all the planning for our wedding. "It's my wedding gift to you."

And as soon as we walked into the little private room at Ralph's Tavern, we could see that she'd done a great job. On a table off to the side stood a small white wedding cake, with *Josh &*

Caleb swirled onto the top. There was one long table set for fifteen people, including two high chairs.

I counted in my head. Five adults and two babies from our house, three from the garage, plus Maggie's catering partner and gay Trey. That was twelve. The pastor made thirteen. "Who are the last two seats for?"

Maggie just grinned at me. "Let's go over the menu?"

"Do I have to? If it's food, I'll eat it."

She rolled her eyes. "Men. If it weren't for women, the wedding industry would crumble to the ground."

"You say that like it's a bad thing."

She tackled me in a hug. "I love you, Caleb. And I'm so happy for you today, I could burst."

I felt a sudden prickle of heat in the corners of my eyes. *Oh, hell no.* I was not going to cry today. With a deep breath, I pushed that swell of emotion away. "Thank you, Maggie. I'm pretty happy, too."

Across the room, Josh was holding Willy, trying not to let her drool on his tie, while Maggie's business partner was adjusting a spray of flowers on the cake table. And Daniel was chatting with Trey, who had come in a minute ago.

Then the priest walked in. When I met her last week, I would never have known she was a cleric, but for the stiff black and white collar projecting from the neckline of her dress.

She was not at all what I expected. I'd not seen the inside of a church since we left the Compound, but the pastors of my youth were dour old men. This one was a smartly dressed, silver-haired woman with sharp blue eyes. She came right over and laid a hand on my arm. "Congratulations, Caleb. I'm very happy to do the honor of marrying you today."

I swallowed hard. Maybe if everyone stopped saying such nice things to me, I could keep myself in check. "Thank you. We appreciate you doing this for us."

She gave my arm a little squeeze. "This is the best part of my job. And it's really special to marry two people who have known each other all their lives."

"I've never spent a day without Josh," I said truthfully. "Never wanted to."

Her blue eyes glittered. "I guess I won't waste any time asking if you're sure about him, then."

"There'd be no point," I agreed.

She grinned. "We can get started whenever you wish."

I looked toward the doorway as three guys from my garage walked in — Joe, Danny and Jakobitz. "Thanks for coming," I said, shaking hands. "I feel kind of guilty getting you guys into collared shirts on a Saturday. But there will be beer and barbecued ribs."

"We wouldn't miss it," Joe chuckled. "I've never been to an all-guy wedding before. It never occurred to me that the food would be better."

"Right?" I agreed. "And nobody will mind if you check the basketball scores later."

"I've got money on the Louisville game," Danny said, shedding his coat.

I laughed. "Of course you do." Looking around, I saw the pastor waiting in front, her hands folded before her.

Josh met my eyes, and there was a flicker of bashfulness in his expression. Apparently I wasn't the only one who was uncomfortable with ritual.

I gave him a brave smile. *Let's just go for it*, I tried to telegraph.

He grinned back at me, and the warmth of his smile was really all I needed to get through this.

I turned to find Maggie in the doorway. "Are you ready?" I asked her.

"Nope," she said quickly. "We're waiting for someone, but I think that's him walking through the front door right now."

A quick scan of the room confused me. We were all here already, at least by my count.

SARINA BOWEN

But seconds later, a familiar face walked into the room, one that I hadn't seen for over a year. "Washington!" I barked with surprise.

He gave me a toothy smile. "Looking sharp, boy!"

I was speechless for a second. But he came over to shake my hand, and his firm grip shook me out of my silence. "It's really good to see you. Didn't know you were coming."

"Told Maggie I wanted to surprise you." He turned around as a pretty dark-skinned lady in a polka-dot dress came into the room. "This is Brenda," he said. "My love, meet Caleb, that troublemaker I'm always telling you about."

"Wow," Josh said at my elbow. He looked as speechless as I'd been. "You're *here?*"

Brenda laughed. "He said, 'honey, we're going to go to a wedding next weekend. There's two boys I need you to meet.'"

Maggie put a hand on my shoulder. "Aw. Let's go, boys. Time to tie the knot."

"Go on," Washington said, putting an arm around his wife. "It ain't every day that I see two runaways get married."

Josh tugged my hand, and together we made our way over to the pastor. She smiled at us. "Are you nervous?"

I glanced at Josh. "Being married doesn't scare me. *Getting* married is a little weird."

Everyone laughed, including the pastor. "It only takes a few minutes, and it won't hurt a bit." She turned toward our little crowd of supporters. "Friends and family who have meant so much to Caleb and Josh this past year, we are gathered here today to celebrate a holy joining of hearts and spirits. Two men who have always been there for one another will declare their union before God and the Commonwealth of Massachusetts."

I'd pasted a rather stiff smile onto my face, because I didn't like being the center of attention.

"Before I read the wedding vows, Maggie wants to say something."

Maggie handed Chloe to Daniel and faced our small circle of friends. "It was fifteen months ago when I got a phone call out of the blue from Caleb, telling me he'd run away from the Compound with Josh. And my reaction was — *finally!* I'd been waiting for someone from my old life to come and find me. There's so much more to life than obedience and subservience. My own journey from that wretched place to where I am now was not easy. But I'm so glad I did it. And I'm so happy to have Caleb and Josh and Miriam to share it with."

Maggie swallowed hard, and her eyes glittered. "Josh and Caleb, it was brave of you to start a new life. Don't ever stop being brave. I know it's hard to stand here and declare your love in public. You aren't used to being accepted for who you are. But what you are is *strong*. And *beautiful*. I just want you to know how proud I am to know you."

Cecilia gave a little whoop, and everyone clapped.

I didn't hear much of the prayer that the pastor recited next, because I was watching Josh. He was stealing looks at all the people in the room, his eyes full of wonder. It calmed me to look at him. Because this was the view I was going to have all my life, now. And it was an excellent one.

"I, Joshua," the pastor began reciting Josh's vow, "take you, Caleb, to be my partner and husband."

"I, Joshua..." He continued to repeat the words she gave him.

"...To be yours in times of plenty and in times of want, in times of sickness and in times of health... In times of joy and in times of sorrow, in times of failure and in times of triumph... I promise to cherish and respect you, to care for and protect you, to comfort and encourage you, and stay with you, for all eternity."

Well, hell. Those were beautiful words. And I wanted to do all those things, too. And now Josh was saying the same, repeating the vows in a clear and steady voice.

And I was so, so not worthy.

SARINA BOWEN

"I, Caleb," the pastor turned to me. "Take you, Josh to be my partner and husband."

My throat was dry like a desert. "I, Caleb..." I pushed forward. "Take you, Josh to be my friend and husband." My eyes were hot, too. This didn't bode well.

The pastor gave me the next lines, and I muddled through. Until "...to comfort and encourage you, and stay with you, for all eternity."

I opened my mouth to repeat those last dozen words. But I made a crucial error, and that was looking straight into Josh's gaze to deliver them. Looking back at me were the steady blue eyes I'd been admiring my whole life. And his handsome face was tilted up toward mine, as if I'd hung the moon. The intensity of all that love just stopped me in my tracks.

There was a silence, because I forgot what I was supposed to say.

Our pastor tried to bail me out. "To comfort and encourage," she prompted. "And to stay with you for all eternity."

My voice broke as I repeated it. And a big fat tear ran down my cheek. *Christ on a cracker*, as Maggie would say. I was crying at my own wedding.

Josh's eyes became round with empathy. But then his lips quirked into a tiny smile. And I freaking loved that smile. So I focused on the sexy curve of his lips. And that was distracting enough that I bucked up a little and held myself together.

The pastor asked Josh if I took him to be my lawfully wedded husband. "I do," he said calmly.

She asked the same of me. "I absolutely do," I said, sounding only a little bit wobbly.

The pastor beamed at both of us. "By the power vested in me by the Commonwealth, I congratulate you on your marriage."

There was a round of applause, while Josh gave me a shy smile.

"Kiss him already," Miriam cried.

I laughed, feeling terribly self-conscious. Josh and I did not do PDA at *all*.

Who knew that Josh would be the first one to shake off our lifelong hangups? He stepped into my space, grabbed my chin in one hand, and planted a kiss on my lips.

And the world did not end. Not at all. The cheering only grew louder.

Not to be outdone, I slipped my arms around his waist and pulled him in. I made it a real kiss. As he always did, Josh tasted like everything I'd always wanted.

Kissing him in front of everyone we knew? It was as easy as rolling off a log.

When I finally stepped back, breaking off the kiss, Josh's face was pink. But he looked as happy as I'd ever seen him. "You survived it," he said, smiling.

"I certainly did," I agreed. He might have meant the wedding. But I meant everything that had led me to this moment.

I survived it. And he was the reason why.

"Now you can have ribs and beer, and then take me to Florida," Josh gave me a nudge toward the family who were waiting to congratulate us.

"I can't wait," I agreed.

The
End

ALSO BY SARINA BOWEN

Looking for more Male/Male romance?

Hello Forever (Book 2 in the Hello/Goodbye Series)

Roommate

The Understatement of the Year

Him by Sarina Bowen & Elle Kennedy

Us by Sarina Bowen & Elle Kennedy

Top Secret by Sarina Bowen & Elle Kennedy

Other Sarina Bowen titles:

TRUE NORTH

Bittersweet

Steadfast

Keepsake

Bountiful

Speakeasy

Fireworks

Heartland

Waylaid

Boyfriend

THE IVY YEARS

The Year We Fell Down #1

The Year We Hid Away #2

The Understatement of the Year #3

The Shameless Hour #4

The Fifteenth Minute #5

Extra Credit #6

GRAVITY

Coming In From the Cold #1

Falling From the Sky #2

Shooting for the Stars #3

THE BROOKLYN BRUISERS

Rookie Move

Hard Hitter

Pipe Dreams

Brooklynaire

Overnight Sensation

Superfan

Sure Shot

Bombshells

Shenanigans

ACKNOWLEDGMENTS

Thank you to Nina for your help and counsel on this project. Thanks to Melinda Utendorf for your assistance getting the manuscript in shape! And thanks to Jay Zastrow for your help and support.

Printed in Great Britain
by Amazon

23301765R00155